GRIMALKIN MANOR

S. ROIT

snowbooks

Proudly Published by Snowbooks in 2013

Snowbooks Ltd.
Tel: 0790 406 2414
email: info@snowbooks.com
www.snowbooks.com

British Library Cataloguing in Publication Data
A catalogue record for this book is available from the British Library.

ISBN 13 9781907777868

For Mom

Preface

He looked about, regarding each of the five Americans assembled around the black vans with a curious gaze and no small bit of caution.

He had no fear of them or the impending investigation. His prudence had much more to do with the fact that he could sense wariness from each person – not only this, but outright distrust emanated from at least two of them. Other emotions shifted and swam in the air as well, such as disbelief and irritation. Only one amongst the party appeared to regard him with some manner of respect, or rather, a possible respect for his talents.

He was still several feet away, but he could sense these things, and as he opened himself a bit further, he noted that the group – for all their misgivings over him – did not feel hostile, not as a whole.

Even had this been the case, he would still have been polite. He was rather accustomed to suspicion, aggression and standoffishness. Had he not spent most of his life as the outsider? As the one regarded with laughter, even fear? This is how it had felt to him much of the time, particularly while growing up in the elite private school his parents had insisted that he attend. It didn't help that after a while even his parents thought him damaged in some way.

Damaged. His mother most often used this word. But then, he didn't care to think of his mother, hadn't since he was eighteen, and he certainly preferred not to think of his father, whom he could easily blame for any damage to his psyche.

This thirty-three-year-old man knew his abilities hadn't been the only thing that made him appear strange to his fellow classmates, back then. He knew well enough it was also the secrets that he kept, secrets that surely caused him to behave in a way they found queer; his gifts merely compounded matters. Before he learned it was better to remain silent about the things he sensed and saw, he'd earned quite a reputation as the school's most disturbed – and disturbing – youth. Growing older had not erased his problems; in fact, growing older added new dimensions to existing difficulties, particularly any time he attempted to get close to someone.

Therefore, it had been some long time since he had been close to anyone, or even made the attempt.

But there was no off switch on his capabilities, and so here he was, about to take part in a paranormal investigation with a group of ghost hunters from the States, ghost hunters with a far more scientific approach than those he'd met previously, or so his patron assured him. They went in as skeptics, not people who attributed every bump and squeak as evidence of ghosts, and so it was perhaps no surprise that they didn't appreciate the presence of a so-called psychic. He knew that at least three of them were figuratively rolling their eyes, and he briefly wondered why he had accepted the invitation of the man who owned the sprawling mansion. He did not dwell long on this thought, however.

He could sense and speak to spirits; it was the first of his gifts that he'd come to understand when he was a child, and it had fascinated him. It still fascinated him, and it made him feel more useful. He believed that his talent must have a purpose, and what was the purpose if not to investigate the other side, to learn what he could learn, to hear what it was the Shades of the once living wanted or needed to say?

As he stood there gathering himself – the Americans studying him, and he staring at them – other thoughts moved through his consciousness.

There *were* those who took him seriously. They had no other choice on those occasions when he couldn't help telling them what he saw when they insisted on shaking his hand or brushed up against him. There were also those who had asked him to display his talents, had insisted that he prove himself, and those were the people he didn't wish to educate. Most often, they didn't appreciate what he had to say. They didn't like what he'd seen. They grew angry and fearful, accused him of trickery, which was preposterous. Most revelations had occurred on first meetings; how could he have known these things beforehand? But he understood. After all, so many people preferred logic, and his displays were not logical.

Having the confidence of others wasn't always good, either. There were those who were amazed with his talents and found him nearly god-like. Zealots unnerved him, no matter the source of their zealotry. It frazzled his sensitive nature.

He took a deep, soothing breath and placed a polite smile on his face, readying himself to interact with the five people he would spend the duration of the night with. He was quite interested in their equipment and their approach, whether they were interested in his ways or not. He possessed a logical and scientific mind himself, and perhaps he could convince them that his methods and theirs were not mutually exclusive. Besides, his talents covered a different type of science, and weren't they themselves in a field many others ridiculed?

Wasn't he amongst the paranormal?

Whatever they thought, there were two things he was certain would be proved this night. The first being that he was no fake.

They would not be able to deny the evidence, particularly after one of them insisted on touching him. He knew one of them would, and he had a very good idea which one it would be.

The second thing he knew – this building was haunted.

He could already feel pulsations along his flesh. He could feel the tingling of his nerve endings and the fingerless caresses.

As he took his first step, a different sensation pulsed through the leather of his shoes, vibrating the very soles of his feet, and he paused.

There was something very unpleasant about this feeling.

1

Zoe squared her shoulders and lifted her chin as she approached the tiny building. Inside was the rest of her team, the ghost hunting team they'd formed years ago. They were having a meeting about a new case, apparently. Zoe wasn't certain what was going on if she were honest with herself. She wasn't the least bit impressed by the phone call she'd received from Jonas. It had been cryptic. Short. This was unlike him. He was a man who got to the point, but he had been *short* with her when she'd tried asking him questions. There was a difference.

A few butterflies stirred in her stomach when she reached for the door handle. Things were not all peachy keen with everyone, lately. She knew that, and so she tried to cut them all some slack. But it was making her tense, and trying to hold her own feelings back all the time just made it worse. During the last case they'd been on, she'd nearly taken Mike's head off, figuratively speaking, and she wasn't very proud of herself. She'd done it in front of the client, right there in the home. Jonas hadn't said much at the time, just given her a cool look. Maybe today he was going to lecture her.

Well. As long as Mike got reamed, too, that was fine by her. Maybe they could all just air their grievances and get it over with, clear the air so they could do their damned jobs.

She stiffened her spine a little more, thinking this was an excellent idea, but first the subject of the case had to be dealt with.

"So what's the deal with this Mr. Smith?" Zoe asked as she strode into the makeshift office, doffing her jacket and draping it over a nearby folding chair. "You made it seem very secretive when you called."

"Last one here, first to start drilling him," Aaron commented with a good-natured grin. "But that's our Zoe."

Jonas turned and looked into Zoe's clear blue eyes. He had known she'd be the hardest sell. She was always cautious, always trying to give him advice. Mothered him, really, though he didn't exactly mind. Most of the time she did it with a light touch, light enough that he knew, *most of the time*, that it was merely because she cared.

But Jonas wasn't prepared to back down when it came to Smith's offer. He needed fresh air and lots of it. Zoe would probably tell him that he was running away, if he gave her the opportunity, but he wasn't going to give her that chance, not this time.

"He wants to remain anonymous, that's all," he said to Zoe.

"He's afraid people will think he's nuts," Brig added, shifting in his black computer chair.

Jonas ignored this and carried on. "He said in his letter he was thinking of opening the place up as a hotel."

"What, are people in England more wigged out by ghosts or something?" Brig's mellow laughter poured through the room. "These days, haunting can be good for business."

"Apparently he doesn't think so," Jonas said, his words accompanied by a lift and drop of a shoulder. "Doesn't matter. It's not the first time someone wanted to remain anonymous. Our job's tracking ghosts, not psychoanalyzing clients."

"Right up our alley, then," Aaron said from across the room, which wasn't exactly far. "Most of the time we don't find much solid evidence, so that should make him happy."

"If that's what he wants," said Zoe, after watching the back and forth, "fine. But *we* should know more about him." She studied Jonas' hazel stare. "Have you even talked to this guy yet?"

"No." Jonas steadied himself for the inevitable onslaught of Zoe's logic. He nearly sighed in relief when someone else decided to add their two cents first.

"Dude, are we going on the basis of a fricking letter?" asked Mike, at last rousing from his near-comatose state on the small and ratty loveseat, the color of which barely passed for crap brown. He pushed a lock of dirty blond hair from his face, and a cloudy gray eye peeked out at Jonas.

"We're here to *talk* about going," Jonas said to Mike, thinking that Mike was like the little brother everyone wanted to keep right on loving, but was increasingly exasperated with. *Or maybe it's mostly me.*

Mike lifted his slender hands. "Hey. Could be a cool place, don't get me wrong. But can we even afford a trip overseas? What about our equipment and all that?"

"I'll get to that, if you guys'll give me a chance." Jonas looked at each of them, the members of his second family. There were times they could get on each other's nerves, like any siblings, but they'd seen and done a lot together, and so were as close as a hot southern night. Because of this, Jonas was fairly certain that at least two of them would accept the assignment with little convincing on his part.

"Anyway," Jonas said, "to answer your question, he's offered to pay all travel expenses there and back, and money on top of that."

"We don't usually take money," Zoe reminded him, her constipated expression reflecting the terseness of voice.

"I know, but –"

Brig's tenor voice cut his team leader's words short. "In that case, what are we waiting for? We've never gone to England either, Zoe, and how else are we going to swing it? The man offered; it's not like we asked." Soft brown eyes shot to Jonas. "Right?"

The big man made a gesture that signaled his agreement.

Zoe folded her arms across her chest. Tightly. "Whatever. So what's the story on this place?"

Aaron got up and handed her the letter he'd been reading. "It's all here. Smith says he'll tell us more when we arrive."

Zoe absorbed the words, the tidy, spindly little words, on the painfully neat paper in her hand. "So we'll meet him for the first time *there*?"

"Guess so," said Jonas.

Her gaze flew to his face. "You *guess* so? This isn't like you, boss. You sound like you've already decided, and all we really have is this." The rattling of the paper in her hand punctuated her statement.

"Stop being such a bitch, geez." Mike rolled his eyes back in their sockets.

"Hey." Jonas pointed a thick finger at him. "Not cool."

Mike lifted his hands in surrender. "Sorry, sorry."

"Besides, she's got a point," Aaron chimed in.

"Yes, I do," agreed Zoe. "A very good and reasonable point."

Brig focused on Zoe. "Smith is probably one of those wealthy recluses, that's all. Not everything is a conspiracy."

Zoe sighed as she placed her hands on her hips. "Did I say it was? You're way too eager," she said. "Don't you think? Sure, it sounds cool, but – "

"Look," interrupted Jonas, his saucer-like eyes moving between the others. "Honestly, I'd like to get away, and I'd like to investigate this place." He gestured to the letter Zoe still held. "It's bigger than most of the job's we've done; we'll really be able to test ourselves. It's old and isolated. It could be a really good case."

"Isolated – and the dude's worried about *ghosts* being bad for business," Mike said. He let go with a derisive snort.

"*Anyway.*" Jonas' gaze begged the others like a puppy. "It'd be nice to get out of Seattle. Like a semi-vacation. We can stay an extra day or two, maybe. It'll be fun, yeah?"

The others exchanged glances. They all knew that Jonas was having a bad time of it lately, what with his wife leaving him, and one of the reasons she'd left was the very thing he was so eager to do. Take off and look for ghosts.

His adoptive brothers didn't want to let him down.

Aaron was the first to respond to the tug of his leader's look. "Sounds cool. I'm in. But still, we're going to talk to this guy first, right?"

A smile broke across the broadness of Jonas' face, making him look much more the pussycat than thug. "Don't worry; of course I'm going to talk to Mr. Smith before we go anywhere. I'm not stupid."

"Most of the time," Mike said, but Jonas didn't bristle. He knew that Mike was teasing. They used to tease each other often. The big man's expression sagged when he thought of how things had been lately. No good joke could cut the tension, and sometimes not even a sharp knife.

Meanwhile, Zoe studied Jonas' face. She'd always liked him, and no, he wasn't stupid; she knew that. If they could all clear the time off from their day jobs, she was willing to support him. Regardless of her protestations, the truth was that even if no one else could get the time away, she'd still go with him. Just the two of them; she was willing to support him that far – especially as she had the feeling he'd go alone if everyone else said no, and she didn't like that idea at all.

Yes, for all her bluster, Zoe often ended up doing whatever Jonas wanted. She knew she was a soft touch when it came to him, much as she tried not to be.

He looked so forlorn all of a sudden, too, which made her decision easier. Unbeknownst to her, the fingers of her left hand skirted the edge of the small, round office table and came close to touching Jonas' arm.

"Okay," Zoe said. "We'll see what else Mr. *Smith* has to say and figure it out from there."

"Mr. Smith," Mike said, though it was a miracle anyone heard him with the way he said it. As if his mouth were full of cotton. "Not very original." Which as far as the others were concerned, was stating the obvious.

"How'd he hear about us anyway? We're not exactly famous outside of this state," Aaron said as they all chose to *ignore* the obvious.

"Are we famous *in* this state?" Brig shot back, and everyone including Zoe relaxed a bit with the small laugh his sarcasm provided.

"Richard told him about us," said Jonas. Richard was Jonas' cousin in Manchester, whom he hadn't even seen for about five years, but they kept in touch by email. Richard was interested in the paranormal, too, but he had to take a business trip – so he'd written in his last email to his cousin – and had decided he'd give the mysterious man Jonas' number.

"Why someone so far away?" Brig asked. "There are people in England who do this sort of thing."

"Because," said Jonas, "he feels more assured the story won't get leaked if he hires out of the country."

"Waaayyy out of the country," Mike said with a chuckle. "Paranoid much?"

"It's not my job to study his mental state," Jonas reminded him – perhaps with terseness he didn't intend.

"So you said. But maybe we should," Mike countered – and having noted the snappishness, attempted humor. "He might have some nefarious plot, like forgetting to pay us."

"Or maybe he's just lonely, and he wants some hot boys and girls to play with." Brig added, diffusing things further. "But don't worry, that leaves you out of it, Mike."

Mike dismissed this with a wave of his hand, and Jonas shook his head, saying, "All right, that's enough. Let's have a serious meeting for a change." His expression softened – an accomplishment indeed, with the fierce, thick bone structure of his face.

This had gone better than he'd expected, at least so far. Zoe might still throw a wrench in the situation. It was time to seal the deal with details of the site.

"It's cool you all seem up for going, but we do have things to discuss," he said.

"A serious meeting? Wow, that's a novel concept," Aaron said, and he sank back into the one good chair in the office that didn't look moth ridden. "Man, one of these days we need to spend some money on this place, by the way."

"Right," Jonas said. "Just as soon as all our equipment's paid off, bro."

"When is that again? 2030?" Mike said, and they all laughed. "We should seriously rethink getting paid for this shit on a regular basis," he continued when the laughter trailed off.

"You know how I feel about that, and we all agreed years ago," said Jonas. The force of his gaze pressed Mike back into his seat.

"Yeah, yeah, I know," Mike replied. Clearly there weren't enough jokes in the world.

~

James Trussart's pale, blue-gray eyes made a study through the rain-spattered glass of the street below. He was holding a neatly hand-written letter which he had read three times in the last few minutes, pondering its contents. The missive, which he'd found tucked into his mail caddy, was addressed to him, yet there was no postage stamp. Naturally, he pondered who might have delivered it, but as he had never heard of the sender, there were no clues in his mind. In fact, he suspected Mr. Smith was a pseudonym – more than suspected, as many people would.

It did not concern him overmuch that his address had been available to a stranger; after all, he did work in various museums, and sometimes for private collectors, acting as a verifier and historian. Occasionally he even did restorations. His name and contact details were listed in certain directories. Perhaps it was someone he had met in passing, someone who knew of his *other* work, who was uncomfortable with speaking of such things. Either that or one of the few people who knew of his talents had been in touch with the mystery letter's author. In the letter, Smith had written that he would prefer to remain as anonymous as possible. He didn't wish for anyone outside of the investigators to know that he wanted his property looked into.

James was dreadfully curious. Few people knew precisely the nature of his...*nature*. Most of his forays were solitary events, and he asked to remain unnamed in the investigations. He knew very well, however, that people were not always capable of keeping things to themselves, and so the fact that Mr. Smith had written to ask him if he might consider lending his *other* talents did not truly startle him. It was a rare thing for James to be startled, in any case – to be startled by another's actions, more precisely.

Perhaps Mr. Smith only knew of his abilities as a medium. More knew of this than about the rest of his sensitivities.

The letter said that if he were interested, to email his response and further details would be given. As he lowered his eyes and looked over the tidily-written words once more, he fixated yet again on one paragraph in particular.

He had limited experience with paranormal investigators. He had read much on the subject, and he knew what manner of methods many employed, but only four times had he tagged along with one of the groups that seemed to be forming overnight, jumping into the fray of the increasingly popular field. Two of the experiences had been pleasant enough, though the young people involved were quite green. They were more congenial than the other two groups, however. More than one person in each of the other groups had mocked him as a psychic, and one person had been overly zealous with him.

A group in Britain, a famous group who televised their excursions, had once attempted to contact him, but he had seen the show and found it laughable. He was not interested in making a profit with his gifts, nor was he interested in being famous – being mocked on a large scale. He was not keen on ripping off the public for a good scare, and he was not interested in further sullying the reputation of legitimate psychics, or legitimate paranormal investigators.

James knew very well that ghosts existed, and he would not be responsible in any way for another like him feeling outcast, ridiculed, and taken far less seriously than he ought to be.

Besides, James, for the most part, was content to commune with spirits for his own reasons, on his own time, though he certainly was not above helping people. He was at heart a decent sort of person. A rather genial sort, most of the time. Only once in his life could anyone ever have said that he had snapped, though he did not see it this way. After all, he had been meticulous, had plotted the entire affair, and he never allowed himself to forget it. He'd gotten away with it, too, brilliant child that he was.

The event had split his being in half, and twenty-one years later, he still could not reconcile these two parts. Only one person in the world knew what he had done. He was certain that they knew, but also certain they would never converse on the subject.

Quickly, he turned his thoughts back to the subject at hand. Ghost hunters. No matter his previous experiences, it still intrigued him.

He turned away from the window, and the fabric of his camel colored trousers whispered like butterfly wings as he walked towards his roll-top desk, on which rested an immaculate laptop. Taking a seat in the smooth, wine-colored leather chair, he set the missive aside and opened up his email, having decided that his curiosity needed satisfying. He set about writing to one Mr. Smith, asking for all of the pertinent details. Should he find the answers satisfactory, he wrote, he would then make his final decision. Before he signed and hit send, he also asked just how it was that Mr. Smith knew about him – even though he was not expecting a straightforward reply to this particular query.

2

Brig's mind wasn't focused on his work. Luckily for him, stocking shelves wasn't brain surgery. It was unlucky for the customer that he'd sent to the wrong aisle for Post-It Notes, but at least no one would die for his mistake. Or wake up babbling incoherently. He was too busy thinking about the trip to England to spare the brain cells needed for making boxes line up *just so*. It hadn't been quite decided yet, but with each mind numbing moment that passed on his shift, he hoped the others would agree to it and be capable of scoring the time off. In fact, he'd already decided he'd tell his boss that he had to go to a funeral or something; an excuse his boss wouldn't debate. Even if they didn't go, he'd take the time off, anyway. He was always up for an extra day off.

But he wanted to go, more than anything he'd ever wanted so far in his life. Brig had never left the country. Heck, he hadn't ever left Seattle. Vancouver, B.C. didn't count, as far as he was concerned, since he could drive there easily. The idea of flying somewhere, somewhere across an entire ocean, made the twenty-two year old giddy. He was glad he'd gotten a passport, just in case he ever won the lottery or a free trip. That optimism was about to pay off; he could feel it.

A box fell unchecked to the floor as his mind wandered further, imagining tidy little villages, rolling green hills, and girls with sexy accents. While he went through the motion of retrieving the box, on complete autopilot, he reminded himself that there might not be much time for girls, but it was okay, because he'd still be in England. The only thing better than that would be if he had a girl to take *with* him.

A girl like Sarah would do. Sarah, whom he spied in the corner of his eye as she walked by his aisle. She was perfect, or would be, if she'd just acknowledge his existence. Just once. Heck, a wave or nod would do.

Sarah gave a little wave, a big smile, and kept on walking when Brig didn't respond.

He refocused on his task, realizing it was the third time she'd acknowledged his existence today, and cursed his own shyness. Sarah was high on the list of reasons – a very short list – that he still worked at Fred Meyer. She was right after the paycheck, in the number two position, but she could easily be number one. Before he could wallow around in the knowledge she'd probably have another new boyfriend before he worked up the nerve to say more than three words to her, he turned his thoughts back to England, sans girls.

He shoved another box on the shelf with fresh resolve. The second his break time rolled around, he was going to call Jonas and tell him that he didn't care who else was going, he'd go no matter what. Maybe having an adventure would strengthen his courage. Make him more attractive in a worldly way. And maybe he could practice chatting up some English girl he'd never have to see again if he made a fool of himself. Then he could try it out on Sarah.

Over in West Seattle, at the Barnes and Noble, Aaron was just finishing his break. He stowed his cell phone in his backpack and shoved it on the shelf before leaving the employee room, popping a breath mint on his way out. He felt good about the call he'd just made, especially since his parents had been so supportive when he'd spoken to them before work. They were always supportive. They had backed him when, after finishing a business degree at the University of Washington he'd decided a nine-to-five desk job – possibly with outrageous over time – just wasn't his thing. Especially not if he had to be stuck in a monkey suit.

Aaron was on his way to becoming a professional student; at least, that's what his parents had said when he enrolled in the Art Institute of Seattle. Graphic arts were his passion, or the passion of the moment. But his parents were happy as long as he was happy, and he made enough money at his job to suit his needs for the time being. When he told them that he had a chance to go to England with his hobby – that's what they called it, a hobby – they'd said that travel broadens one's horizons, especially when you're young, and that he may as well go for it before his semester started and he was saddled with schoolwork.

As Aaron passed row after row of other people's fantasies, making his way to the customer service desk, he smiled. It didn't matter if they knew much about Smith. After all, it wasn't as if most of their clients were friends. They were each strangers who needed someone to take them seriously and help them sort out whatever odd and sometimes frightening things were happening in their homes. This 'home' just happened to be much farther away than they normally traveled. The rest of his team would realize the truth of it and say yes, surely they would.

His decision had left him feeling chipper, something his next customer appreciated.

"Hi, how can I help you?"

The mood in the small, dingy room of a house on Capitol Hill was far more somber. Amidst a fanned-out pile of papers and envelopes on the puke green carpeting, Mike sat, a dejected look on his face. Every paper had lines of short, curt little sentences, outlining services, and beside every line were numbers, numbers ushered in by demanding little dollar signs.

Mike didn't have enough numbers in his account to make the dollar signs stop harassing him.

"Hey, can you scale it back down there? I'm trying to think, damn it."

His housemates' music was mocking him. He could see those dollar signs head banging to Metallica, banging their heads against his, and it was driving him insane. He'd grown to hate Metallica, anyway. It was all they ever played. Since his girlfriend had kicked him out, he'd been waking up and going to bed to the crunchy chords of *Enter Sandman* for five months straight.

"At least pick a different song. Fuck." He brought his fist to the floor, hard, about six times, for all the good it would do. They would just think it was part of the song, if they even noticed.

He grabbed his cigarette pack, feeling even more dejected when he found it empty. He could scrounge up the cash, but he didn't feel much like running to the gas station. He could save money if he'd just quit, but those white cylinders were packed with the only peace he had left, lately. The only thing he could count on, right now. Besides the paranormal group. His home away from... well, this wasn't a home.

His mind wandered through thoughts of Theresa, his ex, obliterating those crunchy guitar chords for the time being. To the girl he refused to think of as his ex, even though she'd sounded like she meant it when she said it was over – and launched his few belongings off the balcony. She'd said she was tired of seeing him give up on everything, tired of watching him self-destruct, and tired of him being gone all the time, hunting things that didn't exist, instead of making something out of himself.

Theresa said that he was a bright guy and could probably do anything he liked, if he'd put his mind to it. If he had the drive. If he *wanted* to. She didn't seem to understand how much it hurt him, her blowing off his interest in the paranormal. She'd seemed cool with it in the beginning. When he pointed that out, she'd countered by saying it wasn't that she thought it was stupid; it just wasn't a real job. He used to have a *real* job, but he'd lost it because he'd taken too much time off, and ever since, he hadn't tried very hard to find another paying gig.

She'd said *Mike, I love you, but we can't go on like this, I'm sorry. You're not even trying anymore.*

But he *had* been. At least with her. At least he'd thought so. He loved her so much he felt he'd suffocate with it. He just wanted her to understand. It was only a bump in the road. This too shall pass.

He crumpled up the empty cigarette pack and sighed. He couldn't talk to Jonas about this. Jonas had his own girl problems. He still wanted to commiserate with his pal, but, Jonas would probably say the same thing that Theresa had, and Mike didn't want to admit that she was right. Thing was, he already knew she was right when she said that since everything seemed to be going wrong, he'd given up. That he'd adopted an attitude of *fuck it. The world hates me, so I'll hate it, and as long as I have you, Theresa, everything's fine.*

Sorry, Mike, but that's not enough. I can't be your everything, and if you won't help yourself, I can't help you.

She was right. He was messing up his life. If he just didn't feel so tired all the time, and so... so depressed, then maybe...

He needed to get away. He couldn't wait to get to England. Three days had passed since their meeting. They had more information about the manor house, and Jonas had talked to Smith a few times. They should make up their minds already and go, just go. Mike didn't care where it was or who Smith was, as long as he could get away from Seattle. Maybe things would look better when he returned. Or look better from far away.

Maybe he wouldn't even come back.

"Fuck it." He got up, grabbed his wallet and blew out of his tiny room (that he wouldn't be able to pay for next month) and rushed down the stairs, breezing past his roommates without so much as a nod as he left the house.

Cigarettes, then Fantasy Unlimited. He could spare a buck or two for the strippers, after stopping at the ATM. He needed bus fare, and there was no point in withdrawing less than twenty or forty dollars. He needed a distraction. That's all it was, a distraction. At least the music would be different at Fantasy's, and the girls were a lot nicer to look at than his stupid housemates.

He pulled out his cell to call Jonas as he walked.

Zoe sat on her small sofa in her Queen Anne studio apartment, thinking as much as she ever did, which was too much. She was thinking that she still wasn't feeling quite right about the trip. About how they hadn't learned much more about the client. She didn't like the near cloak and dagger feel of it – though the others weren't having the same vibes, apparently. Still, she was thinking that regardless of this, she'd promised Jonas that she would go. She was pondering how much she loved paranormal research. Unlike the others, no specific event had led her into the field. She just found it fascinating.

She thought about how bad she felt for Jonas and how she honestly wanted to see that old mansion. About her cat, on whose head one of her hands rested, and her safe little job with Century Link. The safe but not necessarily fulfilling little job.

And, she was thinking about the psychic the mysterious Mr. Smith had insisted be part of their team. She was open to the idea, but she knew that the guys weren't precisely jazzed about it. They thought most mediums were crocks that ripped people off.

They had a point.

Though really, she couldn't include Aaron with the rest of the guys. Aaron was interested in the subject of psychics. He hadn't met one who'd convinced him beyond doubt, but he was hopeful that one day he would. She considered that Mr. Trussart might have some real talent. She hoped so, mostly because it would make Aaron happy, and even she had to admit it would be neat to find someone who could prove they were gifted.

She sighed, sipped at her lukewarm tea, and then closed her eyes, her mind still racing. It was going to be an interesting investigation either way, and hopefully not because Mike decided to be an asshole, like he'd been a lot more of, lately. She wondered what had crawled up there and died this time. Jonas had given him far too many chances already. But… Jonas was a nice guy, and that was that.

Over at the Caffé Ladro in West Seattle, Jonas, who was an electrician by day, wasn't thinking of the investigation. He was thinking of his soon-to-be-ex-wife, who right now was probably getting ready for work, back in their rental house on Fauntleroy. She hated waiting tables, but she made great tips. She was saving to go back to school. That's what she always said, anyway, but she'd been saying that for years. She blamed him for this as well, in the end. He spent too much money on his stupid obsession, that's what she'd said. They should have their own house, kids, the works, not still be renting a claustrophobic space with a postage stamp yard. It was his fault, and his stupid ghost team; it was always about him, him, him.

He thought of how she hadn't always held this opinion, and he thought of how pretty she looked, fresh and dripping, coming out of their shower.

Maybe she was right. Maybe he'd been more attentive to her needs in the beginning. He'd wanted the picket fence, the children. He didn't want it right away, that's all, or so he kept telling her. There was plenty of time; they weren't that old, and he wanted her to go to school, to make herself happy. He wanted her to stop working a crap job. They had money in the bank; they could rent a larger house, maybe even buy a small one, but apparently that wasn't enough. It was never enough. It used to be. She used to think his interest in the paranormal was fascinating. She had supported him. She'd even come along with him on some investigations.

Now she thought it was immature, a waste of time, that he should have outgrown it. She'd said, just the other day, that he loved ghosts more than he loved her. This wasn't true. Jonas loved his wife plenty; he simply wished that she understood, like she used to, or had seemed to, that ghost hunting was important to him, too. That it wasn't a waste of time. That he needed answers – had needed them ever since the event that set him on this path.

He contemplated ordering another coffee, but he soon forgot about that when his cell phone buzzed, and he saw that it was Mike. For all their problems lately, at least Mike understood how important this was to him. He knew that he and Mike weren't so different, in some ways. Zoe understood even better, and a smile snuck up on him as he thought of her. Zoe always supported him, he realized. Then he went outside and answered his phone before he could dwell on it much longer.

3

James sat at the small-yet-adequate desk in the cozy hotel room, his fingers working the keys of his laptop. He had arrived early, in from London, because he wanted to do more research. Some of this he could have done from home, but he preferred settling in well before an investigation, rather than rushing off to a site straight away. He didn't know when the Americans would arrive or which hotel they would stay in, but in the back of his mind he hoped that he would run into them. As it was, it seemed unlikely. It appeared that Mr. Smith might have fashioned it this way – for their first meeting to be on site.

For all his talent, James hadn't read much more than the words on that handwritten missive. This intrigued him. No residuals. It should concern him, also, but he was feeling much too cat-like.

Mr. Smith had told James that he'd informed the American group of his impending presence. Mr. Smith had said little else of this, so for now James busied himself with searching for details online concerning the isolated mansion and the area itself. Curiously, there didn't seem to be much in the way of ghost stories. None of the local legends fitted Mr. Smith's cursory tales. Either the residents were keeping a secret very well indeed – perhaps out of fear – or he and the Americans would shortly disprove Mr. Smith's stories. This was what his benefactor desired, so James supposed it would be a job well done, if a tad boring.

Smith was quite accommodating when it came to travel and lodging. James had not asked for anything above this, nor had he asked for train fare and a pre-paid room, but his secretive contact had insisted. Not only this, but James was to have a rental car at his disposal in order to make the final drive from the village. Equipped with GPS, Mr. Smith had assured him that he'd find his way.

This enigma of an employer was certainly going to great lengths to remain anonymous, thought James. He didn't know that he believed the man would make an appearance at the estate as offered; what he did know was that regardless of Smith's reasons, it seemed a bit odd, this arrangement.

Yet here he was, preparing for the investigation. James and secrets were not strangers. Some people were private sorts, very private, and that was that. Wealthy recluse, this Smith. That explained it, for the time being.

The Victorianesque structure Mr. Smith had described was beginning to seem a phantom itself. James could find no photographs recent or old, nor could he find much in the way of records. Vagaries, it was all so much vagary. He sighed and left off searching the internet, deciding that he would check the local library and then see about public records. This was, after all, a reason he'd arrived a day ahead of schedule, which his benefactor did not seem to mind.

Perhaps he'd also find a nice spot for a bit of orange-spiced tea while he was out.

4

The Americans arrived at the location early. A miracle, since they hadn't been certain the overgrown path they'd driven down was the right one (or that it was even a road) until the mansion's triple steeple rooftop peeked at them from a distance.

As the two vans inched closer – equipment and two human occupants in one, more supplies and three warm bodies in the other – the red-bricked monstrosity revealed more of itself to them with all the grace of a retired burlesque dancer. Her stage: a sprawling, bug-infested lawn of unknown acreage, tended by grotesquely deformed stage hands.

Large, dark, mute trees draped her sides and kept modest most of her veranda. Branches reached like spindly fingers to brush at her face. Yet a patron could still see that she had several sets of unnerving eyes. Shutters, like false eyelashes slept in overnight, decorated those cold eyes and their unwavering gaze. Their dark, ghastly stare.

The skirt of her lawn overgrew itself in places, mostly about her earth-sunken feet, but one could see hints of its former sparkle, ornamented as it was with old baubles of landscaping:

a garden flung here and there, a statue abandoned hither and yon.

The forlorn old gal stared back at them, frigid, weary, uninviting, yet with a phantom spark of her old fire somewhere in those depths, all the same. She seemed a tired old bitch who merely needed someone to tickle the right buttons. Brush and wash her hair. Hem and press her dress – and massage her body just a bit.

The words *Grand Old Dame* came to at least two people's minds as those vans rolled to a stop at the end of a meandering drive. Also the words *Shit, it even looks haunted!* came to someone else's mind as they piled out of said vans, and though there was yet daylight, the sky, which provided a backdrop for the mansion, was sinister with clouds that made for a dramatic darkening of the area. At least, in some opinions, it was. Others considered it normal, or didn't consider it at all.

5

Hands with knobby knuckles rubbed together in anticipation of a good game, a good party. The gesture was so gleeful, one might have thought the owner of these hands was attempting to start a fire and had a good chance at throwing a proper spark from his dry flesh.

"This should be interesting," the old man said to the room. "First impressions are lasting impressions." He chuckled. The sound was dry and raspy. "And so often correct."

He pondered his photo albums for a moment, slyness in the depths of his too-dark eyes. "Particularly in some cases."

He clapped his hands together and scurried into the kitchen. "Food? Drinks? Hmm. What sounds good?"

6

Clustered outside around one of the vans, the five Americans waited for Mr. Smith and the psychic he'd also hired. Just as Zoe had surmised on the flight, her partners' excitement over James Trussart sticking his nose into things could be measured on the tip of one fingernail. Also, as much as she'd hoped to be wrong, Mike was the first to be an asshole about it.

"We can tell him we changed our minds and drive off. Come back later after he's given up and left."

Aaron's gaze slid to Mike. "That's kinda stupid."

"So is having a psychic on this trip," Mike fired back.

"It isn't up to us," Jonas reminded him. "We do what the client wants."

"Doesn't mean I have to like it," Mike replied, with the patience of an old man three hours past his bedtime.

Jonas shook his head with his words. "No, but you're gonna be nice to the guy, got it?"

Mike made a noise somewhere between a snort and a grunt. He looked at Brig. "Hear that? We have to play nice."

"Hey," Zoe cut in. "Just because you don't believe in that stuff, it's no reason to be rude. He might be a good guy."

"Whatever." Mike ambled away from the others, fishing a pack of American Spirits out of his coat pocket, ready to chill out with some good old nicotine.

"Remember, no smoking inside," Aaron said.

Mike waved his free hand. "Yeah, yeah."

"Jonas." Zoe drew closer to his formidable frame. "What time is it?"

"Five minutes later than the last time you asked me." Jonas chuckled and leaned back against the side of the immaculate van. "What's got you so impatient?"

She tilted her head back to get a better view of his face. "Wasn't Mr. Smith supposed to be here by now?"

His shoulders bumped up and dropped. "We're early for once. Give him some time."

"I can't believe we found this place so easy," Brig said, sidling up to them. "I figured we'd get lost."

"Yeah." Jonas turned his head towards his other partner, the real muscle on their team. "So did I. His directions weren't bad. I was relieved to see GPS in the vans, too."

Brig returned Jonas' smile with a toothy one of his own. "Nice not to be driving around in circles, yeah. Especially in a different country. Whatever else we could say about the guy, he's taking care of us." He turned and cast his sights on the rambling manor. "Man, I still can't get over this. Freaking awesome. I can't wait to get started." He spun a half circle, much in the way an enraptured child would. "And just look at these trees. This is the *coolest* place we've ever been."

Zoe's smile erupted with Brig's boyish comment. "It really is amazing. Hell, it *looks* like a haunted house," she said.

"Sure as hell does," said Jonas as he eyed the tilted veranda. "Looks like this place has been empty a long time."

Zoe followed his gaze. "Shame, because you can tell it used to be pretty grand." She imagined lavish, old-fashioned socials, complete with well-meaning matchmaker friends. It almost made her giggle, but thankfully, the guys were distracted. They teased her when she got "all girly".

"Yeah. Maybe Smith will let us see it again when it's restored," said Jonas. He wondered how decrepit the interior was. Smith had said the structure was sound, as far as he knew. They would have to tread with caution, just in case, unless Mr. Smith wanted to pay doctor bills as well.

"Renovations might scare up more activity," Brig said, excitement moving through his eyes, even his limbs, at the prospect. If one looked close enough, they might see the anticipatory shiver. "*Then* he'll invite us back."

Jonas let go with a deep chuckle. "Maybe. Anyway, I guess we could go ahead and start unloading the equipment."

"Now you're talking," said Brig as he rubbed his hands together. "Mr. Smith will just think we're industrious, right?" He nodded in agreement with himself.

"No going in until he gets here, though," Jonas told him.

"I know, I know." Brig headed for the first van, where Mike leaned while puffing away on his cigarette. "C'mon dude," he called out, "drop the cancer stick and let's get the show on the road." As he said this, his hand fanned the air between them.

"Yo, I see a car coming," Aaron said, taking a few steps down the overgrown drive.

All eyes shifted in the direction of the approaching vehicle. A dark blue, two-door sedan with a new-car look. It turned in their direction and crept down the dilapidated, weed-encrusted drive towards them. Mike killed his cigarette by way of booted foot, leaving a black smear, and he joined his four companions as they gathered a couple of feet from the back of the second van.

"You think that's Smith?" he asked. "I figured he'd have a fancier car." Three sets of shoulders shrugged, so Mike backed up and leaned against the van, no longer buzzed about Jonas having said they could unload the equipment. He'd wanted to start even earlier, but Jonas had said they were supposed to wait.

Mike hated waiting.

The sedan rolled to a stop several feet away. A moment later, out stepped a slender, young-looking man, dressed in crisp trousers the color of a fawn, a champagne, button-down shirt, and a close-fitting brown leather jacket that stopped just below his waist.

Mike nudged Brig's calf with a foot. "Look, he's even wearing matching loafers. Sorta girly."

"Yeah, he looks kind of delicate, if you ask me," Brig whispered back. "I hope that's Mr. Smith, because if it's the psychic, he doesn't look like he could last an hour."

At this, snickers erupted in Mike, which set off the same in Brig. The two men were rewarded with an over-the-shoulder glare from Zoe. As her eyes travelled back towards the drive, to the man standing on that drive, she wondered if she were the only one who thought the stranger didn't look old enough to be Mr. Smith, even though they'd never met him.

The man who'd exited the car had paused and was contemplating all of them in return. A standoff, sizing each other up.

He was the first to end it. After smoothing his medium length, pale brown hair, he made a slow approach in their direction. Zoe, not wishing to be impolite, made first contact.

"Hello, are you Mr. Smith?" she asked, though she still didn't think so. This man wasn't at all what she'd imagined, but she reminded herself that it wasn't as if she knew anything about their client. A fact that bothered her more and more about this entire affair.

Yet here she was, even if she couldn't admit to herself the true reason why.

The stranger's response wafted to them on a pleasant tone. "No, I'm James Trussart. I'm very pleased to meet you." He covertly studied Zoe's eyes, noted her long auburn hair and her casual dress. Jeans, white t-shirt and black hoodie.

Zoe noticed that James hadn't offered his hand, though his response had been polite enough. "Oh, well, pleased to meet you too, James." Her hands didn't leave her sides, either. She turned to Jonas, instead. "Um, let me introduce you first to Jonas. He's in charge, basically."

James inclined his head while he studied the bear of a man whose scalp was covered in Velcro-like hair. "A pleasure."

"Yeah, good to meet you." Jonas started to extend his hand, having missed the Brit's reticence with Zoe. When he realized that Mr. Trussart had taken a step back, he dropped that hand and turned towards the others. Puzzled, but not willing to make a scene of it.

"Back here we have Brig," he said. Brig offered a *hey*. "That's Mike." Who offered nothing. "And this here's Aaron." Jonas patted Aaron on the shoulder.

Aaron stepped forward, holding out his hand for no other reason than he was raised with manners. "It's good to meet you, Mr. Trussart."

James dropped his gaze to Aaron's hand. "You may call me James if you like." He lifted his eyes. His hands had remained clasped behind his back the entire time. "Do pardon me, but – "

"Is there something against hand shaking here in England, or what?" Mike asked. Lines of annoyance crept across his forehead.

Aaron dropped his hand as he glanced at Mike. "It's okay, dude, no big deal."

Before James could open his mouth in an attempt to speak once more, Mike persisted. "He won't shake anyone's hand." He eyed James with naked suspicion. "Too good for us or something?"

"Mike!" Zoe wanted to smack him, but she held her place. "Talk about *rude*."

James sighed – not that anyone noticed – as the back and forth continued. *I imagine this could go on all day.*

"I'm just asking," Mike said

"There's a better way to ask," Zoe snapped.

"Oh yeah? Who are you, Miss Manners?"

"Miss Manners would have drop-kicked you to a curb, smartass."

"Think you can do that on your own, Miss Goody-Goody?"

"Guys, for God's sake, stop it," said Jonas. "Making a real good impression here, thanks." He could feel his cheeks wanting to heat.

Mike pushed past Jonas and headed straight for James. "Hi. I'm Mike, nice to meet you." He thrust his hand at the Brit.

"Ugh, you are such an asshole," Zoe muttered. She couldn't help herself. She knew that they sounded like the little kids Jonas had just chastised. She mentally chastised herself for adding to it.

Mike responded with laughter courting his words. "And you have no sense of humor." He nodded at James. "We don't bite. I just want to shake your hand."

"I'm sorry, it's nothing personal, but I really don't wish to," James replied, happy to have the opening. "I am – "

"Why?" Mike interrupted, as persistent as a migraine.

James closed his mouth, bristled by this second rude display. *Good Lord.*

"Miiiike." Zoe's hand was poised to smack him. She was almost beyond caring how it would appear to the stranger. Jonas could give them a double-dose lecture later.

James' sigh was audible to everyone the second time. "Mr. Smith didn't explain about me at all, did he? But then, I rather suppose he didn't know everything about me."

"We know you're supposed to be psychic," Mike said, his arm dropping dead at his side.

"I'm more than that. I'm terribly sorry if it offends you, but I simply do *not* shake hands with strangers, as I was attempting to explain."

Aaron cut in before Mike could conjure up yet another childish retort. "Are you sensitive?"

Everyone's eyes shifted to Aaron.

"Are you familiar with such?" James asked of him.

"Yes. How sensitive are you?" Aaron studied the lovely-looking man with new interest.

James contemplated a moment before replying. They would come to know during the evening, he thought. There was no point in keeping it secret. Especially not if the one called Mike continued to make an issue of things.

"I'm *a* Sensitive, not merely sensitive," he said.

"So you're extremely empathic?" asked Jonas with a lift of thick brows. "Is that what you mean?"

James' attention turned to him. "Yes, that is the gist of it."

"Psychometrics, too, then?" Zoe asked, honest curiosity settling in her eyes. *Bold claims.* "Since you won't shake hands."

This nudged a smile towards James' lips as he looked to her. *They are educated on the subject, it seems. Somewhat, at least.* "Yes."

Jonas pivoted to face Mike. "That's why he doesn't want to touch you, and it would have been nice if you asked him politely in the first place." Jonas then took in James' calm expression, embarrassment sketching itself onto his own face, which made it look like he was being sunburned on fast-forward. "I'm really sorry about that. He's the only one who thinks he's funny most of the time."

Everyone but Mike smiled at the sound of the following breezy laughter. "Yes, well. No harm done," James said.

"So what, if you touch me you can read me or whatever?" Mike said with an expression suggesting James was trying to sell him sand in a desert.

The Englishman retained a cool exterior. "I can. I may see things you don't wish me to see. Feel things you'd rather I didn't." *Or that I'd rather not.* He stared at the mop-headed ragamuffin.

Mike thrust out his hand again. "Go ahead. I gotta see this."

James kept his eyes level with Mike's. "I'd really rather not, if you please. It is much more difficult for me to shield if you touch me."

"Don't blame you," said Brig. With his finger, he described a circle in the air by Mike's head. "Pretty messed up in there."

"Ah, shut up, you," Mike said. He then smiled at James, as if he meant no harm, no harm at all. "C'mon. Let's see what you got." His expression remained as docile as a sleeping kitten's.

"Mike, please," Zoe cut in. "This is really not cool, give him a break. He just said it's harder to shield that way." Bold claims or not, Mike was being a jerk, plain and simple.

Mike, undeterred, made no move to lower his hand, and James continued to study the shorter man's eyes.

"Shields, whatever. Afraid I'll find out you're a fraud?" Mike said, hoping to bait the man. Zoe gave into her urge and smacked Mike on his shoulder, while a swear word from Jonas whispered by them. He shook his head, exchanging a glance with Aaron.

"Mike," Aaron said, "I've read that it's not always comfortable for a – "

"Something happened that you don't wish for them to know," James said to Mike, startling the others with his sudden interruption. "You are keeping a secret; your guilt is tangible."

Five sets of eyes nailed James. Mike, laughing, threw up his hands. "That's so vague, anyone could say some shit like that."

James, having decided that he had no choice but to put the rude American in his place, continued, knowing well that he had touched the correct nerve as further impressions came to him. "You...broke something." His brows creased in concentration. "Something expensive, an item that doesn't truly belong to you."

There was an abrupt halt to Mike's laughter. "More random crap that won't work." Disdain painted his features. "I know how you guys operate. Lead everyone along and try to get us to help you by answering questions and shit."

"He hasn't asked any questions," Zoe said under her breath. Mike glanced at her. "You believe this crap?"

"I'm just saying."

"Maybe you shouldn't."

But James was far from finished. He moved around them, careful to avoid physical contact, and approached the van. After a moment's study, he placed his left palm against the door. Four Americans watched him with genuine curiosity. One with nervous impatience.

"Have you checked all of the equipment in this van?" James said after a long pause.

Mike rolled his eyes and tried not to dwell on the fact that he had been the one responsible for packing the second van. *Bunch of crap, bunch of crap, bunch of crap*. Say it enough times, everyone else would have to see it, too.

Jonas' gaze flicked to Aaron, who was studying James with intensity. Jonas gave up and shrugged. Mike had started it, so why not humor James and finish it, he thought. He was even beginning to hope James might not be full of shit, just so Mike would shut up about it. He knew that what he should have done was grab Mike by the arm and drag him off for a private talk, but it was too late for that now.

Jonas moved closer to the van, not missing that James moved away from him as he did so. "What about the equipment?"

James moved his eyes towards Mike, his features colored with calm confidence. "He packed it. I do not believe that you have checked it recently." His gaze returned to Jonas – who had to admit to himself that this was true. Jonas glanced at Mike just in time to see the younger man's second eye-roll, and then he opened one of the doors, gesturing.

"What should I check, James?"

James' clear eyes, now showing more gray than blue, moved over the contents as he stepped closer once again. Mike grunted as James lifted his hands. It was as though he tested the air the closer he got, and then once he was close enough to the van, his hands brushed invisible currents above the various containers sitting in the back. One of his hands made a swift descent, crash landing on the top of a black container.

"One of the cameras in this case is broken." James closed his eyes and drew his hand away from the container. "It was dropped. He dropped it."

Jonas narrowed his eyes at James and then leveled Mike with a questioning stare.

"Bullshit," Mike nearly growled.

James turned to him. "No. Fuck!" His mouth was itching for a smile as he clasped his hands behind his back. "This is what you yelled when you dropped it, closely followed by something along the lines of Jonas killing you."

Mike's own mouth snapped shut, and he could feel his face growing hot. He wanted to strangle the little fag, shove his fingers in the fucker's mouth — something, anything, to shut him up. Jonas hauled out the black case and set it on the ground. With a glance up to the others, he opened it. Looking back down at the case, he pulled the thermal camera from the padding and turned it over in his hands.

"Son of a bitch," he said. He sounded as if he'd eaten sandpaper. "It's cracked. The screen is frigging cracked all to hell."

Aaron, Zoe and Brig gaped at the thermal. They all then stared at James, none of them knowing what to say, each pondering their own explanations.

Mike flung out his hands in exasperation. "This is bullshit; I didn't drop it," he said.

Hard lines settled about Jonas' mouth and eyes. "Then what happened to it?"

Everyone was staring at him, now. Mike could feel it. They were waiting, just waiting. He shoved his hands into his pockets and attempted a shrug. "It wasn't like that when I packed it."

Jonas' stare hardened, turned to metal. "No? Then how did it get this way?"

"We went over some fucking rough roads," Mike said, but all of his piss and vinegar had evaporated.

"Yeah right," Brig said. "Huge pothole, big enough to bounce the case so hard, even the padding couldn't protect it. Such a big bounce that we slept right through it, too, I guess." Brig hadn't been able to come up with another good explanation, much as he'd tried, and now he was pissed at Mike. Pissed because maybe Mike was lying. Pissed because he couldn't come up with a way to defend his friend. That was Mike's fault, too, damn it. He could only stick up for him so many times before it stopped working.

Before he stopped wanting to.

Mike jerked his head in the direction of James. "Are you gonna believe this pansy over me?"

Brig only stared back at the other man. He didn't know if he believed in James, but he was thinking that he couldn't believe in Mike ever again. This registered in his eyes, and Mike shrank away from it, his attention shifting to his feet.

Brig looked so disappointed in him that it hurt. Mike didn't like admitting hurt, not in front of everyone else.

James could not contain his smug smile. He felt not one shred of guilt over the drama that was unfolding. Indeed, he was somewhat amused. After all, the American had insisted that he prove himself, and so he had.

"It wouldn't be the first time you fucked up," Zoe said, sure that Mike had broken the camera. She would have been certain with or without James bringing it to their attention sooner than they would have discovered it otherwise.

"You shut up," Mike hissed, like the cornered snake he was.

"No. *You* shut up," Jonas said while he rose, and the shroud attempting to cover his irritation flew away. "Everyone just shut up and chill out." He fired a glare at Mike. "You should have told me."

Mike decided that staring at the mansion was better than looking his closest friend in the eyes. He couldn't believe that

Jonas was buying this. That everyone seemed to be buying this psychic crap. But then again, he couldn't offer a better explanation, so he did just what Jonas said. He shut up. His teeth were grinding themselves flat, but he shut up.

Jonas, for his part, decided that they'd already made fools enough of themselves in front of Mr. Trussart, so he let it drop. He figured he'd speak to Mike alone, later. He'd remind him how much that damn camera cost. He'd remind him that they'd been friends for a long time. Remind him how they used to be able to talk and that he'd given him chance after chance. So many chances because they had been friends the longest.

But Jonas was more than beginning to think he'd given Mike his last chance as he returned his attention to James.

"Well. We're not hiding any warts from you, I guess," he said. Mr. Trussart's display hadn't converted Jonas into a true believer, but he couldn't deny the evidence staring him in the face, or that Mike had guilt written all over him. Mike shoving his hands into his pockets before was a sure sign that he was lying. *Not to mention he couldn't look me in the eye.*

James refrained from smiling when he met the other man's gaze. He felt Jonas to be a kind person, and regretted the tension emanating now, the tension between Jonas and Mike. "I shan't speak another word which does not pertain to ghosts and this investigation," he said.

"Hey, it's not your fault," Aaron offered. "Mike pushed. Maybe he learned his lesson." With that, Aaron made a retreat towards the other van. He didn't feel like dragging the subject out. He had nothing more to say about it. "Think I'll get back to unloading, make myself useful."

Brig cleared his throat and rubbed the back of his head. "I'll help you." He took off after Aaron, grateful that someone had ended the scene before he said something shitty to Mike. *This is so not how I pictured this trip, all fucked up already.*

Zoe watched them go and then watched Mike walk down the drive with a scowl on his face, digging out another cigarette as he went. She shifted her attention to Jonas and James.

"We have another thermal. It'll be fine." She hoped her expression was as reassuring as she'd tried to sound.

"Big house," Jonas said, half to himself.

"Well…" Her hand had nearly drifted to James' shoulder before she put a stop to the casual habit. She decided it didn't seem safe, being casual around James. "He may not be able to record things, but if he can see things, then we'll keep the thermal person paired with James." Her gaze found the Brit's eyes. They were pretty, she thought. Pretty, if distant in some way. "If that's okay with you."

"As long as Mike isn't the one in charge of the thermal," James acquiesced, the slow curve of his lips working to ease the remaining tension. "I rather think that he won't appreciate my company, in any event." As he had hoped, his remaining companions laughed.

"I know our first impression wasn't too great, but we're not that stupid, I promise," Zoe said, a sheepish expression on her face. "There's no way we'd pair Mike with you."

"Not to worry, I didn't think that you were stupid, my dear," James said, a fuller smile growing on his face.

Jonas discovered a smile of his own. "At least you're being cool about it. I really am sorry he was such a jerk to you. It's completely unprofessional."

No shit. Zoe wished she could fire Mike herself. But she felt sorry for Jonas. She thought that this might have been the last straw. She suddenly felt a bit bad for Mike. He deserved it, but it sucked. They'd been friends. If he'd just come clean, ask for help, it would be different. She was sure he needed help with something, the way he'd been behaving.

James gave off a light shrug. "It isn't the first time. I should think it won't be the last." He lowered his eyes. His gaze absorbed the case on the ground. "Now, might you tell me more about your equipment? I'm terribly curious."

Zoe liked that idea. Forget the bad scene, and forget Mike. "Yeah, we should brief him, Jonas."

"Sure. It'll give us something to do until Mr. Smith shows up," Jonas said.

James nearly voiced his opinion that Mr. Smith would not show his face. He decided to hold onto that thought just a while longer. Perhaps long enough that the others would voice it first.

7

"Heh heh…about as expected. And right on schedule, so far. I do appreciate promptness."

8

James stood in the tall weeds, for the moment oblivious to the beetle inching up his trousers, and watched the Americans unpack and haul their equipment into the mansion. He had offered to help, but Jonas had informed him that they had a system they could execute in their sleep, having done this together several times. James was relieved at this. Not for laziness, but because he didn't wish to muck something up and gain anyone else's ire.

The Americans were setting up their equipment because, just as James had surmised, Mr. Smith wasn't joining them. He had phoned Jonas with his apologies and instructions to carry on. James had noted that Zoe seemed the most bothered by this turn of events, not that she was surprised.

Regardless, it looked like they were all in it for the night. They'd come all this way, why turn back now? To that end, James waited for the sign it was time to begin.

Jonas had informed him that he was welcome to try a K-II meter during the night. They used them to detect electro-magnetic energy in the air. James had politely replied that he would observe as someone else handled it, voicing that he himself was a walking K-II meter, which had brought a rather warm laugh from Jonas. He knew that the team leader wasn't one-hundred-percent converted, but James did not begrudge this. After all, so far, they'd only seen a tiny slice of what he could do.

Jonas had also offered the use of a slim digital audio recorder, used for what they called EVPs, or Electronic Voice Phenomenon. The recorders could pick up sounds which often escaped human hearing. James had heard such recordings. But this too he had no need of, as he could hear the voices without aid of a device, usually. He had informed the other man that if he could help by collecting hard evidence, he would, but if there were not enough recorders to go around, this was fine.

Conversation of equipment between James and Jonas had come to a halt after this.

James studied the estate as the one called Brig, muscular in a way Jonas wasn't (which not even his brown sweater could camouflage), carried a folding table up to the veranda. It was for the control center in the front room they were setting up, where their computers would show continuous feeds of the night vision cameras they were placing throughout the house. There would not be enough to cover every room, not by far. Often they had their control center outside in a van, but the estate was large, and so they had decided they wanted everyone inside.

James left off watching Brig when Mike joined the body builder on the veranda, and he studied instead the steeple rooftops, thinking that they were the sturdiest parts of the structure. They weren't as weathered as the rest of the house, which caused part of its strangeness. He noted that some of the windows retained glass, dirty glass with a few cracks, and that someone had boarded over the other windows.

As he studied the red-ochre bricks below the middle steeple, he realized it looked as if there had been a fire. It seemed to him, even in the dimming light, that soot clung to the wild ivy that leached from the house, and to the bricks gasping for air beneath it. Mr. Smith had not mentioned this, but then perhaps James was mistaken. He hoped to check this room once he was inside, to satisfy his curiosity.

Before his thoughts could go much further, and before he could focus on the strange sensation that he had first felt through his feet earlier, which was now returning, Aaron approached him. It was then that James brushed the black beetle from his knee.

"Hey." Aaron offered James a smile, which James couldn't help returning. "I was just going to tell you there was something on you." Aaron gestured to the retreating insect. "Anyway, you looked lonely over here."

"Please do not take offense if I say that I wasn't."

Aaron stood expressionless a second before chuckling. He didn't know what else to do. "I can leave."

James replied with a shake of his head. "There is no need."

"Well, I wouldn't blame you if you wanted to stay far away from us," Aaron said.

"I believe it's best to stay away from Mike," James leaned in a bit, yet still out of touching distance, "but thus far, I don't mind the rest of you."

This brought a full, genuine laugh to Aaron, but then his face smoothed once again. "He didn't used to be that way."

James contemplated the tall man's angular features, his green eyes. He said nothing in response to Aaron's comment, nor to the fact he knew that Aaron was about to divert the conversation away from Mike, if only slightly.

"Anyway." Aaron jerked a thumb towards the driveway. "Can I ask how you did that back there?"

With a lift of his brows James inquired, "Did what?"

"How did you know about the camera?"

"Oh, yes." James' expression was congenial. "That."

Aaron said nothing, waiting.

"I could feel that he was hiding something," James continued.

"But can you literally read minds?" Aaron couldn't help asking. He wondered if Mike had been thinking about the camera specifically, or something along those lines.

"No, not precisely," James answered. "Once I said that he was hiding something, the... vibe, shall we say?" James agreed with himself by way of a nod. "The vibration grew stronger, because he then began to dwell more upon his guilt."

Aaron's gaze bounced between James' eyes. "How did that lead you to the van, then?"

Once again, James contemplated Aaron. His questions were borne of genuine interest, he surmised, and he relaxed a bit more.

"His signature – energy signature – was on the van," James explained. "It was more easily ascertained as I stood in his presence." He almost shrugged. "His thoughts, again as energy to me, were bent upon the case. I followed, essentially, the warmest trail. The strongest trail. My focus was upon that one trail."

Aaron's fascination would have been evident to anyone, then, by the turn of his body, the seeming spark in the verdant gaze. Still a cautious skeptic, but he was fascinated all the same. It didn't seem to him that James was fibbing.

"How did you know for certain he dropped it?" he asked James.

"When I touched the case I glimpsed the residual of it happening."

"Is it like a section of film, or something? You mentioned things he supposedly said, too."

"Do you believe me, Aaron?" the Brit inquired. He wanted to hear the other man say it, even if he could sense the answer.

Aaron didn't hesitate. "Well. I think Mike acted guilty after your display. I know him well enough to say that."

James lifted a brow, as if signaling Aaron to continue, and the sandy-haired man obliged.

"I can't explain away what happened. He acted guilty, the camera was broken just like you said, and I don't know how you could have known that beforehand. This was the first time we all met. So unless you broke into our vans back in town…" Laughter percolated in his throat. "Which I suppose you could've, but I doubt it."

James found his next smile easily enough. "No, I did not. I had hoped to run into the lot of you before coming here, but it wasn't to be."

Aaron had hoped the same. "So, you knew what he said because the vision came with sound?"

James confirmed this by way of a nod. "In my head, at any rate. So to speak. The way you hear your own little voice. Not literally every word, mind you, but the sentiment was there."

"Yeah, well. That did sound like Mike." Aaron's mouth began to grow a grin. "That's kind of cool, actually."

A sigh escaped James. "Not always so, mmm, cool."

"When isn't it?" Aaron's grin grew still more.

"Frankly," James spread his hands, "one doesn't truly need or wish to know everything a lover might be thinking and picturing, for example."

Aaron's grin reversed itself. Not because of the other man's words, but because he'd just been thinking that James was very nice to look at. And he'd been thinking something along the lines of what James had just brought up and now wondered if James knew it. He glanced at the tree behind James with a nervous half-laugh.

"I suppose not," he said.

James, who had been gazing at Aaron in silence the entire time, felt something click in his own brain. He felt his face grow a bit warm with the full realization of what he'd said to the lanky man.

"Sometimes one's brain merely dumps random images. It's not as if a person acts on or even believes everything that crosses their minds," James said, attempting to divert the subject while also clarifying it. "It creates confusion, seeing too much."

Aaron studied a few stray needles from the tree. "Not really a fair advantage, either."

James averted his eyes as the other man looked back at him, and he opted for a complete change of subject.

"This yew is surely several hundreds of years old."

Aaron was grateful for the shift. Things had gotten uncomfortable for a moment. "Is that what these are?"

"Yes. I wouldn't suppose you'd seen them in Seattle. There are fewer in America, and not quite like this, as I understand it."

Aaron thought about it and shook his head. "No. I haven't seen trees like these before." He found James' eyes, and having regained his cool, rather liked it when James didn't look away. "Adds to the mystery of the place."

"Indeed." James clasped his hands behind his back, somewhat surprised to feel bark graze his fingers. "As does Mr. Smith's not joining us, I should say."

"I guess he was pretty sick." Aaron lifted and dropped one of his shoulders. He assumed his companion's slight retreat was due to his being a Sensitive. "We'll show him any evidence we collect later. Normal procedure. It's just that we usually get a tour from the owner before we start." Aaron's green gaze shifted from James to the heavy front door of the house as Brig came out through it. "He filled us in on all the stories, though."

James merely nodded once again. He did not believe that Mr. Smith was ill, regardless of what the man had said when he phoned them. Perhaps he was agoraphobic. Somehow, James didn't believe that either.

"Well," Aaron glanced at his new friend – or hopefully new friend. "I'd better get back to work. I *am* supposed to be the tech guy, after all."

"By all means, don't allow me to detain you."

James watched as the tall man debated speaking again and chose not to, then turned and took long strides towards the mansion. When he was alone, James' chin dipped with the smile that hinted at his lips. He'd certainly been quite right about yet another thing he'd sensed when first feeling out the strangers.

9

"The cameras are all set up," said Aaron from his crouch by a brand new wall socket. He was finished with his task of taping down electrical cords. It wasn't just that they were easy to trip on; it was that when someone tripped on them, they tended to bring equipment down with them. The last thing they needed (especially Jonas) was more broken equipment.

"How many?" Jonas asked.

"All of 'em," Mike replied as he flicked on a laptop.

"Okay, that's seven." Brig panted as he entered the room. He'd been hoofing things up and down stairways. Too many steps. "Not much for a place this size."

"A lot more cameras than we ever expected to have, though," Zoe said. She studied what was left of the grand old furniture, which was now moth ridden, moldy, and covered in dust, though much appeared sturdy enough. Not versed in antiques, she couldn't name the pieces, but understanding that they were antiques caused her to reconsider sitting on any of the chairs in the event she *did* break them and catch hell over it.

All she knew was that they must be Victorian or something.

Mike paused in picking and sucking at his teeth. A habit that drove most of the others crazy, but they had always accepted it, because that's what friends did.

"Too bad Mr. Money Bags didn't offer to get us some more cameras," he said and sucked on his teeth some more. *Sssrrrp ssssrrrp.*

"You sound like a damn…cat-fricking-fish, or something," Jonas said. "Anyway. We've got what we've got." He looked over command central, such as it was, there on the table. "We'll just have to cover a lot of ground walking."

Aaron straightened and rose to his full 6'4" height. "At least we have floor plans. Too late to whine about stuff; it's getting dark. We ready?"

Zoe and Mike nodded, while Brig said, "Hell yeah."

"I suppose someone should go get the circus freak," Mike said. Jonas cast a glare at him for that. A look that warned Mike that he was on very thin ice already.

"I'll go get James," offered Aaron.

"There's no need," came a pleasant voice from the direction of the front door. "The *circus freak* is present."

Jonas threw another glare, complete with daggers, in Mike's direction, which Mike didn't see because he was too busy pretending that the snotty English fag didn't exist. Jonas said nothing. He had decided that it was best to ignore the comments. Otherwise, there might be a repeat of the kiddy show from earlier.

James, meanwhile, appeared oblivious to this as his eyes moved about the grand salon. To him, it felt as if the room – the entire mansion – were holding its breath in expectation. She was unnervingly quiet, Grimalkin Manor. No rustling skirts, no whispered promises, not even a soft-as-mink batting of a lash.

He then shifted his full attention to the Americans, who were currently too caught up in their own affairs to notice the strange, pregnant pause of the house and its utter, deceptive silence. He rather envied them this.

Jonas, who'd been watching James when James wasn't watching him, shifted into boss-mode.

"All right," he said. "Brig and Zoe, you pair off and start with the second floor."

Zoe's shoulders sagged. She had wanted to team up with Jonas.

"Mike and I," their leader continued, "will check this floor, first."

Zoe scolded herself when she realized that Jonas probably wanted to have a talk with Mike before the night really got going. This was a good thing. She just hoped that she and the others wouldn't have to pry them apart before it was finished.

James turned his gaze to Aaron. "It would seem that this leaves you and me." He knew that Aaron didn't mind this arrangement, and truthfully, James preferred the idea of spending time with Aaron to spending time with the others just yet. "Where shall we begin?" he asked Jonas.

"Why don't you go where your senses lead you? I'm giving Aaron first shot with the thermal. If you see or feel anything, he can contact us on the talkies."

"Just stay outta our way," Mike mumbled.

James ignored this, nodding his agreement with Jonas, who was certainly far more accommodating than his sidekick was when it came to believing in James' psychic gifts.

Aaron ignored the comment, too, and stopped himself just short of nudging the Londoner. "Hear that? We get the thermal first. Sweet."

James could not help the chuckle brought on by the other man's enthusiasm. Collaborating with him was becoming an even better prospect by the second.

"Whelp." Jonas grinned, something the rest of his American team hoped to see more of. The anticipation of a good hunt improved his mood exponentially. "Rest of the lights out?"

"Yeah, I'll start blowing out the candles." Brig's rough chuckle trailed after him as he set off to do just that. There were a handful of new outlets that worked, but for the most part, the old mansion was as one would expect, maybe even hope for.

Truly "old fashioned".

"Good thing Smith had already started sorting out electrical in this place," Aaron said. "Much easier on the battery budget this way."

"No shit," said Zoe. "And we don't need a generator. Hey, Brig, wait up!"

Jonas' voice boomed after them. "Don't trip over your own feet!" Laughing, he turned to Aaron. "Everyone seems really into this. Cool." He approached Mike, who cast him a wary look. "Let's get on it, man."

Mike made a show of checking and rechecking his gear and then at last trailed after his fearless leader.

After they'd left the room, Aaron turned to his remaining companion. "Don't be surprised if the first scream you hear tonight is human." When nothing but silence met his comment, Aaron attempted to conceal his disappointment. *That joke fell flat.*

He had no way of knowing that James' silence and the distant half smile on James' face that he mistook for a polite – if possibly condescending – way of acknowledging the joke, were actually reactions to private thoughts.

10

The large old kitchen was where Jonas had decided that he and Mike would begin, and it was in some way creepier than what they'd seen of the house so far. But that didn't bother Jonas. He wasn't afraid of houses or ghosts. He was intensely curious, and that trumped fear. Not to mention, nothing had ever come close to being as disconcerting as the encounter in his teens. The thing that had set him on his current path of ghost hunting: a barn, a wheezing series of breaths, and the feeling that something or someone wanted to strangle him. Much more disconcerting.

Still. The room was a bit off-kilter, which in turn would make most people feel strange, and it had an effect on Jonas, or at least his equilibrium.

Mike moved his flashlight beam around the kitchen. He couldn't decide if seeing it in artificial snips of light was worse than it would be during the day, where a person could easily see the crooked crown molding, the battered wainscoting, and the rotting shelves. Shelves which appeared upon closer inspection to be decorated with rat droppings.

"Nice," Mike said under his breath.

"Huh?" Jonas said.

"Just rat shit."

"Oh, yeah. Nice, clean place, isn't it." Jonas turned his attention back to the rust edged sink. There was one window over it, which at one time had been responsible for brightening up the place. But a large slab of wood nailed over it had obliterated all hope of light. Even moonlight.

"So things supposedly move around in here, huh?" asked Mike.

Jonas trained his flashlight on a cast iron pot that perched on the old gas stove, minding its own business. "One of the places," he said.

"What kinda stuff?"

"Did you pay *any* attention when we were talking about this before?"

"Just making conversation, dude." Mike's stomach tightened with the sharp understanding that Jonas was well and truly upset. He wouldn't even talk about the case, which was a very bad sign.

Jonas' eyes paused to roll before recommencing their study of the darkened room. His patience was a bit thin where it concerned Mike. He reminded himself that he was on a job and should be professional. He stilled for a moment and took a deep, relaxing breath.

"There are reports of things moving around the stove, mostly," Jonas said.

"So, someone still likes to hang out and cook," Mike said to fill the following tense silence. He turned on his recorder. "Mike and Jonas, kitchen EVP session," he said into the device. "If there's anyone here, could you give us a sign? Make a noise or say something, maybe?"

Jonas held his tongue firmly in place while Mike attempted to collect EVPs. He wanted to have a talk with him, but they were also here to investigate, and damned if Mike wasn't jumping right on it. *Trying to impress me and make up for before, no doubt.*

"Is there anyone here with us?" Mike paused. "Is there anything you'd like to tell us?" He remained motionless. As he listened, he also thought about how much trouble he'd wrangled for himself. The tension was thick enough to slice with a machete, and ghosts weren't the source.

Mike hit the stop button on his recorder. "Listen, Jonas, I'm sorry – "

"No excuses this time, Mike." Jonas flicked his flashlight beam over Mike's falling expression. "Right now I can't care if your personal life is a mess. You're letting it interfere with professional stuff." He shook his head. "That crap outside earlier, and *man* – my *camera*."

Mike, cloaked again in darkness, appeared contrite, but in his eyes, there was also hurt. His friend couldn't see this, but maybe he felt it.

"I care that you're messing up your life, because I'm your friend," said Jonas. "But you're bringing us all down, and you're distracted all the time. So right *now*, I don't care *why*. You'd better straighten it up for tonight and get it right."

Mike's heart sank to his stomach. He'd kept telling himself that Jonas wouldn't do it, but he knew that was a fantasy. This was it. "You're dumping me after this one, aren't you?"

"Interesting choice of word," Jonas said, peering at him through the minute shadows the flashlight beams cast. "I can't subject everyone to *your* dumping anymore, Mike. I can't take it anymore, either."

Deep down, Mike knew that Jonas was right. Deep down, he felt bad. But he was also disappointed, because he was losing the one good thing left in his life.

"I hope you straighten yourself out," Jonas continued, gentleness finding a place in his voice, at last. "I really do. I'm *letting* you go, so that maybe you'll do that."

Deep down, Mike knew that it was his own fault.

"Yeah." Mike nodded and filled his lungs, letting the air go in a long sigh. "I swear I'll be by the book tonight. And I'll figure out a way to pay for the thermal."

Jonas didn't reply.

"I swear," Mike repeated.

"Yeah, but you can't pay me back for lying, now can you?" Jonas said in a hushed tone. "That's what really sucks. It's not the first time, either."

Mike's eyes squeezed shut and his finger found the recorder's on switch, because he didn't know how to respond in a way that wouldn't come out sounding like an excuse. "If there's anyone in here with us – "

"Shh," Jonas shined his light in the direction of the pantry. "Hear that?"

Mike's ears pricked, his head cocking as he strained for a sound.

Thumpthump

"Yeah," he whispered.

Jonas' large feet managed stealthy steps in that direction, K-II meter in one hand, trusty flashlight in the other. "I'm not getting anything on here, yet."

Thump

"There it is again." Mike moved closer, holding his recorder out in front of himself. "Definitely coming from the pantry."

Jonas' head bobbed. He shoved the small flashlight into his pocket and reached for the door's handle. His hand froze mid-reach when his K-II meter lights flickered. "See that?"

"Yeah," Mike answered in an even more hushed tone than before.

Jonas slowly panned the meter around the door's frame. "I got nothing, now."

"Wait, shh." Mike put a finger to his own lips. After a moment, he turned to his partner. "Did you hear *that*?"

"I didn't hear anything, that time." Jonas edged his meter towards the round knob of a handle. The meter lights danced a spastic dance. "Whoa, okay, that's interesting," he muttered to himself, then spoke to Mike. "What did you hear?"

"Sounded like a whisper, maybe. Barely heard it, so I don't know, really." Mike's ears were still straining to find another sound.

"We'll see if there's anything on your recorder later." Jonas resumed his bid to open the door and did so cautiously, out of habit. A habitual need of not scaring off any possible entities, or having things fall on them or jump out, like an animal. It had happened before.

He handed Mike the K-II meter and retrieved his flashlight to shine the beam into the supposedly empty, grime-laden pantry.

~

They were in a small, square room in the second story, large enough for a single bed, an armoire, and perhaps a chair, though no such furniture remained. Upon shining a light across the floor, one could almost see where such furnishings might have sat, as if sun had bleached the boards in some spots.

There was one boarded-over window, which would have looked out onto the front lawn, could they peer through it. The floor was hardwood and covered in thick layers of dust, save for a ratty rectangle in the middle of the room that once passed for a decorative rug. The cast of the flashlights brought harshness to its former deep-wine hue, which complimented well enough the cat-piss-colored walls. Blessedly, thought Zoe, it didn't smell like cat piss. The room smelled as she expected; old, musty, dusty, forgotten – and moldy. There was definitely an underlying eau de mold.

She sneezed. She sneezed again.

"Bless you annnd bless you," said Brig.

"Thanks." She let her eyes travel around the room once more. It offered little but cobwebs and shadows.

Zoe gave that up and illuminated the floor plans she'd dug out of her pocket. "What's this, bedroom seven on the list of rooms?" She lifted her eyes to find Brig's dark outline. "Huge place."

"Yeah. It's totally cool." He commenced studying the fireplace, of which the house had several. "It's almost got a funhouse effect, too, did you notice? The foundation's settled a lot."

Zoe, having refolded the paper and shoved it back into her pocket, directed her beam towards the boarded-over window. "Do you think it feels creepy in here?"

Brig's laugh was soft as cotton, no trace of mockery that Zoe could hear. "This whole mansion is kind of creepy," he said. "Just like I said, the funhouse effect. I'm wondering if they even used stuff like levels when they built it, actually."

"Yeah, but that's not what I mean." She rubbed the hand not grasping the small light over her arm, feeling the tiny hairs there prickling under her jacket. "I think it feels sort of heavy in here, you know?"

"I do know." Brig squatted, training his beam on the still-ashy fire dogs in the small fireplace. "I think this is the room the girl died in, according to the stories."

"Which girl? There was more than one." Zoe just refrained from hugging herself. She was the only female in the group, and she prided herself on not being a wilting flower. Normally, she wasn't.

"Oh. Uh, crap, so many rooms. The teen, I think. Yeah." Brig was trying to look up the chimney, since Smith had told them odd things sometimes occurred around the fireplaces. Things like strange mists, orbs, and objects tumbling down to land in roaring fires.

This time, Zoe's arms found themselves wrapped around her body. Since they were already there, she gave in and hugged herself. "Horrible way to die."

Even Brig shuddered. "Yeah. Burning alive, that's got to be some scary shit."

"Especially when someone else lit you with an oil lamp," she whispered. "I can't imagine. Her own *mother*. Wonder if anyone knows why."

"Pretty jacked up," Brig said. "Maybe dead women tell tales."

Zoe attempted to process the dull shadows in the room, to little avail. She couldn't seem to center herself, to get a fix on any one thing. "There's a lot of violent history connected to this place, so reports of poltergeist activity make sense. It should feel even heavier, when you think about it." Not, she thought, that she wanted it to.

"No shit. Ew!"

Zoe's body jumped with her nerves and she whirled around after Brig's sudden exclamation. "What?"

"Filthy." He stood up, hand flitting around his face as if flies were swarming. "Cobwebs, soot, you know, all that crap."

Not wanting to admit aloud that she was relieved, Zoe said, "That's what you get for sticking your face up there."

"Ha, ha. Yeah, I know." He studied the scarred wood of the mantle and began snapping a few pictures after deciding the dust from his explorations had settled. "I should've found a way up to the roof before we started on the inside. I don't know if the chimneys are screened to keep crap from clogging them."

"Could explain the objects falling, if they aren't." Zoe cat-pawed her way around the edge of the room, stopping to study what looked like a stain on the wall adjacent to the window. Her free hand drifted to her jacket pocket, reaching for her own camera.

"I'll look in the morning," Brig replied, satisfied with that assessment. "Pretty weird to have dolls falling down chimneys though, screens or not." Another round of camera flashes temporarily dotted the dark room.

"Weird, yes." The amorphous stain pulled more strongly at Zoe's attention the closer to it she came. Her camera clutched in one hand, flashlight in the other, she drifted a bit nearer to it still. "Kids playing games, maybe."

"Maybe. Supposedly no one was ever on the roof." He lit Zoe up with his flashlight. "That anyone knows of, anyway. There are a lot of reports on the fireplaces."

"Uh huh…" The stain. The large, bleeding stain. Something about it was hypnotic, and her camera was all but forgotten, along with its purpose.

"What's that?" Brig asked as he made his way to her. When she didn't reply, he said, "Water stain?" When she still didn't reply, he shined his light right in her face, casting her in stark relief. "Yo, Earth to Zoe."

~

The hall they were in seemed to go on forever, though it was only an illusion. Dark and narrow, meeting doors that were even darker, it played tricks on the eye. It tricked the mind and senses with a feeling of being closed in on. It could make a claustrophobic out of the most well adjusted person. At least, this is what Aaron was thinking as he crept along. He noted how silent it was, as well. As if they were in an Egyptian tomb. Not that he'd ever been in one, but he imagined it would be this quiet. Aaron's mind left off that idea when he spied the room at the end of the hall, which merged with a set of stairs. Somehow that still didn't break up the closed in feeling, but Aaron no longer dwelled on that, either.

"This is a first," Aaron said as he crossed into the small room at the end of the landing. "We've never investigated a house with its own chapel before."

James trailed in after him, not having said much during their investigation thus far. Once inside, he moved left as Aaron moved right – Aaron keeping his eyes on the video screen of the FLIR B300 infrared thermal imaging camera. A swift thought ran through Aaron's head: this thermal and its twin had cost them several grand alone. He was surprised that Jonas hadn't gone off worse than he did when the other turned up broken.

He'd saved and saved for the equipment. Aaron wondered if down there, in that big kitchen, Jonas was chewing Mike up and spitting him out.

Aaron's attention returned to his partner as he felt James' presence in the narrow chapel.

"Private chapels. Less common in America, perhaps," James said. "Insomuch as your structures are considerably younger. Many castles have such."

Aaron laughed. "True. I haven't been to any real castles, either."

"This is something you should rectify, should you have the chance." James took to gazing at the dirty stained-glass window, surmising it had once been a breathtaking study in green, blue, rose, yellow and red; these seemed the general colors of the thing, dulled beneath all of the grime. It was difficult for the moonlight to penetrate, but knowing history as he did, he felt confident those were likely colors, even if he had also decided there was something off about the house. For its supposed vintage, the décor, or what was left of it, didn't add up.

Not that James could put his finger on the exact number that mucked up the sum. It just didn't add up, period. It seemed almost a mock up of what someone *thought* it should look like.

"One day I will," replied Aaron, panning his device about, looking to see if the sensors picked up any unusual cold or hot spots. "We'll have to keep in touch. Then you can tell me the best places to go when I'm ready."

A laugh tiptoed its way to Aaron's ears. It came from the Englishman.

Aaron wasn't certain of the meaning behind that laugh, and so remained focused on his screen, which is what he was supposed to focus on, anyway.

"Do you always investigate at night; always plunge a structure into darkness?" James queried.

"Yes." Aaron decided that the change in subject might be a hint as to what that laugh had meant just before. "It seems like most activity takes place at night, and some of our equipment is best used at night, as you see. Plus, it's generally quieter."

"But of course," James agreed, yet he added, "However, there is plentiful activity during daylight hours, I assure you."

"Oh, I'm sure there is. I know there is, yeah. People are just more prone to pick up on ghostly stuff at night." He couldn't help looking in James' direction. "You know, boogie men in the closet, covers pulled over your head."

A much freer laugh left James. "Yes, I do know."

Aaron dropped his eyes again, feeling a bit stupid, telling himself that yes, it was a stupid joke, and boy, talk about stating the obvious. "I haven't seen anything strange on the thermal, yet," he said, resuming professionalism.

"This is because there is nothing in here with us." Wide, near almond shaped eyes found the other man's form. "Yet."

Aaron considered these words for a time. James had drifted in a straight line to this area, and Aaron realized that he'd actually thought the Brit's senses were pulling him in a specific direction all along. Dark blond eyebrows ascended. James *had* said "yet".

"Do you think – feel – that something will? Join us, I mean," Aaron asked his co-investigator. Both hands on his thermal camera, using the screen to move around rather than interfere with the imaging using flashlights, Aaron did not see the tilting of James' head or the shifting of his striking eyes in the direction of the threshold.

"James?"

A quiet, so very quiet reply followed the speaking of his name. "A moment, please."

Aaron nodded and aimed the sensor in James' direction. His companion's heat signature flooded the small screen. Red, orange, yellow. He shifted it a bit so he could see James to the left, and the cooler blues, greens and grays of the doorway to the right.

"There is a voice," James offered, again so quietly that Aaron wasn't certain he'd heard him correctly, until James spoke again. "Far down the hallway there is a woman, and it is not Zoe."

Aaron had checked everyone's location via walkie-talkie moments earlier, and so did not feel the need to do it again. "Do you have one of the recorders?" Aaron took careful steps closer, attempting to get a read on the hall.

James reached into his coat pocket and produced the device. He found the on switch and pressed it.

"We should go that way," Aaron whispered.

"No need. She will come closer."

Aaron's pulse added a beat to its usual rhythm. Not in fear, but anticipation. "What's she saying?" He stopped himself just short of brushing against James as he vied for a spot by the door where he could more easily capture an image of anything coming towards them.

"Standard fair." Aaron puzzled at the man's following sigh, until James then clarified his previous statement. "*Get out.*"

Aaron just suppressed his laugh. Laughing didn't strike him as something his partner would appreciate just now. "We get EVPs like that all the time. Just like the movies," he said.

"They don't always appreciate being disturbed any more than you would appreciate it," James said. "Occasionally, they are attempting to warn you. It's more difficult for some to relay speech to this side; therefore short and often cryptic statements are what you receive."

Just as Aaron considered telling his companion he knew some ghosts disliked the disturbance, and that he had respect for the dead, he reminded himself that they should shut up and find out what was going on.

He had nothing on his thermal, yet.

"Tell her we're not here to hurt her and that we won't bother her if she wants us to leave," Aaron said.

"I would, however you just did it for me," James replied.

Aaron paused, remembering to give space on the recorder for any disembodied voices. He then asked, "What did she say to that? Anything?"

"She wishes to know what the strange contraption is that you're holding. *It* disturbs her."

Aaron's heart added another beat.

"It's not a weapon," James said into the hall. "It is a modern device, one that we might see you with, in a manner of speaking." A pause. "Yes, a very fancy camera, you might say." Another pause. "Oh, not to worry, you look lovely."

Aaron tore his eyes away from the screen and glanced at James. He was having a regular conversation with a ghost, was he? Aaron looked down the hall. He could not see a thing, not one thing. His eyes dropped again. Still nothing as far as temperature fluctuations.

Aaron knew that ghosts might not always register a temperature change, though often enough people talked about cold spots. But he'd probably be able to see this, he thought. He also knew that anything they'd caught on the thermal they hadn't been able to explain had usually given off heat.

Maybe the ghost wasn't manifesting and James was only hearing it, Aaron told himself. Yet he still felt a seed of disappointment growing inside him. It was possible James wasn't that gifted after all. It was possible James was a faker like others he'd met.

But then Aaron's neck hairs prickled when James took a sudden step back, interrupting those previous thoughts, causing them to flit away like hummingbirds.

11

"Oh shit!" Mike exclaimed and ran out of the pantry.

Jonas, managing not the drop the K-II meter when Mike clipped him as he rushed past, spun around. "What?" He shined his light in the direction of his freaked-out old friend. "What the heck, Mike?" Jonas asked again, while Mike jumped around like the floor was on fire, dumping his flashlight and recorder on the crooked kitchen table. Jonas could only stare as Mike's freed hands commenced flinging themselves all over his own body.

Jonas shot his beam back into the pantry and promptly burst out laughing. "Let me guess." He took a step back inside. *Uh huh, there it is. Hairy sucker.*

"Dude, you need to try and get some control over that phobia. You almost freaked *me* out," he turned and said to Mike.

"I freaking hate spiders, man, you know I do." Mike slapped at his hair, his actions spastic as ever.

Laughter still not able to quite taper off, Jonas' reply carried less weight than it should have. "And you nearly broke some more equipment. Calm down, dude. It's not even that big."

"Fucking spiders – why do there have to be spiders?"

"Look where you're at." Jonas grinned. "Probably a lot of them around here. Hell, a lot of the places we go there are. Probably even more in this place."

Mike's hands flew up in surrender. "Oh, thanks. I didn't need to hear that."

"Like you didn't know."

"I was trying not to think about it."

"Guess you'll be thinking about it the rest of the night, now."

Mike's response to that was an exasperated half grunt.

"Some ghost hunter you are." A smile shifted the bigger man's expression once more.

"Ghosts don't scare me, dude."

"Whelp. If there was anything else in here, I think you scared it away," Jonas said. "Or maybe the spider was doing the thumping before," he couldn't help but tease even more.

"That's it; can we check another room, now?' Mike asked.

Jonas chuckled, but on a dime, became very serious. "We both heard thumping, and the K-II spiked around that door."

Mike was already reaching for his equipment. "Right, got it. We should hang out a while and see if we hear it again." *Be a pro, Mike. Be a pro. You don't leave a room after apparent activity.*

Jonas' smile returned. "Don't worry. I won't make you go into the pantry again."

~

"Hey, Zoe, you okay?"

Zoe's lids fluttered a few times. "Huh?" Her head swiveled towards Brig. "Oh, yeah. Hey, does it feel colder in here to you?"

"Not really." He studied the stain. "You sure seemed interested in this. Have any idea what it is?" He aimed his camera and fired off a few shots at the spot.

Zoe's eyes returned to the harmless looking brown blob on

the wall, which now came to her through residual bright spots. "Looks like water damage." She squeezed her eyes shut. She blinked a few times.

"But from what? Is there plumbing up above or something?"

"I don't remember for sure. I'd have to look at the floor plans again." Zoe rubbed at an eye. "Warn me next time you're going to use the camera, okay?"

"Oh. Sorry. I will." Brig left off looking at the mottled rust-like mark on the wall and studied her. "You know, you were kind of gone there for a minute. Is something on your mind?"

The question puzzled Zoe. *What does he mean, gone?* Instead of asking him, she said, "Not really. Well, I wonder what's going to happen with Jonas and Mike, but that's about it."

"Babe, I think we know what's going to happen."

"I suppose we do, darn it. And it probably won't be pretty." Zoe hugged herself for a very different reason than before.

"Nope." Brig moved away and shined his light around the room, distracting himself more than ghost hunting. "Let's check out the room across the hall."

Zoe considered this. She then reconsidered. "Okay." Content as well as Brig to let the subject die for now, what with the bit of tension it stirred, she turned from the bubbled wallpaper and followed him out.

Behind her back the stain made a silent inhale and then sighed, as if disappointed by the loss of its potential playmate.

~

Aaron found that he'd taken an involuntary step back, but ever the pro when it most counted, he kept his equipment trained on the black hole of a hallway. The temperature had been reading consistently between 60 and 65 degrees with no strange spikes or dips.

Aaron's senses sharpened. He was naturally alert, which was something that made him good at his job. He was not only aware of his camera, but his surroundings, and he was very aware of James.

"What is it?" he asked.

James took another step. When Aaron glanced at him, he was certain James' head was shaking, and that it wasn't shaking in response to his query.

"James?"

"She doesn't want us here."

To Aaron, genuine fear seemed to wind itself through those words, which concerned him. James had appeared, after he'd spent a little time with him, a person not easily flustered. But maybe he'd been stereotyping the British reserve, the seemingly ingrained elegance of the man.

"Did she tell us to get out again?" Aaron's eyes shot back to the hall, desperate to see what it was that appeared to frighten Mr. Trussart.

Urgency bathed James' words to Aaron. "Back away from the door." Aaron reacted to this, backing away even as his eyes told him that nothing was there.

Nothing, yet Aaron felt a sliver of fear slice him all the same.

"James what's going on? Does she want to hurt us?" He was about to ask again, when James cried out. He felt the gooseflesh break across his skin even as he spun around to see James nearly tripping over himself to get away from the door.

No. James wasn't just getting away from the door. He was stumbling back as if something was after him. Right in front of him and bearing down on him. That previous slice to Aaron began to bleed real fear.

"Shit, James..." Aaron nearly dropped his camera, but he had the wherewithal, the instinct, to set it down in a fluid motion before moving in James' direction. Just as Aaron was about to reach him, the altar had stopped James' flight; his lower back pressed to it. As Aaron got closer, he could see that James' hands gripped the edges of it by his sides.

There was no other thought in Aaron's mind just then but to grab the man's shoulders and do something, anything, to help him, because up close, Aaron could see the gray-blue eyes rolling and the lithe body trembling; when he grabbed James, he could feel it, the tremor.

"What is it, what's wrong, what's she doing?" Aaron's heart was not thumping with excitement now. He was truly frightened. He was frightened for James.

What happened next took the tall, thin man more than a moment to digest.

Those eyes stopped rolling about in James' head.

The trembling became more of a shake.

The kind of shaking a body does when a person is laughing, yet trying not to.

James was laughing.

Aaron couldn't decide at first if James was laughing in that way people sometimes do when afraid, or if his brains were about to splat on the floor. He then couldn't decide if a ghost were making James lose his marbles, or if James was just crazy.

And then James looked Aaron right in the eyes.

"Never let it be said that I don't have a sense of humor. You should see your face. Better still, I can feel what you're feeling."

Aaron's mouth opened but nothing came out.

James laughed yet again.

"Oh…you…son of a *bitch*," Aaron sputtered. "You were *faking*?"

James had the decency to stop laughing, or so Aaron thought, when in truth it was the sudden surge of irritation in Aaron which stopped James' laughter.

"Forgive me," James said. "Please – remove your hands." The irritation he could handle. What he did not want was to see more than he should see, and he would if Aaron didn't let go. He would see things more easily, what with Aaron's natural guard having dropped due to the situation.

Aaron almost didn't let go. His fingers almost dug in harder, because in that moment, all he could think was *faker*. Yet as he looked into the other man's eyes, he saw something there that caused him to take his hands away from James' shoulders. What he saw also prompted him to say, "I really thought something was happening to you. You scared me."

After a light throat clearing, James confessed. "Yes, well. That was the idea." James gazed back into Aaron's eyes, thinking that he had been certain the other man wouldn't anger. The longer he gazed, the more he felt this to be true. Aaron wasn't angry. Aaron had been concerned, yes. His surprise, even irritation, was expected. Any moment now…

Aaron started to laugh. "Damn, you're good. You really had me going."

A lighter, pleasant laugh issued from James, drifting through the small room.

"Did you have this entire thing planned, or what?" Aaron asked, his irritation having fled. He could appreciate a good practical joke. He and his cohorts often pulled jokes on each other, and the more he thought about it, the more appreciative he was, having not expected the proper seeming Brit to be a trickster.

Aaron allowed himself another, smaller smile with the realization that James' joke might also mean he had a sense of humor about their skepticism regarding psychics.

"Yes. It is why I led you this way." A smile tip-toed its way across James' face. "I simply couldn't help myself, you were so dreadfully *eager* for something to happen."

"Oh, man." Aaron pointed a finger at the other man. "Maybe I was extra gullible, then."

"Ah, well." James gave off a light shrug. "Perhaps a bit, but gullible only because you are mistaken, obviously. I am not that stuffy."

Aaron couldn't have hidden the wide grin had he wanted to. "Yeah. My bad. You're definitely not. But you know what they say about the boy who cried wolf, right?"

James spread his hands. "I swear that should I behave in this manner again, it will be utterly sincere."

"Well now, I'm not looking for any real possessions," Aaron joked. "I *might* believe you if there's a next time. We'll see how the rest of the night goes." He offered James a full smile, which then wilted as he realized what he'd done. "Did I, uh, freak you out when I touched you?" *I'm just asking in case. Just in case he's legit.*

"Come now. What you mean to ask me is whether or not I felt or glimpsed something you'd rather I didn't."

Aaron rubbed the side of his own face. "Eh…yeah. That."

"No, and this is why I asked you to remove your hands, so that I wouldn't," James assured him.

Aaron nodded. "Uh, cool." He nodded once more. "Thanks. So uh, we should probably get back to real ghost hunting, now." It then registered how close he was still standing to the other man and he took an awkward couple of steps back. "Don't you think?"

"I rather suppose we ought."

"Right. I'll just grab the thermal."

Once Aaron turned, James allowed the mischievous smile to form on his face. Not only for what manner of thing Aaron might not want him to see, but also because he now had physical contact out of the way. He had known all along that Aaron would be the first to touch him and had decided he'd speed it along. It was often much better when he was well prepared and it happened in circumstances of his own making, after all.

Though it was also true that he had a sense of humor and delighted in his victory.

"You know…" of a sudden, Aaron turned back. "Churches kind of freak me out, really." James did not miss the gesture of embarrassment; Aaron's hand flitting up to push back hair which hadn't fallen into his eyes at all.

Nor did he miss the feeling.

He had, however, not gleaned this detail beforehand. This confession just made.

"Why is this?" James asked, quite curious.

James didn't miss Aaron's shrug. "It's kinda silly," the taller man said. The man's gesture hadn't shrugged off the weight of the feeling at all.

"Feelings aren't silly," James replied. "And it seems you wish to tell me, and so I will listen. I shan't even laugh, I swear it."

Aaron moved closer. People always said they wouldn't laugh. But he had a feeling that James meant it. Maybe James could promise such a thing and mean it because of his gifts, he thought; if he truly were that gifted.

"Well." Independent of his will, Aaron's hand smoothed his own shirt front. "When I was a kid, my parents were all about going to church, you know?" He drew a slow breath to continue when James didn't comment. "What I remember most is the devil this, the devil that, and a fiery hell of suffering. Heck, even the angels scared me. One wing always dipped in blood, you know? They were like…God's henchmen."

James nodded his understanding, his agreement.

"Scary stuff for a kid, don't you think?" Aaron asked, feeling a need for his companion to say something, anything. He needed the sound of another voice so his wouldn't seem so nude and alone in a room that felt as if it were also listening.

"Indeed," James said. "Even God is frightening to a child, dependent on how he is portrayed. It's difficult to believe in a God of love when he is portrayed as a vengeful, almighty punisher, who allows Satan his reign; for if he is omnipotent, then certainly he allows it."

Aaron felt a smile begin to form. "Yeah, exactly. And if you're not perfect, your daddy's gonna send you to hell. What the heck is that all about, you know?"

"Love should never be based in fear," James whispered, and Aaron peered at him through the remaining distance between them, which had lessened. When he'd taken the steps, Aaron didn't know. What he did know was that it seemed his words had struck something in his co-investigator.

"A real father loves you, imperfections and all. He doesn't threaten, he encourages. He does not bind you with lies and promises and…"

James' words came to an abrupt halt. Aaron knew very well then that he'd hit something, something deep, something personal. It was the first time he'd felt James had dropped the invisible wall between himself and everyone else – maybe not completely, but it had cracked.

But as good at feeling people out as Aaron was, he still couldn't read minds, and the darkness of the room made it more difficult to read the expressions on his companion's delicate face. He debated asking his next question, a very simple prompt, really, and came down on the side of risking it.

"And?"

The crack in James' wall sealed itself.

"You were telling me something," James said, shifting effortlessly back into the reserved and calm mode Aaron had associated with him from the beginning.

Aaron contemplated these words, but only for a few seconds, willing to make one more attempt. "Yes, but it sounds like maybe you need to say something, too."

"The subject was why you're uncomfortable in chapels, not my opinion of God."

Aaron dropped his gaze to his feet with a slight nod to himself. The subject was closed, dismissed, though he didn't feel dismissed. James had managed to say the words in a way that didn't sound rude. *Besides, why should I be offended?* He continued to study his shoes. *He doesn't know me; he doesn't want to talk about it. It just slipped out before, and that's all. Everyone slips.*

"I guess it stuck with me," Aaron said, lifting his eyes. "I still associate churches with sulfur and suffering and punishment, all that." And even though James had closed up shop on him, Aaron decided to make another confession. "Then there was the thing that happened when I was thirteen, and it's something that led me to do this. To become a paranormal investigator."

James, his features painted with curiosity, asked, "What happened?"

"I woke up in the middle of the night with some creature hovering over me."

The distance between them shortened more. Aaron found it easier to see into James' eyes, though his own feet hadn't moved this time, except to shift in place.

"What manner of creature did you think it was?" James inquired. "What was it doing?"

Aaron could feel his cheeks flushing and thanked the darkness. Then felt them flush a bit more when he remembered it might not matter, given the company he was in. But he'd already said it. In for a penny, in for a pound, is that how it went?

"Incubus," Aaron said. "I'd heard about them. Read about them. Some religious traditions mention them."

"Yes of course," James said. "I've studied demonology myself."

Aaron still felt warm with the thoughts running through his head, even though James was responding only to his words. It had been much easier to tell *Jonas* this story.

"Uh, well," Aaron began his awkward telling of the tale. "Anyway, it, he, whatever, was doing what you read about, I guess. I couldn't exactly see it well. It was a form even darker than the room, you know? It felt like a form." Aaron cleared a nonexistent obstacle from his throat. "There was that heavy feeling, like you can't move, all that, too. It was probably sleep paralysis, but I don't know. It went from nice to scary."

"How so?"

Aaron couldn't decide if it would be better for James to acknowledge the elephant in the room, or keep pretending it wasn't standing right there. *Anyone could probably tell why I'm being such a girl right now.* He'd shared this with Jonas in much more detail.

"I really thought it was going to kill me," Aaron said, skipping the rest. James knew what he was talking about; he didn't need to *say* it. "You know, suck the life right out of me. I started to feel like I couldn't breathe. Like I was choking."

"And then?"

"It vanished. Or I woke up. I don't know. I guess it still seemed real enough to me that I started looking for people who understood, or had it happen, maybe. It was great when I came across someone who said they'd had a similar experience and didn't just think I was a pervert with repressed sexual...stuff." Which maybe it was. Aaron knew all about this as well. He'd asked himself the same questions over and over again, in the years since. Especially why it was it'd been male, and not female. "So. I met other people with ghost stories. And here I am."

"Did it ever return?" James asked, searching the other man's face.

"No. But you know, we moved not long after that. So I always wondered if it was just something in the house. Not like some real demon." A self-effacing laugh left Aaron then, dissipating some of his awkwardness. "But then I'm still uncomfortable in churches, so some part of me must still think demons are real, I guess. That priest was pretty convincing."

"Such a thing, particularly at that age, leaves a strong impression," James said. "Add this to your religious upbringing; why, I'm not surprised that it attached itself to your subconscious, or even your conscious thoughts."

A smile bloomed on Aaron's face. "You really didn't laugh. Not once. I think that's the first time someone made that promise and kept it, at least around me. Even the first person that took me seriously still laughed during a few parts of the story."

A sudden smile found James as well. "This is not the strangest story I've ever heard, and you're by far not the strangest person in this room, sir; neither are you the strangest person I have ever met. In any case, 'strangeness' interests me; therefore, why should I laugh?" His features smoothed, and before Aaron could comment, James asked, "Tell me; are you also afraid of choking to this day? Losing your breath?"

"You really do read minds, don't you," was Aaron's reply. "Well, feelings. Whatever."

"I arrived at a logical enough conclusion," James assured him.

Aaron nodded. "Yeah, but..." he shrugged. "I don't know. Anyway, yeah. The idea of not being able to breathe still kinda freaks me out. I'd hate to die that way."

"I shouldn't think many people would enjoy it," James said. "So you see, you're still not the strangest person in the room." James paused, feeling an honest bit of regret, as he had been all through Aaron's halted telling of the story. "I apologize if my pulling your leg earlier caused undue discomfort. I didn't sense, before, that chapels in particular unnerved you."

"Oh, hey. I wasn't really thinking about it, so nothing for you to sense, right? At least not on that score."

"Mmm. I suppose not."

Aaron's head shook with James' comment. "I was concerned about you, and I was focused on the hunt before that. I don't freak every time I'm in a church. Mostly I just don't *like* them." Aaron laughed.

"Ah. Quite right, yes, I see."

A very different laugh found Aaron. "So what's so strange about you, anyway?"

Aaron's sincere question caused a bit of warmth in James' chest. "Oh, the stories I could tell." Yet James remembered well what happened when others, at first as sincere, had looked deeper; when he had allowed them past his shields.

"But you won't, will you," Aaron said.

James was close enough that Aaron could see the sharp arching of his brow. "Mmm." His brow relaxed. "No," said James.

"Well, all right." Aaron's chuckle was half-hearted. "We're supposed to be investigating, anyway."

"Right you are. Do let us carry on. Oh, and Aaron?"

"Yeah?" Aaron had already started to retrieve his equipment.

"If Satan exists, why would he punish sinners?" James said. "Surely they'd be his favorites." With that, he turned and left the chapel.

Aaron started laughing. A full, genuine laugh. He was still in the throes of it as they made their way back down the hall.

Back in the chapel, the altar shivered, as if missing the heat of James' body.

12

Slender fingertips tapped a methodical, staccato beat on the chair's arm. The long spindly digits lent rhythm to the tune his puckered mouth whistled. Kept good time, too.

Mr. Smith excelled at several things.

He was in a rather chipper mood, Mr. Smith, because the group was in the mansion even now, and they had tucked in for a night of surprises, or so he hoped. If not, it would all be a colossal waste of time.

But he felt confident that his experiment would bear fruit.

Smith was proud of himself for assembling such an interesting set of people. He did so like to pat himself on his humped back. He chuckled as he studied the photographs that sprawled across the table in front of him. To look at them, most wouldn't find them extraordinary, these people. One or two were pleasant enough, physically speaking, but he didn't care so much about that.

A person's worth was on the inside; that's what made him interesting. There inside the skull, in the gray matter, that intricate brain of his.

It could create so many illusions, convictions, and situations... So much to study, to sample.

Darkened, somewhat veiled eyes more closely studied the one called Aaron, a candid photo of him leaving a generic office building in his generic little city. Smith knew what room the boy had been in before exiting the building.

That young man was physically healthy but, deep down, troubled. Smith could glean many things from simply looking at a person, into their eyes, even in a photograph. Knowing where the lad had been made it easy to guess, of course, but a photograph didn't recite words spilled on a couch to a stranger-for-hire.

Did they use couches? he wondered. It seemed so movie-cliché. There was a pause in the tap-tapping as he considered it.

Ah, yes, they sometimes used couches. Just like stereotypes, some clichés were based in truth, and some fit to a T.

Aaron had a secret. But that wasn't what was most interesting; after all, everyone had secrets. His wasn't even the most fascinating secret.

But it served well for the purposes of this expedition.

Besides, Smith always enjoyed betting on how long the most innocent in a group would last.

13

The group reconvened in the main room, standing around command central. None of them had, so far, come across what they felt was paranormal activity. None of them had had a legitimate scare, not one connected to anything other than phobias and practical jokes.

Such was often the case on investigations. They were not glamorous, like the shows; they were mostly comprised of sitting around and wishing something would happen. And they always wanted something to happen, whether the client did or not.

Yes, they came to debunk common claims, but that was also in an effort to show that something else might exist. What every investigator wanted was that one piece of irrefutable evidence, the type that no one could deny. Proof that their own beliefs, experiences, weren't the stuff of fantasy. That they weren't alone, and perhaps, that there was some sort of immortality for humans, after all.

Or it could be as simple as proving one's sanity.

"Well, should we switch up teams?" Jonas asked. "Someone else want to use James' talents for a while, maybe?" His gaze sped to said person, his expression apologetic. "I didn't mean that like it sounded. Like you're some object to pass off. Sorry."

"Not to worry," James said. "I understood your meaning." He also understood that Mike still wanted nothing to do with him, which was fine. He would happily remain with Aaron. He might also stomach Zoe, and Brig seemed a nice enough man, but the Brit had a feeling that comfort would be difficult to find between him and Brig, if they were left alone together.

James didn't want to make the man feel awkward. He sensed that Brig was shy, even with other men.

"Ah, Zoe and I always end up together, anyway," Brig said, much to (not only) James' relief. "Why don't we just keep it the way it is? Unless someone objects."

Jonas glanced at the others. They all wore pleasant enough expressions, congenial masks. Not a one objected. He'd thought Mike would, if only to get away from the tension between them, but no. This suited Jonas. Maybe they *should* work in a frank, full discussion, later.

"Okay," Jonas said. "I know it hasn't been that long, yet, but if anyone needs a pee break, now's a good time to go out and grab a tree. Might not break again for a while."

"Or gee, squat over a ditch?" Zoe quipped, though she felt a little down. She still wasn't going to be alone with Jonas. But she hadn't wanted to complain. Besides, she liked being Brig's partner. It wasn't as if she couldn't speak to Jonas later. Or back home in Seattle. Plenty of time for that.

"I might pay to watch you manage that," Brig said.

"You would, you pervert." She offered him a wide smile and then headed for the front door. "If I catch any of you guys looking, I'll pee in your thermoses later."

"Think I'll grab a smoke," said Mike.

"Hell, may as well go find that tree," Aaron said. "Be right back."

James, now alone with Jonas, gazed at the big man, who turned his attention to one of the computer screens on the table, which were showing live feeds of four other areas in the house. He could feel James' silent contemplation of him. Without looking away from the monitor, Jonas said, "Thanks for before."

"Pardon?"

Jonas made himself look at the other man. "The thermal camera."

"Oh, yes, of course." James wasn't confident that the team leader was very grateful. Grateful it wasn't a secret he'd had to pry out of his *group*, perhaps. "You're welcome."

Jonas studied the feeds once more. "Would you mind watching these for a few minutes? I'm gonna get some batteries from the van."

"I don't mind at all," James said and moved closer to command central.

Jonas spared him a glance. "Thanks." He wasted no time making his way out, and James sank down into a small folding chair they'd brought along, his eyes on the computer screen, but his mind on something else entirely.

Such as the malignant silence. James was not accustomed to absolute silence. He couldn't remember a time in his life unaccompanied by a soundtrack of some sort.

Perhaps silence was overrated, after all. It was so odd, so disconcerting. He didn't know what to do with it. He found himself beginning to miss the dull roar of sensation.

Outside, Aaron stood by one of the old and horrible yew trees, watering its roots. The sound of a dry snap jerked him to attention.

"Don't piss all over yourself, there."

"Damn it." Aaron flicked a hand and wiped it on his jeans. "How about I just piss all over *you*, Mike?"

Mike blew out a puff of smoke. The night was savage in its darkness; the smoke could be smelled but not seen. There was not even an obvious moon in the sky to shed light on the situation or lighten the mood.

"So you're mad at me too," Mike said.

Finishing off with two shakes, Aaron zipped up and turned to Mike. "You mean besides being irritated that you snuck up on me?" He shrugged when Mike didn't retort. "Not really. I just don't understand what's up with you lately, dude."

"I just got shit goin' on, you know?"

"Shit going on. Everyone's got shit going on." Aaron folded his arms across his chest. Maybe he *was* angry. "But we try not to smear that shit all over the place like monkeys."

"Yeah, I know." Mike scraped out his cig against the bark of the tree. Aaron had the sudden thought that the tree didn't appreciate it. But if that were true, it probably didn't appreciate being urinated on, either.

"It's some fucked up shit," Mike said as he dropped the butt.

Aaron bent over to retrieve it, able to find it only because he'd watched it fall, close as he was. A flash of white and tan. "So talk to me. Can't help you if I don't know what it is." He held out the offensive trash.

"How do I know that didn't fall in your piss, man?"

"It's not wet, asshole," said Aaron.

At last, and with a grimace, Mike took the nicotine-stained filter and shoved it in his coat pocket. "Tree-hugging hippie."

"Whatever. It's just good manners, since it's not our property." He nudged Mike. "And you're stalling."

It was Mike's turn to fold his arms across chest.

Aaron stared at him a full minute, or so it felt. "You gonna spill, or not?" he said.

Mike shoved his hands down in his jean pockets and shuffled his feet.

"Dude," said Aaron. "If you can't tell me – us – who can you tell?"

Mike released a held breath. "That's just it. You guys are like family. My only family."

"All the more reason to tell us, if you can't tell anyone else."

Aaron wondered if he hadn't said the wrong thing, then. He hadn't meant to suggest no one else in the world gave a damn. Or to remind his friend that it was probably true.

"But I've totally fucked it up," Mike said.

"Ah, c'mon." Aaron patted his friend's shoulder. "It's not beyond repair."

Mike's head shook and shook. "I don't know, man. Jonas is kicking me off the team after this."

The taller man's brows shot up. "He said that?"

"Yeah. But it's okay. I mean, it's not *okay*, but I deserve it. I know I do." Mike made a show of stretching his arms, his back. "It's for the best. I need to get on with my life, anyway. He's doing me a favor. I can't hunt ghosts forever."

Aaron let his eyes wander over the area, for a moment lost for words, whereas Mike suddenly had an abundance. Putting on a not-so-brave show. Since there were no words waiting for Aaron in the ink-dark night, he looked back in his friend's direction.

"Well. It doesn't mean we can't keep in touch, you know," he said. "Doesn't mean we can't be friends, does it, Mike?"

"I dunno, man. I've got some stuff to straighten out, and…" Mike's words trailed off with a half-assed shrug.

"And what?" Aaron couldn't believe what he was hearing. Was Mike really going to give up the friendships, too? All of it?

Mike shuffled a bit more. "I gotta find a job and help my girl with some stuff. I'll be real busy for a while."

Aaron leaned close, studied Mike's downturned face, a pale flash in the otherwise light-devoid surroundings. He wasn't a mind reader, but he wasn't oblivious to body language and other, more subtle signs. He'd known Mike for a while. His co-investigator was full of crap; he knew that Mike wasn't telling him what was really going on. He wasn't telling him the truth of how he felt.

And he wasn't going to, for whatever reason. Trust issues, embarrassment, Aaron didn't know for sure, but Mike wasn't going to spill his beans any time soon. His posture was so tight that a crowbar would be necessary to pry out anything.

"Well, when you've got time, you can always give me a call," Aaron said, thinking that Mike was afraid. He was afraid that no one would have anything to do with him outside of ghost hunting, and maybe that it'd be too hard to be reminded all the time that he was no longer part of the group.

So Mike was going to dump them first. That's what Aaron surmised, anyway. He understood, even if he were wrong about Mike's feelings, because it's how he himself would feel if it were him. Probably he'd still try to be friends with everyone, but it would be difficult.

"Yeah, I might give you call sometime," Mike said. "I'll see how things go." He gazed into his partner's clear green eyes as long as he could stand and then turned to the tree, unzipping his pants. Not once did he look back while Aaron's feet softly trod through the browned grass and weeds.

Mike took his turn pissing against the tree trunk, still feeling angst over his time with Jonas, now multiplied by the encounter with Aaron. He was starting to feel desperate. Depressed. As the last drops hit the ground, he felt an acute sense of discomfort, which had nothing to do with his urinary tract health.

Slowly, he lifted his eyes to the branches of the tree, which, as if in response, rustled – twitched. Twitched was the better word for it, and Mike had the sudden thought that the tree definitely didn't appreciate being whizzed on.

"Stop being stupid," he said to himself. "Just a tree." Yet before he could tear his eyes away from the branches, he was filled – no, caressed – by the sensation of someone whispering his name.

A feeling, yes. He hadn't heard it so much as felt it, and it lingered there, clinging to him like smoke, or fine silken cobwebs;

just as even the air seemed to cling to his skin, though not in the same way as a hot southern night. Humidity wasn't the cause.

"Hey."

Mike whacked an elbow on the gnarly tree trunk when he jumped and turned at the sound of Zoe's voice. "Ah, fuck!" He treated her to an evil glare. "Don't sneak up like that, damn it. And stop laughing."

Being the one surprised, rather than the purveyor of the surprise, didn't please Mike. The punch line wasn't the same.

Zoe was still laughing while Mike continued to clutch his throbbing elbow. "I didn't sneak," she said. "I said your name, like, three times." Her gaze flicked to his crotch. "I *really* didn't want to see you with your pants down. I'm going to have nightmares, now."

Mike's eyes followed her gaze. He scrambled to do up his jeans while Zoe chortled as if it was the best pratfall she'd ever witnessed.

"Aw, I have two brothers. Seen it before."

"Just…" he finished his thought by way of exasperated grunt.

"I have to say, I wish I could just whip it out and go like that."

"Be my guest," Mike said. "We all know you're hiding a dick in those pants."

Zoe narrowed her eyes. "Lord knows I have bigger balls than you."

Mike was still too rattled for a good retort. He had the impression the tree was still listening. "What're you doing, anyway?"

"Just checking out the place, having a break, same as you." She watched as her companion fished out a cigarette. "Do you have to do that?"

"If you don't like it, find another tree." His Zippo flared into life, briefly lending an orange-yellow slant to his face, which competed with the shadow slicing his nose and forehead on a vertical.

Zoe held up her hands in surrender. She gazed at him a moment through the cloud of blue-gray smoke, which made her realize how close she was standing. She stepped back.

She had him alone. She may as well broach a subject – or two.

"You know, you didn't need to be such an ass about Mr. Trussart, before," she said.

Mike's jaw tightened, his teeth nearly biting the filter of his cigarette off. His eyes became slits. Zoe prepared herself for the inevitable onslaught of his ire. She could feel it rising, a fist ready to punch her. But to her astonishment, it didn't hit her.

"I know," he said at last, not immediately aware how brilliant his answer was, as it closed the subject. Zoe was too stunned to comment. Shock upon shock; first no ass ripping, and now no room for questions. What was there to say to him after that admission?

"I broke the thermal," Mike said, almost contrite, yet loath to admit it. "I was pissed that he figured it out." After a beat, he added, "He's still a pansy-ass fake, though."

Not yet recovered, Zoe could only say, "Whatever." She wasn't just startled. She had softened towards him. Just a bit.

"You'll be relieved to know I'm out," Mike said as he started to lean against the trunk of the tree. Fighting a spinal monkey that he hoped Zoe didn't notice, he was swift to change his position. It had come to him that the tree might wrap its branches around him and pull him inside, through the wood, pureeing him along the way. Like tomatoes smashed through a wire strainer.

He straightened, as if a rod had gone up his spine, waiting for her response.

"Huh?"

"Oh c'mon." Mike took a step away from the tree. "You know I'm fired."

Zoe began to close up, close her body off, as people do. A turn of foot, a folding of arms. But for a second, when Mike took a long pull from his cancer-stick, she saw the look in his eyes. Maybe it was the glow from the cherry, maybe it wasn't. Either way, her stance opened. Her foot turned back in his direction.

"I wondered. But Mike, you know – "

"I know. He's done a lot for me."

"So," she inched closer, "why don't you just tell us what's going on? Or at least tell Jonas?"

Here we go again. Mike turned away from her scrutiny. Were they going to accost him one by one? Was Brig next? He couldn't look at Zoe, couldn't face that penetrating look. That compassionate stare. It was worse than Aaron's.

She was like the big sister, or the mother of the group.

Yes. The mother, and as often as he'd teased about that, given her shit over it, the truth was that he liked it. They all liked that feminine touch on their team. Needed it, whether they always wanted to admit it or not.

"Jonas doesn't care this time," he said.

"That's not true."

"He said so."

"Well." Zoe's brows had furrowed, unbeknownst to Mike. Sure, Jonas was ticked, but he always listened. He was a big softie when you got down to it. "I'm sure he didn't mean it that way. He'll talk it out with you later, when we're not investigating." She was sure of it. It was because they were doing a job, a big, big job, and now wasn't the time for personal crap. But Jonas was loyal. A very loyal friend.

"I gotta get back inside. Make sure that stupid Brit hasn't fucked anything up." Mike stabbed his smoldering cig into the side of the tree in a supreme act of defiance. *And fuck you, too.*

He stalked off towards the veranda before Zoe could make further comment. He did so without once looking back, though he could feel her watching. Watching until the dark negated him. He didn't want to see the tree any more than he wanted to see her standing there. Or to see the tree eat her, or whatever other nonsense he'd started thinking. Because that he'd see, regardless of the black night. He just knew it. It didn't take him long to make his way into the house, though he would never have admitted that he was in a rush.

He pulled up short when he spied the man who'd ruined his life in five short minutes, sitting alone at command central. It didn't matter that he'd broken the camera. This man had outed him before he could come up with a solution.

James looked up from the flat screen to find Mike staring at him. He waited for the words that would soon come. As he returned the other man's scrutiny, James felt the emotions radiating from him, rippling out like disturbed water.

Mike was angry, yes. He had screwed up his own life and wanted someone to blame. James was convenient. He could vent it all at James, blame him for losing his spot on the team, he could –

Mike's shoulders sagged. He let out a breath and then took in a fresh lungful.

"I'm, uh," he looked away, "I'm sorry." He looked back to James. "About before. You know. All that." His eyes shifted away yet again.

James had tilted his head during the other man's awkward apology. It tilted more while he contemplated Mike in silence.

What does he want? I apologized. Mike took a swipe at his overgrown bangs. *Don't tell me the pansy wants me to kiss his ass.*

"Apology accepted," James said at last, straightening his head when he spoke.

Mike stared at the Brit a few seconds longer, then nodded. "'Kay." He shifted his weight from foot to foot and then made his way to a red duffel bag he'd left on a ratty wing-backed chair in one corner of the room. He wasn't in James' eye line, that way. Relief.

James returned to his study of the camera feeds.

"Anything happen while we were outside?" Mike had decided that the silence was worse than being stared at.

"Not really."

"What does that mean, not really?" Mike shoved his cigarette pack into the duffel.

"What at first glance appeared to be orbs was merely dust and insects."

"This place is pretty filthy."

"Ghosts don't appear to me as orbs, in any case."

Mike glanced over his shoulder. "Then why bring them up?" He wasn't going to encourage a discussion on what James could or couldn't see.

"Because the rest of you will see them on the playback. Isn't that what I'm supposed to do, mark anomalies?"

"We know the difference between dust and orbs, dude," Mike said. The tension in his voice was palpable, giving off the vibe that he might snap at any moment. Anyone could have felt it; to the psychic, it was at eleven on the dial.

James turned in the folding chair, which gave him a view of Mike's back. He noted the man's bunched shoulders, the tightness of his entire posture. "Mike, I'm sorry that – "

Mike whirled around to face the other man. "No you're not. So don't bother."

James didn't hesitate, nor did his expression give anything away. "But I am. I'm – "

Mike tossed his hands away from his sides. "No, really, you're not. I wouldn't be if I were you. I provoked you." He lowered his hands. "So don't tell me you're sorry." He shrugged. "I deserved it."

James began to smile. Mike didn't feel like returning that smile. He didn't know how to respond to it. He wasn't certain why he'd apologized to James in the first place. Except that it would make Jonas happy. But maybe James thought that he wasn't sincere. Maybe that's what the smile was all about, and

James was just rubbing in salt with his fake apology attempt.

Mike scowled and set about messing in his bag, arranging and rearranging the extra shirt, a jacket, the cigarettes, batteries, and two flashlights. Certainly, a distraction, but also, a clear hint to the other man.

James turned back to the table. On the way, he caught a glimpse of something in the corner of his eye. Just a glimpse of what some might describe as a shadow flitting by. Except that the shadow was such a dark red it might pass for black.

He said nothing to Mike. He said nothing to the others as they filed back inside one by one. He didn't speak to it at all, because he didn't understand what he'd seen, and most especially, didn't understand why he hadn't felt it. He wouldn't be able to explain it to them.

He hadn't sensed a thing, nothing at all, a fact that disturbed James more than seeing something had.

14

His lips curved at their corners, making little horns, just as in his leathery cheeks, little horned commas formed. The entire effect was less cute than it was disturbing.

Or would have been, if anyone had been there to see it.

Smith studied the images of the one called Mike, which moved before him. That one was quite the piece of work. So desirous of love and understanding, yet unable to take it when offered, because he was too ashamed of his mistakes, his love life, and his financial status.

His bank account carried a lot of zeros, and upon occasion, negative numbers.

Yet it wasn't money that had rushed him to England. It was the guilt of being in love with a woman who sold sex, and the shame of being dumped by a cheap whore. Mike didn't wish to tell his little group about that, but he didn't have anywhere else to go. If he stayed in Seattle, he'd just keep stalking her at the strip club. *Fantasy Unlimited*, was it?

People were ridiculously easy to manipulate, even if one knew only the tiniest part of their personalities. Smith was very, very good at feeling out a personality and adjusting accordingly.

His work was quite simple when the people in question wanted to get away from something. Getting away was more powerful than going towards something.

Always. It was always easier to entice them to run away. Who wanted to face their problems head on, after all?

Not many. Those who did were of great interest to Smith, but they were also so difficult to manipulate. They were the cream in the coffee.

He took another sip of the cooled, coagulated liquid in his crystal goblet and coughed, for the longest time ignoring the ichor oozing from the corner of his mouth. It wasn't troublesome. It was so common that it was rare that he noticed. It ended up on his sleeve by default, as he poured over the pictures; that is, when he wasn't watching his private movie.

He cackled out a laugh of sorts. That one, Mike, he might last a time. He was weak willed, but in other ways tenacious, the poor, lost soul. He hoped this one wouldn't prove the stereotype he might seem at first glance.

15

"He apologized to you?" Aaron peered at the Brit through the side-glow of his flashlight. "Wonders never cease. That might even qualify as a miracle."

James left off scrutinizing the remnants of a four-poster bed and turned towards his companion. "You should know better."

These words demanded Aaron's full attention. He turned to get a straight-on view of the other man. "Know better about what?"

"If you understand him at all, which I thought you did, and if you're as intelligent as I believe you to be, it shouldn't be so surprising that he would apologize."

"Well, I don't mean to say that Mike's such an asshole that he can't…" Aaron paused and reconsidered. "Actually, he's not generally good at admitting when he's wrong." His expression suggested he wasn't comfortable with the words he'd spoken. He had the look of someone who'd had a sip of sour milk.

"Perhaps not, but he does have his moments, and he's not, I think, a bad person."

Aaron shook his head. "Nah, he's not. I still wasn't suggesting he's an asshole. Just…misguided, lately." The sour milk expression vanished. He felt better, sticking up for Mike a little bit.

"Yes, and he also knows that he's in trouble."

Aaron let go with a wry laugh of sudden understanding. "Ah. You think he's going for brownie points." Sticking up for Mike or not, he couldn't deny that James had already figured out a few things about his pal.

"Indeed. Though it was sincere, impressively enough."

"His apology?"

James took three steps away from Aaron before turning to look at him. "No. His desire to kiss me."

The taller man was going to laugh, but the idea that James had sensed something in Mike caused his humor to flee.

"That…might explain why he's so weird about you."

"Aaron?"

"Yeah, that's me."

"Have you not heard of sarcasm?"

Aaron blinked, as if someone had just woken him from a daydream. "Oh. Wait, let me write that down." He mimed taking notes on a pad of paper. "How do you spell that?"

James' laughter danced through the bedroom, lifting the oppressive fog Aaron had felt surrounding him just seconds before.

"Shit," Aaron muttered under his breath, growing serious again. "You're good." He'd not read a thing on the other man's face. He could blame the dark. That idea made him feel less inadequate. Somewhat.

"And this shocks you? I thought Americans perceived us all as repressed, apologetic, and terribly dry."

Aaron laughed once more and took the small recorder from his pocket. "With that hanging in the air, let's do some EVPs. Maybe a live Brit can connect with a dead Brit."

James stopped, his hand hovering just above the marble mantle of the fireplace. "Or French woman."

"Wasn't it all Brits who lived here?" Aaron asked, after pressing record. "Brits who died here, I should say. Lots of death in this house."

"The youngest girl was born in France. She was tutored there and fluent in French."

Aaron moved a little closer to his co-investigator. "I don't remember reading that in the papers Smith gave us."

James turned to face the other man, his fingertips resting on the marble. "That part wasn't in the papers. Only her horrible death by sibling."

Aaron, for the moment, could only gape at his partner.

"And for the record, she loved France and prefers to think of herself as French." A gray-blue gaze flicked to the recorder. "Is that on?"

Aaron nodded.

"Good. She's waiting for her interview."

~

Zoe drifted down the hall towards a small parlor. Or drawing room, maybe. That's what they would've called it, and she was certain she'd seen at least two on the small map.

(Their mother had hated this room.)

"Boring, square room," Brig said as he shined a beam of light into a corner. "I don't think there's anything but mites in here."

"Not even a chair," Zoe commented. "Not that I'd sit in any of the chairs that *are* in this house."

"Poor baby. Sooo delicate."

(Mother had maintained, to her own tragic death, that there was a presence is this room.)

"Am not. I might break it. Worse, I could probably catch some kind of deadly fungus. Just sayin'."

(Perhaps that explained her behavior.)

Brig let go with a hearty laugh. "I can see it now. It slowly spreads across your ass cheeks, like mold on bread."

"Gross."

"You started it."

(She wrote on the walls. She swore the presence answered.)

Zoe grinned and looked in the direction of a boarded-up window. "Oh. I thought we were in the parlor."

"We are." The body builder turned, his flashlight illuminating her profile.

(The rest of the family had humored Mother, her stories. At least, until she started losing it. The others had never felt this mysterious presence. So each swore.)

Zoe shook her head. "We can't be. There's a window here. The parlor on this floor isn't against an outside wall. Duh, and I just realized that if *was* the parlor, then it wouldn't be off this hall. Right? Or am I totally turned around?"

"Honestly, I'm not sure." Brig made his way to her and stopped, following her gaze. "Parts of this house are like a maze. Maybe we're just confused. Or the map is wrong."

Zoe shrugged, though as Brig moved closer to the window, she got a bit of a chill that tensed her muscles.

"I wanted to see if the writings were visible," Zoe said. "That woman swore the spirits answered her in writing."

(They wondered, after she was founding hanging by a rope from her bedroom window, if madness had driven her to suicide.)

"Smith said you could see graffiti. So it must be a different room, 'cause I don't see any," he said, while inspecting the small octagonal shape in the wall. "Weird window, don't you think?"

(Maybe it was the presence.)

"I don't know. I'm not an historian. But yeah, it seems a bit weird for a parlor, either way."

"It's small, more like…I don't know. Bathroom, attic sort of thing? More ornamental than functional."

(One couldn't blame her; she'd lost two children, after all. They were unexplained, strange deaths. But she'd been so short tempered in the weeks prior. Suicide hadn't crossed their minds.)

"Why don't you pry the damned boards loose and see where it goes, huh? Maybe it's not a small window, but a big peephole."

Brig turned and shined his light right in Zoe's face, paying no mind to her protests or the way she shielded her eyes. He *wanted* to blind her for a minute. "What just crawled up *your* ass?"

Zoe was about to toss out a few more careless words, when she paused and replayed her previous diatribe in her head.

"I'm...wow. I didn't mean to sound so..." She offered Brig a sheepish look when he lowered his flashlight. "I guess window talk sucks all my patience dry."

"Pff. Guess so, shit." He shook his head. "This place making you tense, or what?"

Zoe truly didn't know what had come over her. She *just* refrained from holding herself. "Maybe all the stuff with Mike, and this weird client. And being kinda lost. Still, I'm sorry. That's no excuse for biting your head off."

"Eh," Brig shrugged. "It's fine. My head's still attached." Even though he'd never known her to go off like that. Not without a reason. But he let it go. There was, after all, tension in the group right now, and it was a big job. He had some nervous tension of his own, because he wanted to impress this client.

Brig was hoping to make more over-seas trips.

"Actually," he said, "prying that wood off isn't a bad idea, 'cause now I'm curious."

Zoe was quite certain that the wood needed to stay exactly where it was. "We can't. I mean we shouldn't. We don't want to risk pissing off Mr. Smith."

"It's just rotting crap that he'll have removed sooner or later, anyway." Brig wanted to stay on Smith's good side, but even more, he felt a need to see through that window.

Zoe didn't realize it, but she'd taken a few steps back. "But it might be open to the outside, and animals or something could get in." Her mind raced to find a better reason to leave it alone. "And it'll corrupt our evidence. You know, outside noise."

This had the desired effect and was, after all, true. "Oh. You're right," Brig said. "Wouldn't want to contaminate things." He placed her form in his personal spotlight. "You're acting real strange, you know it? First you sound ticked, now you're ready to run from the room."

"Hey, I'm not running." Zoe then noticed how close she was to the door. How much closer. *When did that happen?*

Brig let go with a half-hearted laugh. "Whatever. Take your meds and let's do some EVPs or something, then move on. I don't think much is happening here."

She thought Brig had started to act strange himself. She had thought, for a minute, that he was going to rip the boards from the window with his bare hands, like some insane demolition man.

"Yo, Zoe. You have the K-II meter, right? Get some readings."

She had taken the map out of her pocket and was trying in vain to find the room they were standing in. "Yeah…okay."

Now she's completely distracted – what the hell? Brig shook his head once more, fished his digital recorder out of his pocket, and flicked it on.

"Is there anyone in here with us?" he asked the room. "Mrs. Addison?" He was staring at the pretty window.

Zoe's head snapped up, as if yanked by an unseen force. "Why did you ask that? For her, I mean?"

"Isn't this where they found her?"

Zoe studied the map again. "I…I don't know. Geez. Did someone die in every room in this place?"

She didn't know why she had said that. There had been a few deaths over the years, but it wasn't as dire as her head was making it seem. Four recorded deaths in the history of the Addison family.

That still seemed like a lot for one family, even one as big as it had been. Twelve had lived here, counting grandparents. Zoe didn't really know if four were a lot in those times, and she was beginning not to care.

15

The sound of his nail breaking was sharp as a gunshot and half as loud. He spat it across the room, where it *tinged* off the nose of an old hag done in brass, and ricocheted back to land on top of his clammy, mummified foot.

This gave him no end of amusement. He'd managed three in a row, and snorted with proud laughter each time. Served the old bitch right. She'd been such a nag, nag, nag before he'd had her dipped.

But he soon lost patience with it, and his laughter died on a thin whistle of a sigh. The hag may have been relieved, as well, but one could never tell with that tarnished old witch.

She wasn't much in the way of company, anymore. Sometimes he found himself missing her nagging ways.

Smith returned his attention the goings on of his little group. He was often of two minds when it came to his games, his experiments. Sometimes he wanted it swift, to see how little it took for a group of people to implode. He sometimes giggled with glee when that happened. Most unbecoming.

So was his lack of patience, at times. One would think it went against his nature. But one wouldn't know much, in that case.

Other times, he reveled in the slow burn of a good domino effect. He'd marvel at the stubborn stupidity of whichever person decided to be the hero, the one who would hold it all together. A self-appointed leader.

Smith liked those. So often, the rest of the group plotted behind the leader's back, and sometimes, they even acted on it. Then half argued about what it meant to have gone that far. That they hadn't really meant it, while the proactive ones bragged, being the only ones with balls enough to go through with it.

Dominos. It was always dominos.

Occasionally, Smith tired of dominos and wanted to play a more active role in the demise (or survival) of his test subjects.

It was all so tasty. Decisions, decisions.

He considered Zoe. She might be dessert. Perhaps he should begin with dessert. No, no. That rather left things anti-climactic. Except for the odd occurrence when he happened to be wrong about main courses and desserts, got them backwards.

After all this time, a human or three could still surprise him. If but a little. They could vibrate the silk in spots he hadn't considered.

Perhaps it was senility on his part. If such could affect him. He had no idea.

He could nudge things a certain way, to help ensure the roles, whom to save for last. But again, when dealing with people, it sometimes went awry, because they had their own plans, free will. It was more fun to allow them to shoot themselves in the feet.

"Feet?" Smith laughed at himself and waved a creaky hand. "That girl; I may have overestimated her worth." He stroked his smooth, slick chin. "Though it's more fun to have a woman in the mix."

He nodded, satisfied with his assessment. She'd keep just enough sense in those boys that they might make it through the night. She was stronger than they were, and sometimes, she knew it, deep down, and not simply in an aggrandizing, competitive manner.

"We shall see."

He commenced chewing on his thumbnail, intent on hitting the rat that, bold as a cracked-out whore, had helped itself to his supper.

16

Mike did a thermal sweep of the second floor study's bookshelves. "Whoa. That's a little weird." He sneezed. The room was mustier than the rest of the house. He was beginning to think he was allergic to the place. But as long as there weren't spiders in the room, he could deal.

True, he was uncomfortable in a way he'd never been in any other location, but he didn't want to fail Jonas. The story on the room they were in wasn't pretty. Still, it wasn't as if Mike hadn't heard ghost stories before. And not as if he hadn't lived one repeatedly when he was a child.

"What?" Jonas turned away from the small hearth and took a few steps in his partner's direction. "And bless you."

"Thanks. So check this out. There's a heat signature here that, uh, makes no sense."

(There had been two deaths in this room alone.)

The big man made it to Mike's side and looked at the thermal screen. "What the...You sure it's functioning properly?"

"Yeah, dude. I didn't drop this one." Mike grimaced, wondering what made him think his old pal was ready to laugh about broken equipment. He expected a verbal smack down any second.

None ensued. Nor did laughter. "It almost looks like..." Jonas grabbed the thermal and made a slow back and forth sweep of the shelves. "It almost looks like outlines of books."

(Dad had bludgeoned *his* own dad with a particularly heavy old book.)

Mike shook off the awkward moment of before, thankful that Jonas had ignored it, and peered at the yellowish images on the FLIR. "Yeah, wow, now that you mention it – but what the heck? What would do that? When was the last time there were even books here, and why would they be warm anyway?"

(One of the younger sons had been in the study, reading, when he heard a noise. Thinking it was his father, come to kick him out of a room he wasn't supposed to be in, he'd dropped the book and made for a side door.)

"Good questions. I'm sure there's some other explanation." One that Jonas was already racking his brain for.

"That's freaky, dude. If there really were warm, phantom books. Totally freaky. Especially when you think about what happened in here." Mike reached to run his fingers along one of the shelves. "Freaky." He pulled his hand back as if he'd found a nest of stinging wasps. And squeezed his eyes shut. Open. Shut. They were watering.

(The boy never made it to the side door, so the story went. He had collapsed, just as he reached for the door's knob.)

"What?" Jonas looked at Mike, glanced at Mike's hand. "What happened? You okay?"

"It's just – I just." He inhaled, tried to collect himself. "I thought it would be warm."

(Yes, the boy had collapsed. When his father – who wasn't in the room at the time, so he said – found him later, much later...)

"Geez, you're jumpy this trip, aren't you." Jonas ran a hand over his face. The truth was that he'd been concerned. But he wasn't going to show it. "For a second I thought you'd touched a hot plate."

"It's cold." Mike's gaze was glued to the thermal imager. "How can it be cold? I knew it wouldn't be hot, either, but dude, it's really, really cold, and that doesn't jibe with the reading on the screen."

(…he was dead. His lips were blue, his eyes, red rimmed. As if irritated. Something had irritated his eyes.)

"You sure?" Jonas reached out towards the bookcase. "I think you're just losing it, man." He laughed, though it was a rather subdued laugh. Something was off. Mike wasn't generally such a namby-pamby.

Jonas was beginning to think that the history of the room was bugging his partner. Sure, it was twisted, but they'd heard stories before.

"I ain't lying!"

"Hey." Jonas reached out, gave Mike's shoulder a squeeze. "Chill. I mean," the big man shook his head, "never mind." As if in an act of defiance, Jonas laid an entire palm on the shelf.

He refrained from jerking, from yanking his hand back. It was the most difficult thing he had ever done.

"Told you," Mike whispered. The look on his partner's face hadn't gone by him. As if he had stuck his hand in a viper pit by mistake. "Freaking told you."

"Okay. Well." Jonas drew back his hand, remaining calm about it, mostly for Mike's benefit. Jonas wasn't afraid; he was puzzled as hell. "There must be an explanation."

(Then Granddad had come in.)

"I've never seen anything like that."

The other man looked at Mike. "There's always a first time, and that doesn't mean there isn't an explanation." He gestured to the thermal camera. "Let's totally check that out, make sure it isn't messed up."

"There ain't anything wrong with it." But Mike was already checking, to distract himself from the weird vibes he was feeling, as well as to please Jonas.

~

"Then he left me alone. All alone."

Aaron's eyes moved over his companion's form. James was as still as the marble he leaned on. Tranquil, even as he relayed the words the mysterious French girl was supposedly giving him. She was answering their questions. Well, James had been doing most of the asking, so far. Aaron was doing his duty, holding the recorder. James paused long enough between question and answer to leave room on the tape for the disembodied voice that Aaron hoped to hear later on, when they reviewed the evidence.

The more he hung out with the stranger, the more he wanted him to be legit. Besides, this would also mean there was some cool evidence. Evidence of the other side, which was Aaron's entire reason for being on the team. He needed to know that what had happened to him those years ago wasn't only in his head. That it wasn't some kind of psychosis.

Even if its being real was frightening, being insane was more frightening. Because it still happened, sometimes. He'd lied to James. It *had* happened since they moved from that house.

As Aaron looked down at the digital recorder, to make certain the light was still on, that it was still running, he thought about the conversation in the chapel. He wondered if James knew that he'd lied. If he knew and had let it slide. *That would be cool, if he did.*

"Why was he in your room to begin with?" James asked.

Aaron's thoughts snapped back to the current conversation. James had asked the same thing Aaron had wondered. He waited for the reply.

(Every third night. He visited every third night.)

The pause was longer this time. Aaron remained quiet. Sophie could be getting tired. That was her name, or so James had said. She might not want to talk anymore. Or she was now having trouble getting through.

Or maybe James was tired. Or full of shit.

Why did I just go there? Aaron gave his head a shake, as if to loosen cobwebs.

(She never told anyone. Never.)

Aaron refocused on his co-investigator, who was yet silent. So silent that the American began to get uncomfortable. He moved closer, did so with great care, as one might approach a wild animal. He stared and stared at him. At last, he whispered:

"James?"

Aaron shined his light in James' direction, careful not to blind him. There was no response from the other man.

"Did you lose her?" He moved closer, tiptoeing as if on a tightrope. "James?"

(Sometimes only one night would pass. When he was tense. When they could be alone and he really, really needed her.)

As he closed more of the distance, he saw that James was trembling. Just a little, but it was visible. Aaron paused, uncertain what to make of it. Was the Brit about to make a fool out of him again? Was this another practical joke?

He was close enough now to study James' face. What he saw didn't answer the questions one way or another.

James looked perturbed in some way. Angry, even. Yet in his eyes...

Fear? Then again, he sorta seems...it's like...

"What do you see?" Aaron asked.

No response.

(He choked her, once. Hands around her delicate, pale throat. It left a necklace of bluish dots blossoming beneath her collar, later. That had been most frightening.)

"Hey." Aaron's hand drifted towards the smaller man's shoulder. "James."

And just like a wild animal, James started. After a puzzled look at Aaron, he moved farther away.

"James, what's wrong?"

At last, the other man spoke. "Don't touch me. Don't touch me ever again."

Aaron snatched his hand back, unaware he'd been reaching for him. "Sorry. I'm sorry." He fought the urge to snap at James and leave the room. It was ridiculous how much the words *don't touch me ever again* stung, he thought. Ridiculous.

"Never again. Never again." James backed away. One step. Two, three. "I'll make you stop, I will, I will."

Aaron's personal feelings evaporated. James sounded pitiful, afraid. Pleading.

"James, I…" He didn't know what to say, or what he'd been about to say. But a few more words popped out. "Is Sophie hurting you?"

It occurred to Aaron that maybe this didn't need to be recorded. That whatever was happening now wasn't anyone's business. His thumb had decided this just ahead of him and had already pressed the off switch on the recorder. Just as Aaron began to question himself, to question why on Earth he'd avoid collecting what could possibly turn out to be the most interesting audio evidence he'd ever captured, James took a step towards him.

"Aaron?" he said, his eyes blinking out Morse code.

"Yeah…"

"Aaron?" James took another step and then froze in place. "I was. That was." His chest filled with air but no more words followed.

"You okay?" Aaron was suspicious. But he was also confused, concerned, and dreadfully curious.

"I'm…" James closed up shop. Slammed the door, put up the sign. Aaron could sense it. It was tangible. Even the man's face was blank. This served to heighten his concern. It wasn't at all like the practical joke.

"I'm fine. Let's carry on to another room, shall we?" James said.

Aaron studied his partner and came to a quick decision. "Sure. There's another bedroom we should check out." He didn't even ask if Sophie were still present. He didn't suggest that perhaps she would be in the other bedroom. He couldn't even ask if she was the one his partner had thought was touching him. Or if it was Sophie who was being touched. Maybe that was it... Yet Aaron couldn't bring himself to ask another question about her – or anything else.

"There is always another bedroom," James said under his breath as he headed for the door. Aaron followed, remaining silent. Somehow, this seemed best. Had he noticed, he might have laughed at how soft even his steps were.

(Always careful not to leave marks. Not on the face, anyway. Just that one time.)

As for James, he could still hear Sophie. She had never left. She was in fact, following them. But for James, she had become background noise, like so many other spectral figures. Background noise, because a memory of his own had taken front and center stage and was yet lingering, still had a slight grip on him.

If it was indeed mere memory.

17

Smith settled back into his favorite chair, now ready to continue his observations, since his stomach was no longer pestering, pestering.

And the rat wouldn't bother him again. Ever. That one, he'd save for later, as he did with so many others.

On the way down into his seat, he spread a couple of the photographs around, until he had a better view of Zoe.

He'd been reconsidering her.

Ah, a lovely girl, she was. He did fancy redheads. He understood her, too. She had desires. Desires that might be obvious to the right people, but also other desires no one would guess, not of their little Zoe.

He glanced at the beefy boy, the one called Brig. May as well toss one of those in, he'd thought. You never knew what they'd do, those jock-types. Big on biceps, short on brain cells.

He slid the pictures until he had those two side by side. Not a bad looking couple. Shame both were oblivious to the other, as often was the case. Her gaze wandered a different path, and Brig?

He was just blind. Sweet by some standards, but for all his looks, no confidence. Silly little virgin, afraid a girl would find him lacking.

Probably would, and he couldn't even blame steroids.

Smith chuckled as he bit down, crunching a crispy black shell. When it broke, the good stuff oozed through. He licked at his fingers.

Just a little dessert.

He laughed. It was best that the muscle head didn't see Zoe the way he ought. He mightn't be able to handle her. People underestimated how bright her fire burned. Oh yes, he'd decided he was very interested in how this one would fare, and just what she'd do in any given situation. He hoped she'd prove hardy, because he'd be disappointed for her to give out too soon.

He always did favor the redheads, especially the ones with unpopular fetishes. Fetishes they were somewhat ashamed of and afraid to share, even with a friend.

18

The fine hairs at the nape of Zoe's neck spiked. The hairs on her arms soon snapped to attention. Her feet grew roots, and she lingered, immobile, in the black hole of a hallway. A sliver of ice pressed against the base of her neck and sent a telegram down her spine that said freeze. Stop.

Her breathing was so shallow that she would soon be lightheaded if her brain didn't get more oxygen. Though she might forget the entire event, if she were lucky, and still escape serious brain damage.

Zoe was hoping for such a thing, as she was unable to flee. She didn't feel *alone*. It wouldn't have been an issue if not for the fact that it didn't feel like Brig. She'd said his name twice, with no reply. Besides.

Brig didn't have an evil vibe.

Zoe didn't often deal in absolutes like good and evil. She generally held the opinion that many things in life were gray. That anyone, anything, could go either way.

Except Brig, who was generally a good guy and definitely didn't feel…evil.

It seemed preposterous, but her brain couldn't come up with another word for the thick presence she swore was close, too damned close, behind her. Seconds began to tick by like hours, and (absurd as it seemed to her) the presence had the feel of a Lovecraft novel. Something so hideous it defied description. She felt that, should she turn, Cthulhu himself, itself, herself – whatever – would be standing *right there*. She just knew that tentacles were inching their slimy way across the floor, the walls, the *ceiling*. They were going to slither their way around her body, caging her, until she couldn't breathe at all, not even in shallow sips, and then, ohhh, then, it would drag her down, down, down, to God knows –

"Brig," she squeak-exclaimed. It was all her voice could muster.

Nothing slithered across her neck. Or her feet. Or around her waist. Nothing left sinister, slimy kisses on her arms, or dropped down from the ceiling to cling to her face like those things in *Alien*. The face huggers.

Not a one had gotten her yet. But soon. She was certain of that.

"Brig," she whispered, amazed that she could speak. Hadn't her vocal chords been rusted shut just hours – or seconds – before?

There was no answer forthcoming, save for the groan of wood under feet. But Zoe hadn't taken a step. Her feet-roots had plunged deep into the ground. She hadn't even tried to dig out her pocket flashlight and turn it on (the other one had ceased to function). She didn't want to *see* the thing that defied all adjectives, after all.

Zoe managed a half step. Backwards. Towards the wall. She needed her back up against a wall. It was back there, somewhere. Behind the monster.

She took a half step forward. She swore it was there, the something, towering, breathing down her neck, barring her way to the wall, her potential-new-best-friend the wall.

"Damn it," she muttered. "This is your job. Just...move." Her next words turned into a meditative chant. "C'mon, c'mon, c'mon..."

In frame-by-frame slow motion, she turned her head to look over her shoulder. Jerked it back, convinced something was there. Some black mass of –

"Nothing, girl. Geez." She turned her head once more, this time defiant. Peered into ink on black on void.

There was nothing there. Nothing at all. Not that she could see. This was a great relief to Zoe, except for the part where there really *was* nothing – as in no wall, even. Hadn't there been a wall she'd been about to back herself up against?

Her body followed her head and pivoted around, until she faced the doorway. It looked like a doorway. Her hand delved into her jacket pocket to retrieve the small flashlight. It snapped into life with a press of a switch.

It shone into a room. A room with a boarded up window that seemed more decorative than functional.

Zoe couldn't muster words talk to herself now. She'd left this room some time ago with Brig. They'd been in another room, a bedroom, and then gone into the hall. He had somehow gotten ahead of her, and she'd followed in the direction she'd seen him walk. His voice had trailed off, in the middle of retelling the story about the girl who'd burned to death, set on fire by her own mother.

Zoe had become confused and gotten lost in her own thoughts when he came to that part of the story. According to Brig's telling of it, Mrs. Addison had killed her own daughter. But Zoe thought she'd died *before* her daughter. It was so difficult to keep things straight. Also confusing was, by his math, there were five deaths. She could only come up with four, no matter how many times she counted.

She was lightheaded for other reasons, now. She was usually good at keeping details straight. It was one of her jobs on the team. But not only was she sketchy on the story of the manor, she didn't remember retracing her steps. She didn't know how she'd arrived back where she started. She didn't know why there wasn't a wall where she thought there had been a moment ago, and she couldn't understand why there weren't any other doors in the hallway. She didn't see any when she shined her light in every direction, turning like a lighthouse, light signaling whatever was out there, guiding whatever was out there closer to her....

She didn't like that metaphor.

But she shined it again. Now the light jerked around as if attached to a three-legged hyena's tail, rather than a slow and welcome beacon in the night.

This was worse, but her shaking hands weren't having it any other way.

Baser instincts urged her to flee. But she didn't know where to run. Or from what. Or what to. Logic made a showing and attempted to save her. It tried to explain that she had gotten lost, that's all. Turned around. Such an easy thing to do in the dark, particularly when your other flashlight had gone out.

It made sense. There were just one (or two) problems remaining.

Where was Brig, and why had the floor protested the weight of something she couldn't see, and which definitely wasn't her?

~

At last Jonas yanked his hand back, doing his best to maintain a neutral expression. Difficult to do, because it felt like a box jellyfish had stung him. Or what he'd heard it felt like. The sensation was that of someone running heated razorblades over his flesh, repeatedly – the metal never cooling.

He'd touched the shelf, again, intent on proving to himself that he'd been imagining things the first time.

But the feeling was all too real.

Thank God, there wasn't poison to go with it. So his rational mind said. Even though there was nothing rational about the sensation to begin with. Touching a shelf not covered in glass or spikes – or rigged with electricity or some such – should not result in pain.

"Jesus, dude," Mike said, forgetting all about the thermal. He sounded like someone whose stomach was rejecting his last meal. "What's wrong?" He also sounded scared.

Jonas wasn't keeping a blank enough expression, it seemed. "Nothing. My hand fell asleep. Pins and needles, you know." He made a show of slapping his hand against his thigh, which drove the hot blades in deeper. He looked away, faking a visual search of the shelves and biting his tongue. Literally. If he kept it up, he'd taste blood, soon.

"Uh…that must be some seriously bad circulation you have," Mike said. He wasn't buying it. But he didn't know what to say. Or if he wanted to know the truth. He just knew that he felt nauseous, and he wanted out of the room.

"What time is it?" Jonas made a great show of checking the camera. The pain in his hand had lessened. It was still disconcerting as hell, and it was difficult not to stare at his palm, study it, but it didn't feel as bad as before.

Besides, there weren't any marks. He'd managed a peek at his hand. It almost made his world tilt, because that made even less sense. His brain said that there should be marks. Even though there shouldn't be marks, because all he'd done was touch a piece of wood.

Splinters sure didn't feel like that. Not one single splinter he'd ever had compared.

"It's about twelve fifteen," Mike said.

The big man's brows made a swift ascent. "In the morning?"

"Obviously." Mike allowed himself a laugh. Even to his own ears, it sounded nervous. Forced. He stopped staring at the fireplace and looked at his friend. "You sound surprised."

"Sorta. Because that would mean we came in here about an hour ago."

Mike nodded. "Uh huh." He made no other comment, though he had more than a few observations he could've made.

He didn't like the way Jonas was acting. Or the way that he was feeling. He wanted *out* of the room. He wished Jonas would say they could go, already. He was past caring if it was professional to leave. He couldn't find one shit to give.

Jonas glanced at his hand. At the shelf. Back at his hand.

"It just doesn't seem like it's been that long," he said. Not only had his hand been attacked by who-knows-what, time had evaded him. Passed him by. Left him in the dust.

(He claimed he didn't know when he'd picked up the book, or why he'd ever hit his father. Then he accused his father of killing his own grandson.)

Jonas shook his head and turned a slow circle.

"So what now, boss?" Mike moved closer to his team leader. His feelings of unease were magnified by Jonas' strange behavior. They'd been in the room a while, for sure, but Mike hadn't commented, because he thought that Jonas was homing in on something. He thought that Jonas was recording evidence and concentrating, or communing, or – or maybe drumming up some words to have *The Talk*.

Truly, most of that didn't seem very normal to Mike, but he still hadn't said anything. He didn't want to be an irritation. He didn't want to break the silence and maybe have Jonas decide it was time for *The Talk*.

He also didn't want to find out that something weirder was going on and didn't want to make Jonas think that he thought he was being ridiculous.

Mike was still walking on eggshells and the manor was adding to it. In a flash bulb moment, he realized he was getting annoyed. *Could we get the eff out of here, already?*

Jonas shrugged. Stared at the wall just past Mike. He should report the incident with his hand. Tell Mike about it. It was evidence. Anecdotal, perhaps, but they always made a note of anything out of the ordinary.

It was definitely abnormal.

Procedure: Tell your partner, then the others when they met up again. Record the conversation. He should have recorded his immediate reaction. Everything fresh in his memory, so he could go over it later in a different mind frame. He should do all of this, because it was part of the job, and because none of them ever took such things lightly. They didn't belittle each other's experiences, believable or not.

You just didn't do that to another investigator on your team. Unless you were into practical jokes, but that was a different matter.

Jonas didn't want to talk about it. He didn't know how to explain it. He was more disconcerted than he'd ever been on any investigation. More bothered than the time when he was ten and something had left marks on his back. The thing that had sent him on his path towards real ghost hunting. The thing he hadn't seen, but felt. First the choking. Then the scratching, when he ran.

Back in the present. It wasn't just that it had hurt to touch the shelf – the pain was a ghost of itself, now, which was somehow stranger – it was that for one moment, he could have sworn...

"This place is fucking creepy," Mike said. "Creepy as fuck."

Jonas nodded. As far as he was concerned, Mike had said a mouthful. "Let's take a break. Yeah?"

"I am way ahead of you," Mike replied, his relief evident for the way the words seeped out of him like a tire with a leak. "I have a hate on for this room."

Jonas tracked his partner's movements; Mike wasted no time gathering up his stuff and heading for the door – which was closed. Jonas didn't remember closing the door. Maybe Mike had done it. He didn't remember that, either.

Jonas looked one last time at the shelf that had stung him. He'd lost time, too, so why should the closed door be a big deal, he thought.

He also thought his accusations were off. Sure, he'd felt the pain when touching the shelf, but saying that the shelf had been the cause was his private way of diffusing the situation. Diffusing his reaction. As much as he could, anyway.

Because to dwell on the strong feeling that the wood was… was…somehow a living thing, and not in the *it was once a tree* sort of way, well that was –

Fucked up. Not just creepy. Fucked up. Think I need some coffee. I'm losing perspective.

The big man shook his head at himself and let out a weak slip of a laugh. The idea was absurd. Trees-as-shelves didn't take revenge. Demons didn't possess dead wood, either. He didn't think that they did.

"Boss?"

Jonas snapped from his funhouse of thoughts to see Mike standing in the doorway.

"You coming?" Mike asked.

"Yeah, right behind you." Jonas made a gesture for Mike to carry on. Made it with his previously stung hand. He then had an idea.

"Hey, Mike. I think there was some trace of chemicals on that shelf, or something…"

Yes, of course. That had to be it. Good thing neither man noticed the sudden, effervescent nature of the shelf as they were leaving. How it almost bubbled. How those minuscule bubbles were black in the dark. And how they weren't necessarily liquid.

19

"Ah, Jonas." A black and brown spotted finger separated him from the rest, like moving pieces on a chessboard. "She loves you, you know." A laugh like dry leaves skittering across a sidewalk left him. "Or you don't. Everyone else does, though. I wonder..."

Smith hoped he was right about her feelings for Jonas. About how much she felt for him. Jonas himself wasn't all that interesting, but he'd been the easiest to manipulate. Dangled half a carrot, and here he was. The man had been so desperate to be away from his life in Seattle. Away from his troubles.

And close to Zoe. Jonas might not be secure in the idea that she loved him, but that hadn't stopped him from fantasizing about her. He'd always wanted her. Lust had nothing to do with love.

More leaves blew from Smith's throat and out his mouth, along with a thin line of spit that dangled there, so ready to drip onto the likeness of the big man, but not quite reaching. Jonas really was one of those incorruptible types, of which so few existed. He'd had so many opportunities to act on lust, but he hadn't, not once.

Poor boy. Stupid way to live life, in Smith's opinion. Why, it wasn't living at all! One should grab life by the balls and squeeze until someone squealed!

Smith's hands came together in a sharp clap of sound and that line of spit vibrated; he was so tickled with himself. Oh yes, he amused himself to no end, sometimes; he was so damned *clever*.

He studied the face captured in time on good ole Kodak paper and, at last, flicked away the gooey string attached to the corner of his mouth.

Soon Jonas would wish he'd acted on more of those impulses. Indeed, he'd wish very hard for it, silly sop.

20

Aaron and James had found another bedroom. It appeared on the map to be a bedroom. Neither man was quite certain of this when they looked around upon entering. It was bereft of furnishings, void of character. Stark. Unsettling because it was forlorn in its vacancy. Its abandonment. Somehow, it didn't seem that anyone had cared for the room, even at the height of its glory.

No. It never had glory.

But neither man was speaking about it, neither was interested in discussing what the room had been. Silent agreement voted it a bedroom.

James was, for the moment, trapped in his head, with the ghost of something from the past. A ghost not connected to the manor house they were investigating, and not literally a ghost at all.

That was what James hoped, and so far, his hope had proved good.

Still, he'd rather face real apparitions than remain trapped in the flashes of memory he couldn't quite shake. Hadn't been able to shake ever since his encounter with the French woman. He knew that it was because her story had been too familiar. Too personal. He knew that, much as he tried to deny it at times, guilt drove him to the dark corners of his mind.

The conviction that he'd do it again drove him to the corners behind the corners.

A whisper managed to reach James all the same.

"Do you hear that?"

(The Father had wandered into the bedroom on the third night.)

The Brit turned his head in the direction of the voice, tired of living in corners for the time being, and grateful that Aaron had managed to bring him back into the light. The why didn't matter.

"What is it?" he asked the American.

"It's like a – a low hum. Sort of. You don't hear it?" He moved about the edge of the room, with James' gaze tracking him. "Before you ask, it's not any of my equipment."

James glanced at the devices in his companion's hands. "I was not going to ask."

(He'd seen a figure, outlined in candlelight.)

"I think it's coming from this direction." Aaron moved along the edge of the wall farthest from James. "I can't remember what's on the other side of this wall. What the other room is."

James, curiosity piqued, took steps in the other man's direction. "There is scarcely any electricity, let alone working appliances."

"I know, I know. That's why it's weird. I was just wondering, though. Maybe…maybe wind through a window?"

"Would you like me to check the other room?" Even as he asked, James moved towards the door.

"No." Aaron whirled about. "Wait."

(It occurred to him that it wasn't anyone he knew. Even the outline didn't match a family member. More importantly, it didn't feel like a family member. One could tell the difference. Because you got to know your family, really know them.)

James did so, his eyes on the other man. He made no comment. He didn't need to ask if Aaron were all right. He knew the other man didn't want him to leave. That he'd feel abandoned. He knew that Aaron's flesh had broken out in tiny bumps. If not literally, James could imagine it well enough.

"I'm here," James said.

Aaron would've run a hand through his hair if his hands hadn't been full. As it was, he glanced at a spot near his feet before turning away to face the wall once again.

"Dang," he said, a bit embarrassed but thankful James had stayed, whatever he might have picked up through his emotions. "Now it doesn't seem like it's coming from here."

"You can still hear it?" James moved closer, his ears deaf to this mysterious hum.

"Yes." Aaron walked to a corner and moved along the next wall. He sighed. "Not getting any thermal hits. Nothing else seems strange. Oh," he looked across his shoulder, "could you turn your recorder on? Maybe it'll pick up the sound."

(There was a strange sound starting up, in his head. Was it in his head? The vision of the outlined silhouette blurred – or seemed to.)

James had already produced the device and pressed the switch. "Recording," he said.

"Thanks," Aaron said. "So…you really can't hear it?" he asked in a low whisper.

James listened. He cocked his head, out of habit, straining for a sound. He wanted to say yes, to put the other man at ease. He wanted Aaron to feel validated.

But he couldn't bring himself to lie. Not even to himself, because the truth was, the silence bothered James more than ever.

"I'm sorry," James said. "But no."

If Aaron were honestly hearing something, James felt that he should be, as well. Unless the other man had the hearing of an owl, which was doubtful. But he didn't believe that Aaron was making up stories.

He could sense the truth of Aaron's discomfort. The sound, the room – that was the cause. It wasn't the sort of nervousness that came with weaving lies.

Aaron made a slow turn away from the wall and attempted to focus on James. "I can't figure it out." He opted for a shrug, but it came off more like an attempt to fold in on himself. "Maybe something'll show up on the recorder later."

"Shall we move on, then?" James inquired, aware that Aaron was trying to talk himself out of the creeping sensations up and down his spine.

"Umm…" Aaron paused. He shouldn't leave a room with possible activity. It wasn't protocol. It wasn't good investigation technique. They were trying to catch evidence, after all.

But he couldn't shake the awful, dark, strange feeling that –

(The figure, it had a…)

"Yeah, let's go," he said, the debate in his mind, over.

James nodded. "Lead the way."

Aaron sucked in a lungful of air and tried to gather his wits. The hum: it felt like nerves in his brain were buzzing. Like things were crawling around in there. Things that didn't belong.

He shook his head a bit too hard; at the same time, he took a step and stumbled – just a bit. James hadn't moved, had been watching, and therefore, reached for Aaron on an impulse.

But he missed his mark, because his mark sidestepped and kept heading towards the door.

"I'm cool," Aaron said. "I mean I'm fine. Must be a loose floorboard."

"I knew what you meant," James whispered as he turned to follow. He knew many things, no doubt, though he wasn't able to anticipate what happened next. He didn't have time.

"Oomph." The sound rushed from James when Aaron backed into him, running roughshod over the soft loafers and more delicate flesh beneath. James put his hands up in self-defense when the other man kept moving, both now doing a backwards shuffle, like a couple of drunk, frantic beetles.

"Aaron, what in bloody hell – "

"Something out there – I heard it, felt it."

(Impossible! It had a…)

The something appeared before them. Abrupt, rushed.

"Shit! You scared the hell out of me." Aaron stopped treading on James' loafers, much to James' relief. "Zoe?"

"This is what caused you to run me over?" James said, a bit offended, if also amused. "A harmless young lady?"

Zoe was oblivious to his words, indeed, to anything but the question on her mind.

"Have you guys seen Brig?"

(They found him dead in that very spot, his face a frozen expression of confused fear.)

21

The three of them stood in the absolute silence of the long hallway. The flat, featureless darkness. Two of them thought it seemed darker than the rest of the house, even with flashlights, but neither would speak such nonsense aloud.

(They had always been so close...)

The third had a few other ideas of what was *in* the dark, but also refused to speak to it aloud. That might make it real.

"You probably just got turned around," Aaron said.

Zoe fought off a shiver. "I don't know. Maybe. Seems like I keep running into bedrooms." *Didn't I just leave a bedroom, damn it?*

Aaron worked up a laugh. He was still disconcerted, and the vibe from Zoe wasn't helping. Nor was the sense that he could see shadows in the blue-black of a hall behind James. It was too dark to see shadows, he thought. And they weren't blips he was catching in his peripheral, the type that disappear when a person turns their head to look straight at them. No.

They were straight behind James.

Aaron vomited up a chuckle, and he realized his companions were staring, waiting for him to follow up that laugh with something useful.

"Funny you say that," he said to Zoe. "James and I were just talking about how there's always another bedroom."

James studied Aaron and with success, fought the urge to look behind himself. It would only disturb his companions more. Intellectually, he knew that nothing was there.

The logic of the manor was beginning to escape him, however, and he felt increasingly open to his companion's every nuance of emotion. He didn't like it. It made him uncomfortable. It was like an itch just below the skin, which he couldn't possibly scratch and, even if he could, was afraid to. Doing so might peel said skin away, leave him raw as a peeled grape.

Zoe glanced at James, noting his silence. It disturbed her almost as much as the lengthening hall. It was. It was getting longer. *Get a grip, girlie.* "Yeah, too many damned bedrooms." In a sudden fit of agitation, she added, "I'm fucking sick of this place; can we just go? I hate this mother fucking house."

The two men continued to stare at her, James with a neutral expression that served to annoy her and Aaron with a look of surprise. This too, irritated her.

(Gotten along so well, so very well...)

"What?" she said. "What?" she repeated, this time to drown out the sound of tiny...tiny... *like scurrying rats? Great. Just great.*

"Hey, hey," Aaron said, reaching out to touch her shoulder. "C'mon, it's not that bad. You ticked at Brig?" *Why are we all ignoring the elephant – or ghost – in the hall?*

Zoe reasoned that must be the answer for her sudden outburst. Yes, it was. Brig had traipsed off and left her alone in the dank blackness of the unwelcoming room, in a house that would spit them all out if it could. She was sure it would. It hated them as much as she was starting to hate it. They were like fleas pricking at its skin. Ticks, spreading disease and trying to suck the life out of it. Parasites. The manor viewed them as parasites.

She snapped to when she realized James was looking at her with the queerest expression on his face. She wondered where her thoughts had gone sour, and why. It wasn't her first investigation, after all.

"Well." She shifted her gaze to Aaron. "Yeah, he left me."

"How is it you didn't notice his leaving?" James asked.

Finally, he opens his mouth, and to what, make accusations? Zoe thought. "We were investigating. I turned around, and he was gone."

James held up his hands in surrender. Or to ward off the wild woman. Zoe couldn't decide which it was, as she looked at him. She lifted her hands, rubbed her face.

"Sorry, James." She looked to Aaron. "Maybe I need a break. It's just that I've been wandering around without a light, trying to find Brig and not trip over anything." Even her small light had given up on her, abandoned her, and left her alone in the dark, the wee bastard.

"What about the walkies?" Mike asked, striding up out of nowhere, startling at least two of the others. He got right in Zoe's face, as if he were searching for gold in her pores. "Try that, smarty?"

"Of course I did!" What frigging slime pit spat him up?

"Dude." Aaron gave Mike a gentle nudge. "Chill. Where'd you just come from? I didn't hear your footsteps."

"Down the stairs. I made plenty of noise." Mike waved a hand. "Where's Brig, and how did Miss Manners manage to lose him?"

"You say that like it's my job to babysit him," Zoe shot back.

"You're not supposed to abandon your partner."

James took a step back, his face a study of careful neutrality. Aaron was riveted to his partners. He'd seen them give each other shit, but never with so much vitriol as seemed to infuse their current tones.

"I didn't abandon him!"

"What the heck's going on?" Jonas' voice boomed down the hall in their direction, bounced off the walls. "What's all the shouting? You trying to wake the dead for real?"

(Tension began to fill the rooms. Everyone was always so tense.)

"Your girl went off alone," Mike said. "Left her partner."

"I did not. You don't even know what's going on," Zoe said, thrusting her finger in his chest. If it had been a knife, he'd have been gushing blood. "You waltzed up, stuck your nose in, and laid into me."

"Hold up, hold up, Geez," Jonas said. He grabbed the fighters by an arm each and pried them apart. "I don't know why you're making such a case out of this, guys. Just chill."

Aaron and James exchanged a look, which gave Aaron a little thrill. Because it made him feel as if he and the Brit had connected – or something. Like they were in on the same joke. Both had chosen to stay out of the fray as much as possible. James in particular wanted little to do with the argument, as evidenced by his closing in on the wall behind him. In that moment, Aaron began to reach out to him.

But the air in the hall thickened, and he lowered his hand, redirected his gaze back to his team.

"She's supposed to stay with her partner," Mike was saying in reply to Jonas.

"Dude," said Jonas. "You act like she dumped him in a ditch after dissecting him for lunch." His gaze moved to Zoe. "What happened?"

She filled him in, her words zooming out as if they were racing each other. It kept Mike from interrupting and made James dizzy. Jonas just managed to hear the important bits.

"And I looked for him," Zoe finished. "If someone wants to go with me now, I'll keep looking for him."

Jonas made an intense study of the woman. "Why are you so freaked out? He couldn't have gone far."

"She's wiggin'," Mike said. "Totally spooked. I can tell."

Jonas pointed a finger in the direction of Mike's face. "So were you a few minutes ago. Now you're just being a shit."

Aaron could no longer keep his mouth from opening and the words from tumbling out. "Jesus, you're *all* wigging."

James agreed with this assessment, albeit in silence. Though this did nothing for an unease that was working its way through his nerve endings. Discomfort that had nothing to do with the emotions in the hall – which should have a few more doorways, but didn't, he noted. Uncomfortable with that assessment, he refocused on reducing his cohort's emotions to white noise, background static, courtesy of years and years of practice. And it was working.

Until Mike spoke up, yet again.

"Hey." He took a step in James' direction, pointing an accusing finger at him. There were many fingers flying about the hall, James thought. "If you're so special, you can tell us where he is."

(They began to argue three, sometimes four times a week, and these arguments took increasingly sinister tones.)

Aaron's eyes did a slow roll, while James' brows lifted.

"Pardon?" the Brit replied.

"You can feel him out," Mike said. "Whatever. Catch his brain waves. His," he wiggled his fingers, "ooo, vibe."

Zoe's hand went to her forehead. "Oh my God," she muttered. "It's a kiddy circus."

James merely stared at the American in silence, for a time. To his amazement and growing discomfort, no one else spoke. Not even Mike. He just stared back. They all stared like dogs waiting for the bacon he was eating to fall on the floor. James would have preferred Mike to continue harassing him, if nothing else.

He didn't wish to say what was on his mind. Instead, he said, "It doesn't work that way."

Zoe appeared crestfallen. Aaron shifted beside the Brit, but held his tongue. Jonas looked away, and Mike's stare burned into the stranger.

"Oh really," he said to James. "Now it doesn't work that way."

James moved away from the wall he'd been about to hold up, not knowing when he'd backed closer to it. "I am not a trained seal."

"Nah, you're a pampered poodle," Mike retorted, and with those words, boxed the other man in with his body. "A pampered, prissy poodle."

"Mike!" Jonas snapped. "Good God, what's gotten into you?" He looked over the group. "All of you? Seriously!"

(It had nearly come to blows on more than one occasion.)

Only Aaron and Zoe acknowledged that Jonas had spoken at all. They did so with a look and nothing more.

James was still attempting to hold his ground against Mike. He was the proverbial deer in headlights.

"As you like," he said. James was repeating a mantra in his head. *He will not bait me, he will not bait me, he will not…*

"What the hell is that supposed to mean?" Mike was so close, he could taste the others man's breath.

An answer was not his to have, because just then, Mike felt himself jerked backwards. He whirled around to see his old friend, Jonas, not glaring at him, but looking at him with wide, surprised eyes. Yes, his old friend looked shocked, though the way he pulled him had been anything *but* friendly.

"What the fuck, Mike?" Jonas studied the other man's eyes. "Seriously, what the fuck?" Jonas no longer had a thought for how it looked to the outsider, to the man from London. The situation was too far gone as it was, and Jonas was intent on Mike.

Someone else answered before Mike could come up with a good excuse, which was a reprieve, because nothing came to him.

"It's this house," James said. "It's making all of you tense." There was more to it, but James was surprised at what he'd already said. He was worried enough about the reaction to those words, let alone what they might all say if he elaborated.

Simple seemed best, for the moment. Besides, he couldn't quite explain it, and even the skeptics wanted him to have the answers.

He didn't. Sure, houses often contained residuals. Places held left-over energy from past events, people – particularly if the emotional imprint was high. The Americans would know this.

Yet James said nothing else, because what he was currently sensing wasn't the same. It didn't feel...well, it didn't feel, and yet it did, which made no sense as an explanation. They wouldn't accept it.

"No shit," Mike said, not understanding there was meaning in what the Brit *hadn't* said.

Zoe grasped her own biceps. Her fingertips promised a row of black marks in the coming days. She understood. Understood how *she* felt, at least. Tension was a given. There was something wrong with the house. She kept thinking, when she'd been looking for Brig, that something was wrong with the house.

But she wasn't going to say it. Not yet. Let someone else be the crazy one. James had a good start. She'd let him carry on. It wouldn't be the first time others viewed him as the odd one, the freak. Right? That was fine by her. James didn't have to work and live with these people. She did.

Not that he'd done much but state the obvious, but she held hope that he'd carry on and be the loony in her stead. They expected him to be the drama-queen, after all. To be full of shit.

Jonas spared James a glance and then returned his attention to Mike. "Whatever it is, you need to calm down." He glanced at Zoe. "All of us do. You'd think Brig had run off or was murdered or something, for God's sake."

(One night, there were blows. Very bad blows. Bloody, bruising blows. Apologies weren't swift.)

"Don't say that," Zoe blurted.

Aaron held up his hands. "Okay, guys. I don't know what got in the water, but let's just take a breath, get our crap together, and look for Brig. He probably wandered off to check out some other part of the house. It's not like he hasn't done it other times; it's just a bigger house." He turned towards Mike. "He's done it to you, before, so I don't know why you're making such a case. Chill out, okay?"

Mike tossed out his hands, shrugged and turned away, suddenly intent on a small side table that he didn't remember being there before.

James held his silence, glad they'd forgotten him. To any outside observer, the group would seem to have turned on a dime, making much out of nothing. They'd have seemed like very different people than the ones who'd set out on the investigation not so long ago. Like people who were ready to decide whom to eat first.

Jonas sucked in a breath. "Well. If everyone's finished, then, let's go find Brig and get on with this case."

"All that over a piss," Mike muttered. "That's probably all it is. He went for a piss."

"Well you're the one who made a federal case out of it," Zoe said. If words could kill…

"Don't even start again," Jonas said. "Jesus. Let's just get back to investigating." He was already heading for the stairs. "While we look for Brig, I mean."

"I'm right behind you," Mike said.

"No." Jonas halted, turned, and looked Mike in the eyes. His gaze telegraphed that there was no room for argument.

"Zoe's coming with me. The rest of you do whatever you think is best."

Zoe's stomach did a flip. She tried not to look too eager when she caught Jonas up. It was obvious that he was agitated. He didn't even seem to care who did what, so she knew quite well that he was flustered. Not that he would appreciate this being pointed out.

Mike glared at Zoe and turned away, feet rushing him past Aaron and James, towards the other end of the hall. He thought it was the right way to go. There should be a set of stairs, according to his map. The first set that went to the third floor.

Aaron and James exchanged another meaningful look, while Jonas and Zoe headed down their chosen steps. Mike was heading up the other stairway.

"You are not going it alone, are you?" James felt compelled to ask. When he had moved to the other end of the hall, he didn't know. It seemed to him that the three of them had wound up at the end of said hall without taking a single step.

Mike slowed, but he kept ascending. "I ain't a little girl."

"Of course not," James conceded. The sense that he needed to stop Mike was strong. It started in the center of his body and flowed like thick liquid through his limbs. Liquid that threatened to solidify. "But I don't feel it's a good idea for you to be alone."

Mike stared down at him from the first landing. "You can feel Aaron up, for all I care. I got work to do."

Aaron felt the heat rise in his cheeks. He cursed himself for even thinking to be embarrassed. He also cursed Mike and wondered if something really had gotten into the water, because everyone was acting like a shit. Everyone but James.

The psychic made one last attempt. "It's not safe."

"Whatever. I gave you a chance to find Brig, but oh, it doesn't work that way. Which means it don't work!" Mike took the next steps two at a time. James lowered his gaze, counting the lines in the wood flooring. The counting distracted him from thoughts of how it had – seconds ago, it seemed – been far too dark to see the flooring at all.

His mind raced, but he would say no more. He knew that Aaron was looking at him. That his companion's thoughts were racing, as well.

Aaron cleared his throat. Cleared it again. Once more, and he'd sound like a Model A cranking up in sub-zero temps. "Well."

"Yes. Well," James agreed.

"That was fucking weird."

James' nod was absent, automatic.

"What did you...?" Aaron reconsidered his question. Perhaps he didn't want to know. He opted not to voice the rest of his thought.

"Nothing," James replied, nonetheless.

It was Aaron's turn to nod. He wasn't getting an answer right now, whether he asked aloud or not. Later he'd wonder why he didn't press the psychic for answers concerning a friend's safety.

"Where to, then?" is what Aaron asked.

James drifted towards a door he didn't remember seeing before. He had a feeling there was a small set of stairs that wasn't on the map. He had a thought that they should study the maps again before taking these stairs, but he couldn't seem to stop himself. "Away from here."

Aaron hesitated, but not for long. He decided he felt much safer with James and would rather be with him than anywhere else.

It wasn't long after the two had found the stairwell and begun to descend that Mike reappeared in the hallway. He directed his light up and down the area, flashed it across doorways, looking for someone. Anyone.

The hall was too long. Too dark. Too quiet. Was anything ever this quiet? Even a graveyard? He didn't think so. Even if he were to wear earplugs, there wouldn't be such absolute silence.

It gave him the willies.

So did the gaping doorways, which to him were like...like missing teeth in a sinister grin. The sort of smile that promised pain and suffering. Torture and a slow death.

(No swift apologies. But the blows had brought a swift death.)

He wasn't as brave as he had pretended to be. He was unsettled. But, as much as he wanted to call out for the others to wait up, tell them he'd changed his mind, pride demanded silence. By God, he wasn't going to let that prissy little foreigner think he was scared, or that he might be right.

Even if the prissy boy had a point, and maybe he wasn't such a bad guy. Mike wasn't going to admit it to his face.

He fidgeted, there in the spotlight he was casting. Debated. Argued with himself some more. Paced a few steps, careful not to come to close to those missing teeth. The creaking of the floorboards crept through his feet, traced a slithery line up his spine, and gave him a goosey shudder.

"Damn it," he swore under his breath. "Stop being such a pussy."

Mike retraced his steps, his stride defiant. The house would not defeat him, damn it. Neither would the others. He was going to get the best evidence of the night, or debunk the suspicions on his own.

Ratty, unwashed hair covered the wan expression when Mike hung his head, feet feeling their own way back up the stairs. If he could do either of those things, maybe Jonas wouldn't kick him out of the group.

They were all he had, after all.

22

Zoe let her fingers glide across the cool, satiny surface of the marble statue. They'd come across it in what the map suggested was a living room. Sitting room, that's what she thought they used to call it. *So many rooms – no wonder they needed so many names,* she thought. Even if several seemed to have the same purpose. None of it made sense to her.

She looked up into the face of the figure that towered over her. In the second it took her to recoil, she wondered why she'd ever touched the foul thing. It was disturbing. The most disturbing thing she'd ever seen up close. But she couldn't look away. It wasn't in a train wreck sort of fashion. It wasn't morbid curiosity.

She felt as if she *could not* look away from the black marble sculpture.

Black. She hadn't even known there was black marble. Not that she was any sort of art connoisseur. She liked new, shiny, clean things, Miss Zoe did.

The statue's face – in the loosest sense of the term, she decided – *was so hideous it defied description.*

A nervous giggle escaped her. Ran right off without her consent.

"What's up?" Jonas turned away from (yet another) fireplace to look in her direction.

"Nothing." She fanned the air with the hand not clutching the mini Maglite. "Just, this dude – I mean statue – is weird."

Jonas glanced at it before turning back to his own private investigation. "What's weird is some of the stuff left in this room. I'd think maybe it was worth something, you know. Why leave it behind?" He studied what he thought was an expensive silver platter. She turned back to the statue.

"Yeah…" *Worth bashing with a sledgehammer, maybe. Bash its smarmy nose right into its diseased brain and make those beady bat eyes fade out, be vacant like they're supposed to be, instead of…*

Alive

…following me around, even when I'm not moving. Heheh. That doesn't make sense.

"You doing anything useful over there?" Jonas cast a second glance in her direction. "Zo?"

"Yeah. Yeah I'm gonna get some readings, sure." She produced her K-II and waved it around Cthulhu's face. *No, not him, but one of his ardent followers. He'd be much uglier, even uglier than this thing.*

But it was more than the fact the marble male would lose every sexiest man alive contest in the universe; it was that he managed to look especially vicious. Brutish. Cold-hearted, seedy, and slimy in a way she thought that bottom-feeding, wannabe mafia thugs, were. Which was no mean feat, considering it was only a statue. The artist must have been a real piece of work himself.

Who could make such a thing? Self-portrait?

She let out another giggle. The cold-hearted part, at least, made sense.

Jonas didn't turn around this time. "Have you been smoking something?" He chuckled, but this belied his unease. She sounded like she was losing a few cards out of her deck. It was out of character.

Zoe was still waving the K-II around. "I wish I was smoking something." She wanted to turn away from the big marble guy. But she didn't like the idea of him being behind her. She almost giggled again when she realized that she'd been fingering his thigh before, and was now looking for electromagnetic energy in the area of his crotch.

"You're doing better than David, so why the attitude, big boy?"

"What?" Jonas lifted his brows at her. "What are you talking about?"

Zoe backed away from the seemingly animate piece of – again loosely termed – art. "Um. Just amusing myself. This room is boring."

"Whatever." Jonas shook his head. "Let me know if anything comes up."

"Something on this statue already did!"

Any other time, he might have laughed. But the woman didn't sound like herself. Goofy was one thing; he couldn't describe what this was. Like some sort of temporary madness.

"Um. Anyway." Zoe backed up some more, all of her giggles evaporating like liquid helium. She was certain the ugly marble bastard was leering at her. Daring her. Ready to dislodge a foot and take a step in her direction.

Spying.

Jonas was oblivious. He wasn't even facing her or the statue. He'd started thinking about Mike again, and the outburst in the hall. Then he'd started thinking about his hand. Almost as if to himself, he said, "Do you think I'm doing the right thing?"

The words didn't reach anyone but Jonas, though the marble man might have heard, or so Zoe would've believed, if someone had asked her later. Her retreating form had picked up speed in the face of its gaze. That leering, nasty, maniacal, ne'er-do-well face.

"I don't know," Jonas said. "It seems like the right thing. But I thought coming here was good, too, and now I'm not so sure."

Back, back, until she stumbled, dropping her light. Jonas turned at the sound, just in time to present his chest for Zoe's face to smack into with an audible oomph.

"Whoa, what the...Zoe, what's gotten into you? What's wrong?" His arms, of their own accord, went around her. He wasn't without protective instincts, after all. He cared about her state of mind, no doubt about it.

Zoe considered not looking at him. Considered keeping her face somewhere between his pecs. It was warm. Safe. Cozy. Strong...

Too many feelings moved through her at once. She was relieved, but embarrassed. Scared, but safe. She wanted to laugh, yet she was intimidated by the damn statue and was certain it was coming after her, though for some reason, Jonas didn't notice it.

This embarrassed her even more. Why couldn't he see it? He wasn't seeing it, or he'd be scared too. Or, at least, swearing at the strangeness of it. Right?

"Hey," he said, with more concern in his words. "You okay?"

She shook her head without lifting it. Then decided that she was acting like a little girl lost in the woods with a big bad wolf chasing her – instead of a grown woman doing a job – so she nodded. Drew her face away from his warm, wonderful chest and looked up, into his eyes.

He looked so concerned. It was a nice feeling. Such a nice thing that she wanted to milk every second of it. But no. That would be cruel. That would be something his wife would do.

That's not fair, or nice.

"I'm okay," she said. "I got...well, that thing creeped me out. There. I said it. I'm a total girl."

Jonas gave a little shrug. She felt it, because he hadn't let go of her.

"Everyone gets spooked sometimes." He directed his gaze past her, towards the offending piece of marble. "Now that I get a good look at it, I don't blame you. That thing's ugly as sin."

Sin. It's swallowed everyone's sins, and that's why it looks like that.

Zoe almost smacked herself. "Totally ugly." She didn't turn to look. She knew very well where it was. She didn't need to see if her flashlight had landed in a way that illuminated the sinful face of the tall, hulking marble man, casting it in an evil slant.

More evil.

Jonas was seeing this well enough for two.

"So..." He let his arms drift to his sides. Nothing rushed. They had enjoyed their brief stay. He had liked holding her, if he were to admit it. "We should check out the rest of the room."

Zoe stared up at him a moment longer.

"Shouldn't we?" he asked, and her stomach tilted.

"Yes." She forced herself to turn, to walk towards her flashlight, which was indeed casting its beam at the face of the fake man, the demon marble, made possible by the fact it had landed on one of the giant's feet, between its obscene toes in such a way as to make the perfect angle...

What were the odds of that? Well, I'm not going to test it and find out!

Jonas could see that Zoe was scared of the thing. It was in the tightness of her movements, the slowness of her advance on the figure, the wary glances she cast up its body.

"Want me to get that?"

"I got it, Jonas, but thanks."

He had a sudden thought that a rock hard foot would crush her delicate, pretty hand. "Nah, I got it." He started in her direction.

In a great show of bravery, Zoe reached for the Maglite herself. Forced herself to do it, not wishing to fall apart in front of Jonas like some amateur. As if mocking her, the light clattered away, rolled onto the other foot. She had to reach again, to get closer.

"Zoe…"

"I got it, I got it." Her fingers found purchase on the black aluminum, and she snatched it away from the toes, convinced they were about to wiggle, further taunting her.

She turned. Jonas was closer than she'd realized. So was the statue. Right behind her. "Um, see?" She held aloft her prize. "Got it." She fought the urge to throw herself into his chest again.

"Cool." He glanced up at the unnamed masterwork. Decided that it was too hideous to have a name. "Let's get moving."

Thank God, she thought. "Just say where."

~

Aaron took wary steps, following James. For most of the evening, Aaron had trusted this interesting and somewhat odd man. He didn't know why; it was just a feeling. He tried to operate from his gut; it was right, always right. It was when a person second-guessed that things ended up skewered. That infamous little voice was so immediate, so damned critical.

Aaron's little voice was pestering him about the Englishman. Giving him grief. Niggling, niggling, but over what, he couldn't decide. Or maybe it was that he couldn't abide the nagging.

James was hiding something. This wasn't news. Aaron had ascertained that factoid hours ago. That didn't mean the man wasn't trustworthy. Everyone had secrets, and they didn't share them with people they'd only just met. Had James dumped his life story on their first meeting, the American would trust him less. He'd also have died from boredom, possibly. Was anyone's life story compelling enough for a novel-sized retelling, an uninterrupted campfire sitting? No doubt, there were some of those in the world, but Aaron hadn't met them.

Though... he thought it likely that the Englishman had some fascinating stories to share. When one considered James' talents, the kind of upbringing he may have had...

Unpleasant, perhaps. Clearly, judging from other moments in the evening, James had some unpleasant memories, yes.

Aaron left off thinking of such things when he saw where he'd followed, what the end of the path was. Where the stairs had come to an abrupt halt and dumped them.

The hush of words left him, without thought. "This wasn't on the maps."

James stepped farther into the room. That's all it was; a chilled, moldy, damp, dirty, vacuum-sealed room. That's the feeling both men had. That the air was stale. That they were breathing air that people of times long past had expelled from their lungs.

He couldn't understand why it was so cold. His breath left visible traces when he exhaled. He didn't sense a presence, so much as a weight. The atmosphere was dense, thick as molasses in an East Coast February.

"What is it, a...a cellar?" Aaron asked, not yet comfortable with the idea of moving from the final step to the floor. His foot outright rebelled at the idea.

"Oubliette," James whispered. Not so much in response, but a thought verbalized without premeditation.

"What?" Aaron tried to step down. Both feet refused. There was something about the floor they didn't like, didn't want to touch. Aaron decided to stop arguing with them for the time being.

But then James' sharp inhale caused him to jump. Just a little. He was about to ask another question when James made a partial turn, revealing his dim profile.

"Oubliette," James said with much more volume and purpose. "It's a French word. From the verb oublier, to forget."

"So it's like, a forgotten room?"

"In a way, yes." James eyed his companion in his peripheral vision. "Oubliettes were dungeons accessible only by a hatch in the ceiling. Or floor, depending on where you stood."

"Then there shouldn't be stairs. Right?"

James shook his head. "No. But it's precisely what the room feels like, reminds me of."

Aaron shut his eyes, his brows creasing. He could not imagine what happened in such a room. The mere idea threatened to turn him into a claustrophobic. Brig would've been freaking out and running away before they'd gotten halfway down the stairs.

Brig...weren't they supposed to...something about Brig.

"Clearly, this is not an actual Oubliette," James was saying. "There are stairs, as you pointed out. It defeats the purpose of the forgotten prisoner. Unless they were added later?"

"You're right, though. It feels like that kind of place." Aaron ventured a peek through a well-directed beam of light. "Maybe that's just the power of suggestion."

James shifted his attention to the far wall. "I'm a marvelous hypnotist."

Aaron's reply fell back down his throat, never standing a chance against the little voice in his head.

Then why don't you compel everyone to hand over their money and their pants?

It surprised him. His darker, sarcastic thoughts were increasing, where it concerned James. He didn't understand why. The man hadn't done anything to him. He hadn't brought him harm, or meant any with the earlier joke. His warning to Mike had been congenial, and he'd sounded concerned.

Genuinely, Aaron thought. Therefore, there was no reason not to like him, to trust him. So far.

Except…what was he warning Mike about? What did he think would happen? Why didn't Aaron ask?

He ordered his feet to move, at last making it off the final step, and came to James' side. "It's damned quiet in here. It makes some sense, since there aren't any other doors and we're underground, but," he peered through the soupy air, "I don't know."

"One would think a bit of sound would travel down the stairwell."

"Yes."

"Strange, indeed."

Aaron observed James a while longer, before turning on his recorder. He didn't ask a question of the room, just let it run, listening. For what, he didn't know. They never really knew. They hoped for something, anything to come across, that's all.

Maybe not just anything.

Aaron quivered in his shoes. "Really cold in here."

James nodded his agreement. There was no reason to divest his new friend of whatever self-comfort he could muster. At least, he held hope that Aaron was a friend, of sorts. As much as one could be in a short time. More friendly than the others felt towards him, is what James wanted. Just one friend in this sad little situation.

Inwardly, he sighed. He hadn't had many friends. If any. He couldn't imagine why he was thinking such thoughts, now. He doubted that he would ever see the American, again. They'd go their separate ways and…

James' scalp crawled, as if he'd contracted a sudden, Guinness-record-breaking bout of lice. This was torture enough on its own, fighting the mad urge to scratch until his nails left trenches, but with it came such a profound feeling of dread, James almost collapsed under the weight of it.

Aaron didn't pause to think. James was halfway in his arms before comprehension that he'd moved struck. "Shit, you're like, turning gray. What's wrong?"

James swayed out of the other man's grasp, out of his reach, stumbling forward. "Pl-please…don't."

"Sorry, I'm sorry." Aaron took an instinctive step towards him, regardless. "But you look like you're going to be sick. Like you're going to faint."

James held up a hand in a signal to stop. To give him space. Bending nearly in two, his hands then went to his knees.

"James…?" Aaron couldn't stand by and do nothing, though he had little choice. He considered it the hardest thing he'd ever had to do in his life, to stand by and watch someone so clearly suffering.

He then admonished himself, thinking that it wasn't about him. James must be feeling twice as bad. Three times. Even in the side glow of the flashlight Aaron had dropped, James appeared blanched.

"The air…" James, though he despised the taste of it, inhaled. There was no other recourse. "The air here has a foul taste."

Aaron had no concept of this. Yes, it was stale and had a sort of old piss smell, amongst other things, but he wouldn't have called it foul. Not the way James just had, as if speaking of something utterly evil.

"Do you want to leave?" Stupid question. Sure he does. "C'mon. Let's go."

"A moment."

"I'll get the stuff, and we'll just get out of here, pronto."

"Please, could you stop talking?" James attempted to straighten himself.

Anger flashed in Aaron, swift and bright. "Screw you, too." He tossed a hand out. "Who are you anyway? Legolas? Ooo, the air here has a foul taste." A derisive snort chased after the words.

James folded in on himself once more, the onslaught of emotion in the American's words absorbed, because he was vulnerable in that moment.

"You know something," Aaron went on. "You know shit that you're not telling."

With great effort, James responded. "Don't be a hypocrite." He took in a measured bit of air through gritted teeth. "Each of you is keeping secrets, every last one of you. Do not think that I am oblivious to it." After another sip of air, he managed to right himself, using the borrowed anger to his advantage. "I may not know the details, but the feeling oozes from each of you, like you're all ruptured fountain pens." He made a vague, all-encompassing gesture. "And I can sense that you're all afraid to speak up. That you're all pretending it isn't real, which is a bit ironic, don't you think? Considering it is, after all, your job to hunt what others insist doesn't exist."

As swift as it came, the anger fled. Aaron stood, staring at the other man, abashed.

"You wanted evidence, and yet you all shy away from it," James said. "Most of you believe me to be full of shite, yet you keep expecting me to have all of the answers. Well, sir, I don't, and so I haven't said a word about this house."

Aaron, his cheeks warm, discovered his voice. "I'm- you're... you're right. I mean, speaking for myself, anyway, and well... the others are acting weird, yeah. I'm sorry. I'm really...I like you and..." he looked away.

"You don't know what came over you?"

To Aaron, it sounded like an accusation. No. A sarcastic rebuff. "I..."

"But of course."

Another rebuff. He deserved it, he knew. Though he honestly didn't know what had come over him. He wasn't going to say that, however. He wasn't going to make the excuse James expected of him.

"If you are quite finished," James said, walking past him, towards the stairs.

Aaron made no reply. Didn't move. The situations with his first time partner and old time partners had him paralyzed, not simply in thoughts.

James moved up the first step. The second. He paused and clasped his hands, laced his fingers together. Tight.

"Aaron, do please forgive me," he said and pivoted in place to face the other man. "I can only say that I was overwhelmed and couldn't handle..." James closed his mouth. This was a reason he didn't have friends. It sounded like he had his own lists of excuses much of the time.

"You don't know what came over you?" Aaron whispered.

James lowered his gaze. "Actually, I do. But touché."

A breeze of a laugh blew through the room. Aaron's laugh.

"It's difficult sometimes to sound diplomatic when I'm – "

"As raw as a victim in a burn unit?" Aaron cut in.

James arched a brow. "Pleasant visual. It does drive home the point, however." His shoulders, previously rising towards his ears, relaxed, along with his brow. "I wish that I could offer you some facts, Aaron. I wish that I didn't feel so lacking in control, just now. I need a moment, perhaps."

Aaron, at last able to command his own limbs, moved in his direction. "It's not professional, but to hell with it. Let's get out of this horrible room. It obviously has a bad effect on you." He gave off a sheepish look. "Us." He gathered up his light, his recorder. "Shit, this job is messing with all of us, seems like."

"Fair enough." James was beyond elated to be leaving the dungeon. For that's what it was. That's what screamed at him.

In fact, the entire manor had begun to project dungeon at him, but he wasn't going to tell Aaron that. Not just yet. His remarks on secret keeping hadn't been admonitions, only statements, conveying that he wasn't the only one. That he knew, and had some understanding.

He couldn't speak his thoughts aloud until he'd sorted his own feelings on the matter. The last thing he wished for was more arguments and misunderstandings.

~

Mike wandered down yet another hall. Does this house have enough fucking halls? And into another bedroom. Probably a bedroom. Does this place have enough fucking bedrooms?

He couldn't be certain what it was. There wasn't any old, rotting furniture. There weren't any defining features, except a fireplace. It meant little to Mike, as over half of the rooms in the manor had fireplaces.

He panned his camcorder slow and steady on the off chance he might capture something. Anything. He was determined to come back with evidence. Something more than spiders in a corner. A shudder worked its way through Mike's bones. He didn't appreciate where his thoughts had gone.

He snuck his way around the edge of the room, looking this way and that, thinking how drab it was. How dull and lifeless. Boring, tasteless. Big house like this should have better-looking décor, he thought. Sure, it was old, decrepit, left to rot, but still – shouldn't there be something left of its former glory? Smith had installed some electricity but hadn't cleaned up the place first? There wasn't even a hint or promise of old Victorian wallpaper.

Maybe the previous occupants had left the room to its own devices long before ditching the house, he reasoned. Mostly, these thoughts were the ramblings of a troubled mind, which was attempting to ignore what was really going on and focus on something simple. Mundane. It didn't want to think about lectures, or hairy, too-many-legged-freaks, or people with more money than they had a right to possess.

"Fuck you" money that Mike would never have.

He let go with a snort at this thought and took a bold few steps to the center of the room.

"Bet you didn't even work for the money to build this fancy place, did you?" Mike's gaze attempted to penetrate the darkness to either side of the small recorder screen. "Probably inherited it. Yeah. I bet you did. Just like Smith probably did, stupid fop." He paused long enough to wonder where he'd heard that word. One of those boring, nothing-but-talk movies his ex made him watch, most likely. Because she was trying to gain a little culture.

"So how about it?" His feet described a circular path on the floor. "Did Daddy die and leave you all his cash?"

Some called it provoking. Anger the spirits, dare them to come out and talk, to defend themselves. Mike hadn't particularly been one for such tactics, in the past. But he was frustrated and likely on his last mission, so he no longer cared about the moral arguments against provocation.

"Fat, lazy bastards, sitting in your posh house, doing nothing." Mike walked to the other end of the tiny room. "Man, why did people make their bedrooms so small back in the day, anyway? If I had that much money, I'd have a huge bedroom." He laughed until he snorted. "Not much going on in here but sleep, eh?" He stared at the night vision of the screen.

There was no reply to a single one of his outbursts. No footsteps, no feeling of eyes on him, and no thick atmosphere. Not even a temperature fluctuation.

"Either you're a bunch of loser ghosts, or this is just a big fat waste." Mike lowered his camera and peered about the room. "But, that's what Smith wanted. Just ghost stories with no ghosts. Bad ghost stories. Seriously, your stories are not very original."

He wasn't going to think about the room with the phantom books and angry shelves. He wasn't thinking about it at all when he noticed that the previously unremarkable, moldy wallpaper appeared to brighten, like someone turning a dimmer switch back to its higher setting. The paper blossomed pale yellow in the center of the wall as he looked at it through the camcorder screen. It bloomed brighter and wider, spreading out along the wall, until the yellow petals reached every corner. Until they bled into one, coloring in every spot.

As he turned a slow circle, a whispered expletive leaving him, he witnessed the same happening on each of the other three walls.

To his nose came the scent of yellow. Yellow like a daffodil, tulip, or perhaps a yellow daisy. He didn't know. Just yellow – it smelled like yellow.

"Oh my God." A smile spread across Mike's face. Something was finally happening. Something not scary. Something he was recording and he could see it, even, with his own eyes, when he looked up from the screen. "Look at this, guys. Look at the walls. Is that crazy, or what? So cool."

His smile widened. He liked the color. It was a happy color. It chased all the bad thoughts away. Like a warm, summer day, with a light, cool breeze coming off nearby water. The buzzing of fat bumblebees in clover came from the other direction, and the prickling of the hairs on his neck warned him…

Warning him. A hand went to the back of his neck, startling him. For a second, Mike hadn't realized it was his own hand. It seemed that the hair there really did feel prickly.

Then, as if electricity had flooded the room, the hair on his head began to rise. He could feel it. A storm was coming, that was it. That's how he remembered it feeling when he was a child in Iowa, standing outside, late July, and a beautiful summer day would swiftly turn dark, the sky pregnant with sinister, green-black clouds.

There's a banger coming, get in the house, Mike! Sure to be lightning!

Except that one time when he hadn't been anywhere near home, but instead, out exploring, and he'd come across a cave in the bluffs and had no choice but to run inside, because his mom had always said that when your hair stood up like that, it was best to get inside, watch the pretty lights from there.

So he'd run inside.

He'd run inside, not thinking much about how far or fast, since a clap of thunder rang his ears at that moment. In his dash to safety, he'd run face first into a silken, sticky phantom. He couldn't see it, but it was all over his face, stuck to his lashes, to even the hair that fell over his eyes. The hair his mother was always threatening to cut.

He'd swatted and rubbed, plucked at and shook, but nothing would get rid of the damned web. But worse, oh, worse…

The spinners of the web. The tickling of their legs, too many god damned legs, and there were hundreds, or so it felt like. He'd run into a nest of creepy-crawlies and they were making their way down his neck, into his collar, down into his shirt, millimeter by excruciating millimeter.

Hairy legs, shiny black legs, brown legs, spindly legs. Legs, legs, legs. Prickling his flesh, miniscule steps, prickle, prickle, and prickle.

He'd screamed and spun a circle, grabbing and slapping and flinging his arms about in hysterics, like a man on fire.

They were creepy-crawling their way across his face, trying to get up his nose, and they were shuffling down the front of his shirt, and over his arms, leaving his skin ready to peel off his body and flee ahead of his skeleton.

He'd had the urge to scream again, but the fear they'd get into his mouth sealed his lips shut, and it came out more a strangled whimper. The last thing he wanted was for those evil, nasty things to tickle their way down his throat on thousands of legs and set up camp in his stomach. Lay eggs there, or whatever it was they did. It couldn't be good, whatever they did down there.

They'd lay eggs, and one day his stomach would burst open, and thousands upon thousands of translucent eight-legged baby freaks would swarm out and finish the job, devouring him outside in, inside out.

The grown-up version of Mike in the dingy room screamed and dropped his camcorder. Why his mind had gone to that horrible place, he couldn't fathom, but he had little time to ponder it, when he saw that the happy yellow wallpaper was curling on its edges. Every edge, curling black, like leftover zigzags smoldering in an ashtray.

With the visual came a sound. Difficult to discern, at first. It was soft. Like a lover's caress. Just a rustle, if that.

He backed slowly towards a corner.

The rustle came once more. Over there, a rustle. It wasn't the rustle of leaves.

Not the rustle of fabric.

What is it, Mike asked himself. *What makes that sound?*

His flashlight stabbed the darkness, making a bull's-eye on the wall opposite. Revealed to Mike was a small stain. Rusty brown, muddy.

It looked as if it were growing.

Grew.

Mike rubbed his eyes with the heel of his empty hand. This achieved the blurring of his vision long enough to make him think the stain had moved across the wall.

His eyelids blinked in rapid succession.

It had moved, hadn't it?

Was moving.

So was Mike. First, his feet had taken him another step back, until his heels contacted peeled wallpaper and cracked plaster. They had then moved him a step forward, curiosity and the voice in his head reminding him that he was getting the only evidence of the evening. Amazing evidence that urged him closer to a stain that he didn't remember seeing before.

The camcorder. He remembered that he'd dropped it. He was swift to retrieve it. It wasn't broken; this much he could see when he glanced at the screen and aimed it in the direction of the wall blob. Thank goodness for small favors. It wouldn't do to break any more of the equipment. He was in hot enough water – no need to bring it to a boil.

The voice in Mike's head told him to shut the flashlight off to cut the glare, to allow night vision its reign. The evidence might be better that way, less corrupted, especially if it were paranormal and not simply his eyes deceiving him.

Or his paranoia. He cursed himself when admitting this, when he conceded that he was frightened, he really was. He had been mesmerized before, perhaps. Too stunned to register an emotion. But events so far had gotten further under his skin than was healthy. The others were right, before, when they said he needed to calm the fuck down, and he was trying, really he was.

Maybe the fag – no. *James*. That was his name. Maybe James had been right. He wasn't a bad guy. Not really. He might have been right to warn Mike about going it alone.

No. Now he would get the best evidence of the evening!

The stain swelled and relaxed, swelled and relaxed, as if it were breathing.

To hell with that fag! I'll show you, all of you. You'll be creaming your jeans when you see this footage, and Jonas, he won't fire me if I get the best evidence we've ever captured!

Mike took slow steps closer to the amoeba on the wall, doing his best to ignore the bumps on his body from which every hair protruded. He tried as well to remain present – to ignore that childhood memory.

An exceedingly difficult task as he was so ready to fling his arms around like a mad man.

23

They had all found themselves back at command central, once again. Not by virtue of connecting through walkie-talkies, nothing staged, nor agreed upon; they simply found themselves gathered there.

As if pushed in that direction. Implied compliance. Led.

Pushed is how they might have described it, had they time to think about it, later. Had one of them asked the question of another investigator.

Jonas and Zoe. Aaron and James. Entering from different parts of the house, they had arrived in the room at the same time. Precisely.

After five minutes of standing around, each pondering personal secrets, one of them at last decided that something else was odd.

"Where's Brig?" Zoe asked. Never mind that she realized neither she nor Jonas had mentioned him – she didn't think – the entire time they were supposed to have been looking for him....

One of her hands fluttered to her forehead as she tried to remember.

"We…" Aaron paused. How could he possibly have forgotten about Brig? The oubliette was stressful and strange, but how could he forget? "We didn't see him."

Jonas looked at each of them, wondering if he had lost time again, but he refrained from checking his watch. "Maybe Mike's seen him?"

Aaron reached for his walkie-talkie. "Let's see." He pressed a button. "Mike, check in, please."

A static response mocked him. He tried again.

"Mike, it's Aaron. Where are you?"

More white noise.

"Wait," Zoe said. "I think I hear someone."

Everyone in the room listened hard. Each began to nod. Save James.

"Yeah, maybe that's him, can't tell," Jonas said. "Maybe the batteries are dying."

"Or there's interference?" Aaron said. "Sounds like interference."

"Could be ghosts," Zoe offered, snapping from her reverie. "That happens around ghosts."

They all looked at James with expectant eyes. Held breaths. He could sense their desire for an affirmative answer. It would explain everything and make them less uneasy. Ghosts were better than their darker thoughts, of which they were beginning to have several.

He dearly wished to step back and away, but he held his ground. "I don't know."

Before anyone could make a remark in return, Aaron lifted the walkie once again. "Brig, check in."

"For God's sake, he's not answering, don't you get it? So stop fucking asking!"

All eyes moved to Zoe. James was the only person in the room not surprised by her hysterical interjection. He'd felt it coming, unlike the others, who had never seen Zoe lose it. Not on an investigation, and they'd known her to be polite in personal associations, as well. This was the second time, now.

Not that Zoe shared all of herself, for them to know her well. There was a wall between her and the world most of the time. It was so meticulously constructed, as to be invisible and so, her co-investigators never noticed it.

Jonas was the first to snap out of his shock. He moved in her direction and reached for her hands, taking them in his. Gave them a reassuring squeeze.

Zoe looked up into his eyes, her own moistening. He didn't say anything, just held her hands, and it made her feel several things she couldn't sort out, or didn't want to sort. Or shouldn't.

"I'm…I'm sorry," she said, and lowered her gaze. "I don't know what came over me."

"You're scared," Jonas said, without recrimination. It was a simple, compassionate statement. One that caused a lump to form in Zoe's throat.

"Where are they? Where're Brig and Mike?" Aaron turned to James, who had done his level best to seep into the woodwork. "You must be able to sense *something*, anything. Can't you?"

The question was so sincere. So full of hope. James looked into the other man's eyes, eyes that reflected those emotions, and wished dearly that he could give the answer that would set Aaron's mind at ease.

"I can't," he said, and the words tasted bitter. "I can't sense them."

A forced wave of sound left James, then, forced out because Jonas had slammed him up against the wall without warning, without pity, and most of all, without thought.

"You're a fraud! Just another frigging fraud, Mike was right."

Where Zoe had shocked her friends before, now Jonas had shocked everyone in the room. It took more than a moment for Aaron and her to register what had just happened. James' body vibrated and hummed to the tune of Jonas' anger, which flowed through the big man's touch, paralyzing the Brit – who had been blindsided for once in his life.

James was bordering on nauseous by the time either of the other two people in the room stepped in.

"Hey, whoa!" Aaron grabbed a beefy arm belonging to his team leader. "Back off, okay? You're freaking him out. Shit, you're freaking *me* out." He didn't know what to think. He didn't know what to do. He'd never seen his boss so angry.

Jonas didn't back off. He grasped the lapels of his captive's jacket and shook James as if he were a push-me pull-me toy.

"You can't do jack," he bellowed into an increasingly white face. "That crap with the camera, it was a trick."

"Dude," Aaron tried pulling on that arm, but it was like arm wrestling the hulk, "it was broken, just like he said." Perhaps he could reason with Jonas. Surely he'd have to listen to logic.

"He did it," Jonas said, without breaking eye contact with James. "He did it himself."

"When did he do that, huh?" Aaron dared a small push at the broader-man. "He didn't have access, Jonas." He gave him another shove, hoping to gain more of his attention. "Dude, this isn't like you. Chill, okay, and we'll have a civilized talk." *Oh my God, this is all going to hell.*

Narrowed eyes moved to Aaron. "Civilized. You've been hanging around this guy too long already," Jonas said. "Gonna ask him on a date when we're done?"

"Jonas please, please let him go."

The plea was soft, plaintive, and feminine. Zoe had woken from what she thought was a bizarre dream, in which Jonas had lost his mind and become the killer in a bad slasher flick.

"This isn't you talking," she said. *It can't be. He's stressed, that's all.* "You're not a bully, Jonas." *He'd always seemed a big old Teddy bear to Zoe.* "But right now, you're acting like one."

Her voice sluiced through the muck in his brain, through the reddening haze of his anger, and diffused it. Jonas could feel his hands, arms, gaining weight; his fingers loosened, his arms lowered themselves, and he made a slow turn in Zoe's direction, the understanding that he should be embarrassed slamming into him. He should be more than that. In the silent moments that followed, he had time to feel ashamed.

James began to melt, so it appeared to Aaron when he looked. To slide right down the wall. Once again, he found himself wanting to reach for the now fragile-seeming man.

He didn't. He was afraid of what might happen. That maybe he'd make it worse. Or that James would admonish him again; tell him not to touch him. Not ever. So Aaron stood still, unable to digest what had happened, anyway. If he moved, the world might tilt in the other direction, and he'd be sick.

Jonas managed to meet Zoe's gaze, which to his relief was full of compassion, though beneath it there was confusion. They were in the same boat. Jonas was confused as to why he'd lost so much control of himself. Nothing about the night was proceeding in normal fashion. It was like one long, horrid Monday.

"You're right. It's not like me. I'm really, really sorry," he said. He knew that he should apologize to the outsider. That he was making his remunerations in the wrong direction. He was shamed twice over when admitting to himself that he couldn't face James, just yet.

Zoe merely nodded. She looked to James, who had moved away from the rest of them and stood hugging himself, his back to all of them.

She couldn't blame him. She also couldn't refrain from voicing the opinion that had popped up in that dream that wasn't a dream. An opinion that repeated itself.

"It's not James' fault. He can't sense them, because they're not in the house," she said.

Aaron felt himself nod his agreement. It had occurred to him, as well. Before Jonas had had his brush with insanity, Aaron had expected James to reveal that truth.

Green eyes flicked over the Brit's back. Just a glance.

Perhaps James hadn't intended to mention that little fact, after all, Aaron thought. But this time he felt no irritation, impatience, or anger over the secrets. As James had said, they were all keeping them. As he looked in Jonas' direction, he also thought of how they were all going a bit crazy.

Crazy. Yes, they were slowly going bonkers. Some faster than others, perhaps. Maybe he was being dramatic, but Aaron couldn't help himself. It was the proverbial something's in the water, except no one had been drinking the water.

Maybe it was an airborne virus.

Aaron felt a zap of anxiety. Had a sudden urge. He rushed towards the front door.

"Hey," Jonas said, grateful for a reason to look away from Zoe and her questioning gaze. "What're you doing?"

"If they're not in the house, then they're outside, duh." Aaron reached for the doorknob. "Someone needs to look." Anxiousness set up camp in his stomach. He was certain something was wrong, other than the obvious.

Even more certain when he tried the knob and it wouldn't turn.

"What the?" Aaron jiggled, wrenched, and twisted at the round metal handle, but nothing budged. "It won't open." His ministrations became more frantic.

"That's impossible," Jonas said. He strode towards the door. "It's just stuck; give it some muscle."

"What do you think I'm doing, huh?" Aaron pulled and pulled. Nearly placed his foot to the door for a better advantage. In fact, he was lifting his right foot as Jonas reached him.

"Here, let me try." Jonas nudged the other man aside and grasped the knob, tight. "Wuss."

It was an attempt at humor, but no one laughed, particularly not when Jonas tugged, hard, and nothing happened, other than a loud protest of wood and hinges.

To James it was as if the door had cried out. A cat with a smashed tail, a rat in the grip of a stone hand. He covered his ears, though this did nothing to block it. The sound came again, louder, when Jonas yanked, harder. A wailing of tiny beings, thousands of them, protesting the separation of their joints.

"Damn it," Aaron swore and beat his fist on the wood. "Stupid old shit. You'd think it would break." He turned and headed for the hall, the one that led to the kitchen.

"Wait." Zoe flinched at the sound of her own voice. "Wait, don't leave." Trepidation. It worked its way through her limbs. Her nerves. "We should – "

"There are other doors, and I'm going to check them," Aaron said.

"I'll come with," Jonas said. It was a good excuse to get out of the room, and he wanted it.

"But…" Zoe appealed to James with a look. Her hopes fell short, when she saw how closed up he looked. Like he was curling in on himself.

"We'll be right back; you two just stay put," Aaron said as he walked away, with Jonas catching him up and right on his heels.

"They'll all be sealed."

James' breathy words startled Zoe. It hadn't seemed he was ever going to speak again, and she wished, now, that he hadn't. The words were ominous. Because she knew what he meant.

"What do you know?" She rushed to his side. "Huh? What do you know about this house and, and…" She didn't grab him; she wasn't going to be like Jonas. But part of her wanted to. She wanted to shake him until reasonable explanations fell out of his ass. As it was, she ended up shoving him.

James did nothing but repeat himself, essentially. "The doors won't open."

Zoe studied his face as if trying to see through to his bones, or through them into his brain. What she saw instead was that he appeared lost. Lost in his body. It didn't make sense, the descriptive, but it was all she had. That, and as she peered closer, the idea that he was in a trance.

Maybe it was the same thing.

Her ponderings were cut short when the other two men came bounding back into the room, their ire preceding them. One didn't have to be a sensitive to notice it.

"Everything's sealed tight." Jonas rubbed his head, something he only did in a fit of nerves, of upset. She'd seen him do it the night he confessed to her that he was getting divorced.

He'd told her first.

"How can that be?" Zoe asked.

Aaron turned to James. "Maybe he knows."

Wherever James had been for the last several minutes, Aaron's words, his tone, appeared to lead him back. He looked at the American, bewildered, at first, then with a strange sort of resignation.

As if he knew precisely what was coming next – this time.

"I know what you know," James said.

"Oh yeah?" Aaron moved closer. "I think you know more."

James closed his eyes with a sigh that carried the weariness of a much older, world beaten man.

"You show up, act all secretive, and all kinds of weird crap starts happening," Aaron said.

James opened his eyes to gaze upon the man he'd come to like in such a short time. What kept him calm in the face of Aaron's confrontation was that he felt that the other man liked him, too. That he wasn't honestly suspicious.

He just needed someone to direct his frustration at, if only for a moment, and of course, a stranger was always first choice.

And so James didn't take it personally. Another thing he had much practice at, in his lifetime.

"Let us think on this, Aaron," he said. "How could I lock the doors from outside and yet be standing here?"

"Hidden passage," Aaron fired back. "This place is like a maze. Maybe you know more about it than we do. You're from this country; we aren't."

"Yes, of course," James said, unable to quash the instant bubble of sarcasm. "All Brits are given blueprints for every mansion and castle upon birth. Just when was I out of anyone's sight, by the by?"

Aaron grasped at another straw. "You found that room."

"Maybe he knows Smith a lot better than he says," Jonas said, ignoring James and Aaron both. It would make sense, and he wanted it to make sense.

"You guys…" Zoe looked at each of them. It could explain a few things. She wasn't sure what to think, but… "Hey, James. So you and Smith are playing a joke, right?" She pushed out a laugh. "One big joke. Aaron told me how you pulled that joke on him earlier."

Aaron searched James' eyes. A joke. He'd like that to be true. Except there was another problem.

"He'd never get Mike in on it," he said. "Mike couldn't stand him."

"I don't know what's going on or who knows how it happened, and right now, I don't think I care." Jonas strode to a broken down old chair. "Right now I want some freaking air."

"What are you doing?" Zoe gestured at the chair.

Without answering, the big man grabbed the back of the chair with one hand, and an arm of it with the other. Most of it was in a state of rot, but the wooden arm still looked solid. He wrenched at it. It popped off almost too easily.

He didn't bother to pause, to look at the others, instead nearly ran to the large front room window. He swung, like a professional baseball player, and connected with glass.

It should have been a home run, but it wasn't even a base hit.

"What the…" Jonas looked in disbelief at the unblemished glass, while the others in the room (save James) gasped. Jonas swung again.

And again.

The reverberations raced up his arm, began to hurt.

"That's not possible." He spun around, and looked at the others. "What is it, special glass? What the fuck is going on?"

Aaron raced to the window and looked not at it, but through it.

"Is someone out there?" Zoe asked as she hugged herself. Hard.

"Where're the vans!" Aaron turned an accusing look on James. "The vans are gone!"

The Brit began to shake his head.

"They can't be gone." Jonas looked through the dirty glass. "How can they be gone?"

"James…" Zoe inched towards him. "Listen, just tell us. If you and Smith are up to something, just…just tell us."

"So I can wring your neck," Jonas snarled, as he pivoted in the direction of the stranger.

Zoe held up a hand. "That's not helping." She made another appeal to James. "No one's going to wring your neck. Just let us in on the joke, and we'll forget the whole thing."

"I have no idea where the vans are and I have never met Mr. Smith." James held his hands up in a gesture suggesting he was warding the others off. Protecting himself. "I understand your need to point at me. I wish I could help you, I do – "

"If you're not up to something, then what the fuck is going on?" Jonas said. "Why won't the doors open, where are the vans, and what's up with the bullet proof glass, huh?"

"Wait, wait." Aaron ran both hands through his hair. "Maybe it's just Smith. It's Smith's doing." He turned and touched Jonas on the arm. "James is trapped in here, too. Smith is playing tricks on all of us."

Jonas studied his friend.

"James is a victim of whatever this is, just like us." Aaron nodded. He preferred this idea. He didn't like expecting the worst in people. He wanted to believe that most were good, decent types. "I don't think he wants to be stuck in here any more than we do."

"We never met our client," Zoe said. "We never checked him out. I don't want to say I told you so, but it's all been really weird." She glanced at James, and back to Jonas. "James was hired just like us." She didn't want to think she was in a room with a – to use a phrase James might employ – royal wanker.

Jonas shook his head in disbelief. "So now you're all on his side."

Zoe let out sound of frustration. "I'm not trying to be on anyone's side, okay? Why does it always have to be about sides? God, now you sound like Mike, who probably took off in a fit. We know you're firing him after this."

Jonas lifted his hands up. "Mike doesn't even know where he is, why would he – "

"Forget that," Aaron said. "Zoe's right. We need to stick together and figure out what's going on. Find Brig and Mike. Maybe they're playing jokes. If they're not in the house, then they could've locked the doors."

Aaron wasn't feeling as comfortable with that logical explanation as he would have liked. Door locks could be broken. He didn't think they could break through these doors.

It was as though the house wanted to keep them.

Aaron wanted to slap that thought straight out of his head.

"Yeah...maybe," Jonas said. Then he laughed. It was a weak laugh. One that fizzled out before it ever really started. "It would be like them."

Jonas had felt like the door was resisting him in a more personal manner than a simple lock, when he'd gone after it. That it was, in some way, pulling back. But he didn't want to say that aloud.

Then there was the problem with the window. Mike and Brig playing jokes did not explain the unbreakable window.

He wasn't going to say that, either, especially since they hadn't.

"Oh, duh! Phones. We were so busy ripping into each other we forgot the obvious. Let me see if I can get a signal." Zoe went for her purse, snatching it up off the command central table. She found her cell, but after one look, her expression fell.

"No bars," she said, giving it a go, regardless. "You guys?" She held her phone next to ear, her expression slipping the rest of the way to the floor when the device remained silent.

Aaron had already retrieved his from a pocket and gone through the same motions. He gave her a shake of his head. "Nothing."

"Mine was in the van. I forgot it in the van," Jonas said.

They looked to James.

"I did not bring one," he said.

"No cell? What century are you living in?" Jonas dismissed that with a hand wave and plopped down into a folding chair, which protested with a teeth-grating squeal. "This is messed up. If Smith is behind this, what does he want?" He looked up at Aaron, then Zoe, as they'd begun to gather, to huddle up around him. "Why would he do this?"

Once again, the others turned their eyes on James, who had not moved from his spot, many feet away.

"I'm so lost," he admitted. His eyes grew moist. A moment of weakness, on display, and at least two Americans softened towards him. "I've been confused all evening. I don't understand this house or this...this..." he gave up in his search for a word, his hands, arms, spreading.

Aaron walked towards him, and stopped a few steps away. When he spoke, it was gentle, coaxing. "It's okay. Maybe it's time we all just started talking like rational people and stop hiding shit."

He looked to his friends, nailing each with his gaze. "All of us have stuff to admit, I think. So let's get started and see if it helps us figure anything out."

24

They'd all told their little secrets. Told them fast, as if needing to get it over with, now that they'd decided to stop hoarding them. Or most of them. Not everyone was as forthcoming with their information as they appeared.

Each had drag-raced through their stories, their words serving as vehicles. They all felt some impending sense of doom, and confusion over why this investigation should be so different. It wasn't just that others had been less eventful.

Other investigations didn't prompt deceit and forgotten friends.

They stood, staring at each other, not certain how to react to certain details when it was all finished. Jonas' stung hand. Aaron's strange humming and following paranoia. Zoe's certainty she'd sensed Evil. In any other investigation, the Americans would've laughed and said they'd all managed to get the haunted house spookies.

James confessed that he'd connected with one bona fide ghost in the lower levels, and that he'd felt a literal crushing sensation in the dungeon. That what was so strange about the evening was how he couldn't get a read on much of anything.

One secret he yet kept for himself. He had never shared it with anyone, and would be damned if he would now. Nor would he offer anything remotely connected to it that might give it away.

It didn't matter; it wouldn't bring back Mike or Brig.

Jonas made a study of his hands, his nails. He let his gaze wander around the room. In a swift motion, he rose and grabbed the folding chair he'd been sitting in and ran to the window he'd sparred with before.

"Jonas!" Zoe crossed the room in his direction, but was too late.

Jonas slammed the metal into the glass, glass that should've shattered, or at the very least cracked to draw an icy looking web.

Instead, the chair had rubber-balled off the window, and Jonas had almost taken it to the chin as he stumbled back.

"No way, there's no way!" He looked about, his eyes wild, and spotted a smaller window. He rushed it, chair and all, a near growl leaving him as he closed in on it.

It was a repeat of the other display, only this time, he took the resulting bounce-back in the mouth.

"Oh!" Zoe rushed to him. "Jonas, are you alright?"

Ignoring her in his frustration, he dropped the chair and stalked away, wiping at his mouth as he did.

Tasting blood.

"Fuck me," Aaron whispered, his voice hoarse with growing fear. "Are we trapped? For real, are we trapped?" He began to pace. "What are those made of, anyway?"

James snuck his way into a corner, his mind swimming, his skin crawling. He needed to get out. So much of his life he'd wished and hoped, even prayed, that he could once, just once, not feel the things he felt. Not take in everyone else's emotions. Not have to listen to dead men's tales.

Never had he considered that one day, he'd want this talent back if it left him. It was unsettling. He didn't know what to make of it or how to process the feeling, or lack of thereof.

Though, lack of feeling wasn't accurate. Oh, he could feel, just not the things he needed to most, in the situation. He'd reached out to the window while they were telling their stories, when no one was looking, but his touch had told him nothing. There was no residual, no story to unfold.

If someone had tampered with the windows, he should have sensed it. In lieu of live people, he should sense spirits, the poltergeists having a go at the team, but he couldn't.

James snapped out of his reverie with a very real feeling that Zoe was staring a hole through him. He met her gaze. She was afraid. He decided then, that he wasn't going to mention the bit about the window if he could help it.

It wouldn't assuage her fears. It would only feed them.

They both started at the sound of Aaron's expletive and turned just in time to see Jonas about to make one last attempt with the chair. None of them were able to stop him, though stopped he was.

What brought him to a halt was a sound none in the room could describe. A sound that wasn't human yet carried undertones of humanity, all the same. It raced along their spines and raised the hair on their bodies. It brought gooseflesh and shivers. It rushed the blood through their veins until they could hear it pounding in their ears.

The chair clattered to the floor.

"It's not going to let you out."

Jonas left off gawking at the chair, his attention snapped to James after the monotone words.

"What?" Lines creased his forehead as he looked at the Brit. "What did you say?"

Zoe's spine danced a jig.

James' face was a study of neutrality. "Don't hit me. It hurts."

More lines formed on Jonas' face, deepening around his lips. "What are you talking about? No one hit you." His gaze dropped. James had probably thought Jonas was going to hit him before – and might still do so at any time.

Jonas was thoroughly disgusted with himself.

"I don't like being hit," James said.

Jonas held out his hands, palm up, an appeal in the gesture as well as his eyes, when he brought himself to look at the other man again.

"I won't hit you," he said. "I'm sorry about before. I didn't mean to scare you; I really didn't."

Aaron had been watching James since the first soft words had come out of his mouth. He scrutinized the blank expression.

"It's not James," Aaron said. "I mean, he's not talking about you, Jonas." He shook his head. "It's not about him."

"Huh?" Jonas looked at his young partner. "Then what? You think he's channeling something?"

"It's kind of like the stuff before, that Sophie person," Aaron said. He moved closer to James. "Is that you, Sophie?"

Zoe turned away. She couldn't bear to watch. The lack of expression on James' face was unnerving, and though she couldn't explain why, she didn't think it had anything to do with this Sophie.

It was more sinister than that; she just knew it.

Aaron made another attempt. "Sophie?"

James blinked, his eyelids fluttering as if a cloud of black smoke had wafted into his face.

"What?" He swiped at his eyes and did his best to focus on Aaron. "What did you say?"

"Um," Aaron's gaze wavered, "were you hearing Sophie again?"

An expression of bewilderment painted the canvas of James' face. "No. Why?"

Zoe interrupted their attempt at conversation. "Hey." She drifted in the direction of the central table they had set up, her eyes fixed on a particular piece of equipment. "Isn't that Mike's camera?"

Jonas followed her gaze. The camcorder had a bright orange sticker on the side that bore a single black bolt of lightning. He couldn't remember where Mike had gotten it; he'd probably told him once, but that didn't matter. What mattered was that everyone had considered it Mike's camera from the day he slapped the sticker on it.

"Yeah," Jonas said as he reached the table. He'd been pulled towards it, in a sense. "So he must've been down here."

"But when?" Zoe reached, brushed her finger along the edge of the sticker. "I didn't see it sitting there before."

Aaron joined in. "We were too busy arguing to notice."

Zoe wasn't convinced. "No. After that, we all checked the feeds and stuff. One of us should have seen it." She looked up at Jonas. "You didn't." Her gaze flicked to Aaron. "Neither did you. How about you, James?"

He moved his head side to side. No.

"Maybe…" she snatched the camera off the table and walked to him, *"you can get something off this? Touch it and see."* Her gaze dropped and lifted. She felt bad for asking, but she needed to know. Someone needed to find an explanation for something, anything. *"Please?"*

James stared at the offered camera, knowing well that he had little choice. It wasn't that he didn't wish to help. The house was causing him to question his abilities. Also, he'd done something to confuse the Americans, if the way they'd looked at him just moments before was any indication. He had no idea what he'd done, or what he'd said that had prompted Aaron to question him the way he had.

It was discomfiting. Even when he channeled spirits, he tended to keep a sense of himself, or so it had always been before.

James hesitated just long enough that Zoe almost asked him again, but he then lifted his hands and waited. She realized he wanted her to deposit the machine into his waiting arms. His posture, his expression, they were nearly laughable. He looked like he was waiting for her to dump a pile of dung on him.

Pity that a laugh wouldn't suffice to massage her and lessen her tension.

Camera contacted palms, and James squeezed his eyes shut, preparing for an onslaught or perhaps worse, a lack of vibe, no information at all.

It might have been nice to be the hero for a change, but it seemed someone or something was conspiring against him, for he felt nothing but the cool surface of the camcorder, the metal and plastic. Lifeless metal and plastic.

He did have an idea, which struck with such swiftness and certainty that he rushed to the table, stopping just short of banging into it. His shins and thighs would thank him for this later.

"You can play it through this. Play it on the monitor where everyone can see."

25

His cackles sent the roaches scurrying for their darkened lairs. The ones that weren't a garnish, that is, though some of them yet twitched.

"Weak-minded boys. All it takes is just a little push, just a little disorientation." He snaked his way through his kitchen, a set of bat beady eyes searching the shelves, the cabinet doors. "And you, dear James, how much longer are you going to last? I hadn't counted on your best talent." After plucking the spice he wanted from inside the sink, he slithered his way back towards the table. "Shall I change the odds? Shall I introduce a new dilemma?"

Smith grabbed his bowl and tipped the bottle over it, watching as maggots wriggled their way out and plop-plopped onto the contents of the bowl.

"You're all about to hop on the crazy train." He laughed and choked on it. Ichor lurched up through his throat and sprayed into the bowl. At this, he merely shrugged.

"Where did I hear that? Crazy train…"

He turned and, bowl in hand, made his way towards what passed for a living room. A living room in dire need of dusting, vacuuming, and fumigation. Copious amounts of bleach might also have been nice, but none of this was Smith's way, and besides, his housekeeper had been bronzed.

"Mike, Mike, Mike." He sank into his chair. "Anger and pride will get you every time." A bit of cancerous meat went into his mouth. "Zoe...to think, all this time you've wanted to see something, and now..."

Smith laughed, coughing up more ichor. Good thing he'd gathered a group of people to sip. Time was running short.

26

"Jonas!"

Panting.

Whimpering.

"Someone...anyone out there? Damn it!"

A crash, after scuffling. Scrambling feet, scattering footsteps. Another crash, perhaps into a wall.

Breaths, pulsing and throbbing like a racing heartbeat.

"Shut it off," Zoe managed to say. A barest hint of a whisper.

White and black Converse-clad feet flailed, kicked and slid, half in, half out of frame.

Anxiety was tangible, even through the corrupted playback. It crawled, slithered, and wound its way through everyone's nerves, limbs, spines.

"Off...shut it off..." Each of Zoe's words tasted like bile. The bile so ready to launch itself from her mouth.

Jonas and Aaron's attentions were stuck on the playback, much more than morbid curiosity keeping them focused. This was their friend. This was something they couldn't believe or understand. They were in shock. They were confused.

Appalled.

Frozen in place.

James had turned away from Mike's pitiful wails. His pleas for mercy.

His abrupt silence.

All sound had been sucked out of the recording. At first, none in the room noticed this. They thought he'd met his terrible end and had stopped screaming. A final gasp of life, taken by something they couldn't see, just out of frame, thus making it all the more horrible. Lurid.

Their imaginations worked overtime, a thousand hamsters spinning a thousand wheels.

It made Zoe sicker, though somehow, she managed not to vomit. Green blossomed around her edges when she realized that the playback no longer included what she imagined were fingernails on wood, and rubber, the rubber of his sneakers, squeak-sliding along the floor and contacting solid walls, or, or...Cthulhu himself. The monster that would be sticky rot, maggot slime, sucking, poisonous tentacles and...and...

She slapped her hands to either side of her head.

She'd wanted them to shut it off, but not the audio only. It seemed impossible, but it was worse without the sound, the last twitch of a foot before it flew out of frame. The following spasm of fingers on a hand that shouldn't twist the way it was. It shouldn't be in the frame at all; it wasn't possible.

Then gone. Like the Converse, it was gone.

But the sound came rushing back like a freight train, and Zoe came out of the folding chair with such violence it flew back and skittered across the flooring and came to rest against the broken antique wingback. The two chairs huddled together, as if afraid of what other harm might befall them due to the crazed giants in the room.

"Shut it off! OFF!"

Zoe's shrill demand spliced her partners' attentions in half and chilled James from his scalp to his toenails.

Jonas switched the playback off as fast as he was able without breaking any equipment.

"Okay." Zoe rubbed her face. "Okay, so. So where…where was that? What room? We…we need to see if…" she rubbed her face again and took a deep breath. That breath shook so much she needed another to gain oxygen before she coughed more out.

"There must be another way out," Aaron whispered. He was still stunned. Scared. Off kilter, uncertain as to what he'd just seen.

"We're not leaving Mike in here. He needs help," Zoe said. "And Brig – what if he's in trouble?"

"I didn't mean," Aaron waved his hands, and started over. "We'll split up. Two look for Mike; two look for a way out."

"What about Brig!"

"Fuck this, I'm getting out." Jonas rose and started walking away, without so much as a courtesy glance at the others.

"Hey!" Zoe trotted after him. "What about us? Where are you going?"

"C'mon, Aaron," Jonas said.

Aaron stared at the big man's back. "But…"

Jonas turned, coming face to face with the woman he'd sometimes wished was his girl in the last few months. He felt guilt over that, but not for what he was about to say or do.

"You and James stay here in case Brig comes back. Aaron and I will try to find a way out. There's a tunnel on the map; it might lead outside sooner or later."

"But – "

"We can go get help."

The room seemed devoid of air for Zoe, then. She looked up into those big, dark eyes and knew that Jonas meant it. That he wouldn't be swayed.

"Leave them here?" Aaron said. He drifted towards Jonas. "Why don't we all go, then?"

"Brig might come by." Jonas repeated. "He's probably just turned around. And maybe Mike'll show up."

James studied the three strangers huddled several feet from him, in their own little group. They'd forgotten him for the moment. Normally he wouldn't mind. He'd wanted the wall to swallow him up just a few moments ago. Problem was, he now felt that the wall would be happy to oblige.

"C'mon Aaron." Jonas turned away. His strides were long and fast. Aaron stood, stunned. He glanced at Zoe, an apology in his eyes, confusion in his expression. What he read in *her* eyes spurned him on.

After catching his boss up, he remembered the Brit. The new friend he'd made…or had started to make. He looked over his shoulder, unable to stop moving, because Jonas was walking at a swift clip, and he didn't want to let Zoe down.

One more look at those blue-gray eyes, just one more look. The idea that it could be the last time sent a wave of fresh fear through his being. He told himself he was being morbid.

"Sorry," Aaron whispered to James before disappearing down a dark hall.

Zoe had followed that green gaze. Hers were the only eyes on James now.

"I didn't want Jonas to go alone," she said, feeling a need to explain. Grateful that Aaron had somehow understood.

"I know," James replied.

"He was going to go alone."

"I know."

"He's doing what he thinks is best."

James nodded.

"They'll come back."

It came out a statement, but James felt the question hanging in the ether.

A question he couldn't answer. Though he nodded again, all the same.

27

"Flashlights working?"

"Check."

Zoe nodded in his direction. She let out a thin stream of air and sucked it back in. "Ready?"

"Like you, I can scarce stand to sit here and wait a moment longer." James looked away and back, a tentative smile forming. "Well. I could, but not if you leave me."

She tried her best to return his smile, small as it was. He was all she had, just now, and she was sure he meant well.

Didn't he?

"They went down, so we go up?" She lifted a brow at him. She was nothing if not practical.

James agreed. "Seems as good a plan as any."

"Okay. Let's..." Zoe's words died with the sudden shift of her companion's attention. His head had snapped in the direction of the stairs closest to them.

"That eager to go?" she said, calling up a small laugh, which answered. It was much too nervous a sound to do any good, though.

James appeared not to notice. His head snapped in the other direction, the direction Jonas and Aaron had gone. Zoe thought it was a wonder it didn't pop right off his neck.

"What is it?" She took steps towards him.

He turned and moved. Not down the hall. Not to the stairs. He moved, with the grace of a dancer, to the front door.

"James?" Thoroughly confused, Zoe could do little but trail after him like a lost puppy hoping for scraps.

Once close to the door, James closed his eyes. Inhaled. Zoe realized he was sniffing the door. In a sense. Or the air around it. She wasn't sure. She'd never seen anyone do what he was doing. Okay, he wasn't actively *sniffing*, but...

James stepped back, a look of disgust bathing his features.

She was hesitant to ask. "What...James, what?"

"Don't you smell it?" He turned his gaze on her. "Sulfur."

Zoe's testing of the air was much more obvious than his had been. Her nostrils flared. Her inhales were short, raspy bursts. She shook her head.

"No?" His brows lifted. "Rotten egg scent."

Zoe shook her head again. After making a big show of inhaling once more. "Do you sometimes pick up phantom smells?" She didn't want to think about the common associations with sulfur. That was just silly.

His nod was absent. He was distracted, yet again. This time Zoe followed him towards the hall Jonas and Aaron had gone down. She didn't bother to ask what he thought the smell meant. She didn't think he'd answer. She was more interested in his current trajectory, anyway. *Yes, let's go that way*.

James offered some words, at last. Not that they clarified much.

"The kitchen is this way, correct?"

Zoe nodded. Then remembered he couldn't hear a nod. "Yes. But there's more than one room off the hall. Dining room," she conjured a mental image of the floor plans, "um, parlor and... smoking room? That doesn't seem so different from a parlor, but whatever. I mean really, what's the difference between a sitting room, parlor, and smoking room, other than wanting to sound rich, maybe."

"Smoking rooms were for the men," James replied, like some sort of automated historian.

Zoe clamped her mouth shut. She was blathering, anyway and didn't want to carry on with it. She sometimes did that when she was nervous. One of those people who had to fill uncomfortable silences. Brig would've teased her.

A sense of loss gripped her for a moment, two. She'd give anything to hear Brig tease her as they walked down the hall, but it was not to be. *He can make up for lost time after we find him*, she told herself.

"So are we going to the kitchen, James?"

He kept walking.

"I guess so," she said. "And I guess I'll keep talking to myself."

On he walked.

"Right." Zoe sighed and followed.

What else could she do? She sure as hell wasn't going to sit and wait for him. Alone. All alone in the room where they had last heard Mike, screaming. She'd thought of staying and checking for what the other feeds had recorded, but after watching Mike...

She couldn't stomach the idea. Not yet. Blessedly, James hadn't mentioned it, either.

"Hey!" Zoe stumbled back. Her fingers flew to her forehead. "Ow, crap. What is wrong with you?" He'd rushed back in her direction with no warning, and she'd run smack into him.

"Pardon...I can't..." James surrendered to silence, which added to the list of things that unsettled Zoe.

"You can't what?" She grabbed his shoulders. "What? Spit it out."

His eyes widened, making them whiter than was normal. Another thing added to Zoe's list. It startled her. She didn't

188

think anyone's eyes could open so wide. She then noticed the tremor running through his body. When she looked at her hands, and saw where they were resting, understanding smacked her in the face.

The tremor was James attempting to hold it together. Wasn't it? She'd touched him, and it must've been like a kettle boiling over. All over him.

"Oh, wow, I'm sorry." She pulled her hands away and held them up, to show him that she'd stopped touching him. "I didn't mean to...I'm sorry. Are you okay?"

His reply was as tight as his posture. "No."

She stepped back to give him room. Let out a sound that was a cross between a frustrated grunt and a sigh of resignation.

"I don't know what to do here, James. But we need to do something. Look for them... we need to..." She shook herself. "But something made you stop, and it scares me, and..." A sound, like someone sitting on an inflatable raft and forcing air from it with a teeth-grinding whine, made its way out of her.

Pure frustration.

"I cannot go that way," James said.

Zoe could only gawk at him. The statement was so final. It left no room for debate.

"But..."

James came unglued from his spot and moved around her, making his way to the front room.

"James!" Zoe held her place. "We have to do something!"

"I am not stopping you." He reached the middle of the room. Pivoted in place to face her. "But I cannot go with you. Forgive me."

"You-you...Asshole! You'd let me go off alone?" For all the bluster, her words lacked sting. Frustrated as she was, part of her understood, and the other half of her hated the admission. As much as she wanted to defy that little voice and be angry with him, it was a half-hearted attempt.

"I'm sorry," he said.

She stomped her foot, but even that lacked the necessary resonance to convey true anger. Inside, she was beating herself up.

Angry that she didn't have the guts to go it alone, not even for her missing friends.

28

"Tut, tut. We couldn't have you getting ahead of the game, James, dear. It wouldn't be sporting." Smith rubbed a hand over one of his brittle thighs. A thigh that was softening, finding new life, as the evening wore on. "You have more talent than I expected. Why, you and I aren't so different, when you think about it. But I can't have you getting ahead. It wouldn't be half as tasty."

His cackle echoed off the walls.

"Ah, but how lovely of you to try your hand at playing hero. I hadn't expected that, either!"

His grin was full of half-rotted, venomous teeth that, even now, were regaining some of their dark luster.

29

"Did you hear something over there? I think I heard, like, whispering."

A great yawning silence replied from the center of the deepening dark.

"Jonas?"

His whisper rebounded off a shadow, mocking him.

Aaron peeked through the slender beam his failing flashlight cast. He could hear breathing. His own. He didn't hear the whisper any longer, or maybe he did, and it was in his mind. It was the tunnel, playing tricks on him.

"Jonas?"

Aaron's hand began to tremble. It was so dark, even with the light, the light that kept threatening to betray him, dimming, sucking up the last bits of juice from batteries he swore he'd put in it only fifteen minutes ago.

He did what any intelligent person would do in the situation. He whacked the thing against his palm.

"C'mon, you bastard." It teased, gave him a brighter flash, offering its wares for sale.

"There we go."

It dimmed.

"Arg." He did his best to use the wan beam. It was better than no light, and he needed to find Jonas. Fast. Before the light gave up on him completely.

But instead of moving he stood, a sliver of ice pressed to the base of his skull, wondering why Jonas didn't answer. Where did he go? He'd been there, just a moment ago. Hadn't he? There were only two ways in and out.

Weren't there?

Aaron's entire spine began to chill when he realized he didn't know for sure. Jonas had the map, and Jonas hadn't said. Didn't he have a map?

Aaron wasn't sure now. He reasoned that he should turn around and go back exactly the way he'd come, and then he'd arrive at the entrance. This was a good idea. Before his light gave up the ghost.

But he should find Jonas, he told himself.

They hadn't found Brig or Mike. *What makes you think you can find Jonas?*

"I can't leave him."

He left you.

"Well…No, he's just turned around."

One way in and out.

"Two…"

One. He left you. Turn around and go back.

"Yeah…" Aaron turned on his heel and walked back the way he'd come. Just in time, as his flashlight waned, waned, and died.

He'd keep going straight. Slow and steady. Perhaps not so steady, but the intent was there.

To keep himself company, there in the dark, he had the sudden and, he thought, brilliant idea to listen to some playback on the digital voice recorder. For an investigator who had spent time in many dark places, it was easy – muscle memory. He fished the player out, found a retrieval point, and pressed play.

James' voice disturbed the stoic silence of the tunnel. A few seconds revealed that it was the session with Sophie. This sparked enough interest in Aaron to take off the edge, to calm his shiver, at least a bit.

The Londoner's voice whispered along the walls, and Aaron found himself wondering if he were all right. He and Zoe, were they still waiting? Were they holding down the fort, or had they gone off alone?

He hoped James was okay. He wanted to talk to him again. He wanted to compare notes. He wanted to walk out of the damned spooky mansion with him and have James make another of his dusty, dry jokes.

All would be right in the world, if James...

Aaron had a sharp and painful realization. There were no other voices on the tape. James, asking questions. Silence. Question. Silence. Question...

Temper rousted out any lingering fear. It didn't matter that closer study of the playback may prove fruitful; Aaron dwelled on the fact that no woman's voice filled the gaps between his cohort's queries. There should be words, crisp and stark, he reasoned. James was having a full out conversation.

"Damn it." It hit him like a strike to the cheek and left the burn, the sting.

Aaron trudged on to the rhythm of fraud, fraud, fraud. How far, how long, eluded him. Particularly when he found himself – somewhere at the end of the fifth playback of the recording – in a room.

A room that shouldn't exist. It shouldn't be, because, as he emerged more and more from his brain fog, he understood that he recognized the room. He knew where he was, because there was one distinguishing feature that shone...

30

Zoe's eyes moved over the small bundle that was James, huddled up in the corner as if he could make himself disappear. She felt a twinge of sympathy.

Jonas and Aaron had been gone for a long while. There had been no contact on walkie-talkies. They'd tried. Several times.

Brig hadn't shown up. No Mike appeared. James didn't seem physically able to leave command central. She wasn't certain she had enough energy left to spare for feeling irked, however.

She was still using it against herself.

They had, to pass time and find clues, listened to some of the playback on the recorders. But they'd found nothing, heard nothing. It was both a relief and a damned shame.

James pondered whether Aaron had had time to listen to anything. Whether he'd decided that James was full of shit, since Sophie didn't appear on his tape. James didn't know why this idea had struck out of the blue, though it gave him hope. Because just maybe he was picking it up from Aaron himself, this idea, which meant the young American was alive.

Yes?

Zoe didn't know what to think, feel, or believe any longer. She wished it would all go away, that she'd wake up in her small but comfortable bedroom, never having come to England.

"I know what you're thinking." James' sudden hoarse whisper chased the image of her bedroom away. "You're suspicious of me." With good reason, he knew. Besides the lack of evidence on the tapes, he hadn't been very forthcoming. Even for a stranger.

She shook her head. "You really *are* confused. I'm scared and worried, is what I am. And I hate myself for being too chicken shit to search this disaster zone of a mansion."

Cool blue eyes scrutinized her. "That as well. One doesn't negate the other."

Zoe let out a sigh. Suspicious? Fine. If she were being honest, she was. Yet she would not go off the deep end. Because she still couldn't figure out how he could have managed locking the doors or how he could have done anything to Mike, since he was with Aaron, and...

Still. There wasn't anyone else around.

"Yes, I'm suspicious," she conceded aloud. "So, since we have nothing better to do, I'll ask some questions. How well do you know Mr. Smith?"

"As well as you," James replied.

Zoe's head began to shake and shake, until she willed it to stop. "But how do I know that for sure? You're as much a stranger as he is."

James drew a breath and let it out in an audibly languorous exhale. "Fair enough. It's normal to be suspicious of me, someone you'd not met before tonight."

"You haven't offered much about yourself, even though you've been here all night."

James arched a brow at her. "Chit chat hasn't precisely been on the agenda, most of the evening." After a short pause, he added, "There is also the fact that I haven't been teamed up with you, and when I was with the group, well...I don't believe this requires further explanation."

Zoe placed her hands on her hips. This was good. This was what she needed, to focus on something else. Something that might make sense. "Fine, but you didn't offer much before whatever it is that's going on." Her eyes narrowed. "Except maybe to Aaron, but he's not around to ask." The accusation in her last words startled her.

She didn't want to think of Aaron in the past tense. Why would she do that? Zoe gave herself a mental shakedown. *He's fine he's fine he's fine – everyone is fine.*

The Brit's gaze fell. His words tiptoed out. "I know more about him than he does me. I like him."

"You didn't like Mike," she shot back, suddenly wanting to pummel him until he confessed. To what, she didn't know. Maybe she never wanted to know. It might be better not to. If he had some master plan, he'd already pulled it off so far, so what chance did she stand? The thought frightened her more than finding nothing on one of the feeds had, when she'd distracted herself with rewinding and going over it, after all. No clues had surfaced. No sign of Brig or Mike. No sign of any of the team.

It made no sense.

Once again, Zoe readjusted her mental state with extreme prejudice. She did not want to go there. Not right now.

James met her glare with a wearied gaze.

At that moment, he looked so pitiful in her eyes that she felt a bit of shame for her previous urge to beat him up. "Never mind," she said. "But about Smith…"

"I don't know anything about him at all, really," James offered, knowing the subject of his personal life didn't matter in the end. "Though I was never surprised that he chose not to show his face."

Zoe gaped at him and then sank down where she stood, landing on her ass and not giving it much notice. "Honestly, neither am I," she said. "We shouldn't have accepted his invitation. I had a bad feeling all along, but Jonas…"

Jonas. *Oh God, where is Jonas?* Zoe bit back the tears that wanted to well up in her eyes. Right now, she wanted to be numb, comfortably numb.

"And yet you accepted," she heard James say.

Her return words were another accusation. "So did you. You've got all these, these, gifts, and you accepted, too."

"Yes. I did."

"Why? Why did you?" A fire kindled in her belly.

James uncurled from his semi-fetal position and leaned back against the wall, placing his hands on his knees. "You wish to blame me for your being here." He offered a slight nod. "I can accept this, even though my refusing would not have hindered you. You need someone to blame, then very well. Here I am."

Zoe pounded the floor with her fists. "Damn it, why do you have to be so fucking congenial about it?"

"Because you need it, and arguing will get us nowhere."

With his words, she sagged, deflated in her rise to anger. "So…really. Why did *you* come?"

His laugh held no humor and bordered on sick – the only word for it that satisfied her.

"I've no intricate explanations. I'm too curious for my own good, upon occasion," he said.

"But…" Once again, her head shook itself in lieu of words.

"I never met him and therefore had no chance to read him," James explained.

"But you said you weren't surprised he didn't show up," Zoe said. She'd blame someone for something, yes, she would, and since he was being so tolerant of it, then fine.

He offered to take that blame, she'd accept. It was just good manners.

"No. But I certainly had no idea that any of this would happen," James said.

Zoe tried a different way around the same subject. "Didn't you get a letter?"

"Ah. You're a clever girl. I knew you'd come round to that."

Zoe simply stared at him and waited for the answer she wanted.

"Yes, a handwritten one, no less." James, having seemed so small and fragile moments ago, appeared to relax into the conversation. "It's not an exact science. A letter doesn't give me a person's life story, and perhaps his mind was bent on the sincerity of the words being written." One of his shoulders lifted and dropped without ceremony. "Perhaps he did not pen the letter at all."

Incredulous at his shift in demeanor, and finding it more and more difficult to vent at him, Zoe said, "But you think he set us up, too, don't you."

"Someone arranged to have the vehicles spirited away, vehicles which he provided. It is his mansion, we are here on his terms, and perhaps we're fools for it. But then, who would imagine this scenario?" James offered her a slip of a smile, which she found odd.

But Zoe pressed on.

"It doesn't explain what's going on in this house," she said, for her own benefit more than anything else.

"*I* can't explain what's going on in this house."

His admission frightened Zoe more than everything else that had happened. Even in her imagination. He'd mentioned before that he was at a loss, but this was in the quiet, alone time between them. Nothing stood between her and the words. There was nothing to distract from or soften them.

And he'd admitted to being at a loss twice. Two times, now. That made it worse. More real.

She couldn't be angry with him for being in the situation. He hadn't forced her to make the trek from America, and she didn't grasp how or why someone would go to such elaborate lengths for a sick joke, or...

Maybe she was naïve, she told herself. He could be in on it, yet for reasons she couldn't explain to herself, she didn't believe this.

She was angry in general, though. Because she wanted him to have the answers. He'd proven his gifts and she'd hoped, so strongly hoped, that he would have a logical explanation for everything. She needed this to cling to, as it was better than a nameless fear.

"There aren't any other people in this house, are there?" Zoe asked. He might not have *all* the answers, but surely, he had a few. He'd had plenty of time to sit and regroup. They both had.

"No. There haven't been. We've been the only warm bodies here this evening," James replied. "Meaning the team we began the evening with. Nobody else that I sensed."

She was glad he understood her poorly worded question. This was what she had wanted – and yet not wanted – to hear. She continued her line of questioning; she could do nothing else.

"Ghosts? Are the ghosts here powerful enough to..." *do whatever it was they were doing?*

Zoe tensed as James appeared to fold in on himself again, as he seemed to shiver like one of those tiny, little dogs people carried around in handbags. "This house..."

Zoe held her breath.

"This house..." James' hands flew to the sides of his head and pressed, as if his head were about to burst. "I can feel its heartbeat. Hear it breathing."

Zoe shuddered when he gasped.

"I'm not certain what's in my mind and what is real any longer, I don't think." He hugged his knees to his chest and whimpered. "This house feels...it's *alive*."

Zoe flew to her feet. "No. No, no no." She began pacing a tight circle. "There's an explanation, there has to be. That's... that's just..."

"Insane."

Zoe stopped cold and looked at him after he said it.

"Yes, it feels insane, and this insanity is making me ill," he said.

Zoe took a closer look at him and for the first time noticed that beads of sweat were breaking out on his face. In fact, she realized he looked flushed. A sharper pang of sympathy and the ingrained desire she'd always had for mothering people hit her. She moved to him, kneeled before him, and only managed to stop her hand when it was less than an inch from his face.

But she could feel the heat long before her hand came so close to his flesh.

"My God, I've been so unfair to you. This must be so overwhelming," she said. Her eyes caressed his features, drawn and tight as they were. "It literally makes you *sick*." Surprise registered in her eyes when he laughed.

"Thankfully, it's been some time since I was in a situation which made me ill," he said.

She longed to touch him, to hug him. Hell, she needed a hug, too.

Her surprise grew when he lifted a hand to hers and pressed her palm to his burning cheek. After this, tenderness moved through Zoe's eyes.

"It'll be okay. It will," she said. Levity, she would try for levity, and she wanted to believe what she was about to say. "It'll be like the movies. The sun will rise, the evil will be banished, and we'll all walk out of this piece of shit house."

"You Americans do love your happy endings, don't you?" His eyes, so pale now, searched hers.

"There's nothing wrong with a happy ending. Work with me here, okay?" *Please*, she thought. *I can see that you don't believe we're walking out of this place, but let's pretend, James.*

Softness found a place in James' eyes. "The sun will rise, its rays blinding and glorious, piercing the windows, shattering all shadows, and we'll walk out into the fresh morning air. Just down the road, we'll see an automobile. They'll offer help, and we'll ride into the village for a warm bath, bed, and food. Oh, and tea. I'm stereotypical in that."

Zoe found her first smile in what felt like an eternity. "Eloquent. The end."

"Yes, because they always roll the credits before the debriefings and padded cells."

A laugh snuck its way through her. "A padded cell sounds pretty good right now."

He squeezed her hand. "Certain medications might prove rather lovely just now, as well."

"Three hot meals."

"With jelly?"

They both laughed. But Zoe's humor fled. Her next words were no joke. She meant them with all her heart.

"We'd be alive."

"Yes. Alive," James agreed.

"Why did you really come here, James?" she asked in a soft voice. Talking was good; she would keep talking. Whether or not the subject was dark, it kept her thoughts from racing away to fouler places. Strangely, speaking made it feel less real.

If only for a time.

"I wanted to help, and...I understand having secrets. Mr. Smith's secrecy didn't alarm me. I meant it when I said that I am more curious than is healthy," her companion said.

"*You* have a secret."

"Don't we all?"

"I'll tell you mine if you tell me yours."

He let go of her hand and turned his head.

Zoe sat back on her heels, uncertain. She opted to keep talking, because the silence was deafening, uncomfortable.

Frightening.

"I'm in love with Jonas. That's the biggest reason I'm here." Replaying in her mind what she'd just said, laughter accosted her. "As if you didn't know, I suppose."

As she'd hoped, he turned his head back and looked at her. "I'm likely not the only one who did," he commented, then amended for her benefit, "Does."

She warmed her hands on her thighs, shaking her head. "Maybe not. The real secret is – I never thought his wife deserved him. I always thought I'd be better for him. Sounds catty, probably. I never said that to anyone because he loved," a golf ball wanted to rise in her throat, "loves her. If he was happy, then I was happy for him."

Why am I compelled to use past tense? It's not so dire. It's not! It's the stress.

"Then you are a good friend, my dear," James said.

Her fingers twined the strings on her jacket.

The others were dead. She'd heard James' words. He too, had used past tense. Still, she almost thanked James for trying to comfort her, however small the way.

"So. I shared," she said. "Sorry it wasn't anything, I don't know, less obvious and boring. Something more dastardly." She worked up a chuckle. There was another secret. One that almost shamed her. One he might find more interesting, but no. She wouldn't offer it. Not even if…if it might die with him.

"I killed my own father."

Zoe's gaze snapped from her fingers to his face. He was joking because of what she said. He had to be. She'd play along. "Oh yeah? How'd you do it?"

"Hunting accident, this is the official record." His gaze penetrated hers.

She felt herself fidgeting. "Rifle?"

"Indeed."

Zoe noticed that he wasn't sweating as much. His body was relaxing again, too, as if it were all so…

"You're not joking," she whispered. "Oh my God, you're not joking, are you?"

"No, I am not. This doesn't do much for your being suspicious of me, now does it?"

How can he be so blasé about this? she thought. *He just told me that he killed his father!*

"Amazingly, it happened nearly exactly as I'd imagined so many times. I had falcons for allies. They came to love me more than him." James' gaze drifted. It was as if he were going to another place, transported in his mind. "They were my best friends. I was dreadfully sorry about his mount, however. Broken leg."

Zoe's thoughts were stutters even before her next words found purchase. "Y-you…how…"

"His steed galloped in the precise direction I had mapped out time and time again, the falcons flying just where I'd trained them to, and, oh, dear. The horse fell, pinning him, and his rifle discharged as they went down." One of his hands cut a graceful path through the air with those words.

Zoe was still attempting to catch up, her string of words blundering their way out. "He, well then it was, you didn't – you're telling me a story. Hah hah, scary story. Let me guess, he comes back as a ghost to haunt you."

James' focus returned to her in an instant. "Oh yes, I'm telling you a *story*. A *true* story. Blessedly, he's never haunted me literally."

Zoe's jaw nearly unhinged itself in its sudden drop.

"Would you like to hear the rest?" His head bobbed in agreement with himself. "His gun discharged, and while he lay there, I assessed his position, approached him, and much to his surprise, shot him myself. To be certain he was dead, mind you. I then switched rifles. I was very precise, very careful; I'd gone over it several times, the positioning. After this, I only had to get back on my own steed, work up the tears, race back to the house, and display frantic behavior." He held up his hands, wiggling his fingers. "We always dressed properly for hunting. Gloves, everything. A second shot made no difference if anyone had heard it. He had fired before me at a hare, I would have said. We had a good bit of land, so it wasn't necessary to explain it, in the end. I'd been rather certain no one else would be about, and I was correct." A phantom of a smile formed on his face. "Terribly thorough, indeed I was."

Zoe was stunned. Stunned didn't even cover it. She was many things, none of which she could work out as she gaped at him.

"Of course, it's not perfect. A very observant person may have discerned that there was something odd about the death shot, and they might have questioned, but…" he shrugged. "It was never investigated."

Zoe's eyes had started to water, because she'd forgotten to blink.

"I was a brilliant and precocious child, my dear." He patted her hand. His brows began to knit themselves. "I believe my mother was suspicious, but she never said a word." His following laugh was as dry as dead leaves. "One could say that it was the only thing she ever did for me. Though really, she cared little more for him than me I think, and she didn't care for me at *all*. She benefitted greatly from the will. My part was placed in a trust."

"You did it for the *money*?" Zoe nearly vomited up the words.

James' lips dipped into a deep frown. "Good Lord, of course not. I didn't give a damn about the money. I was twelve; I couldn't have got my hands on it, in any case. If I'd wanted the money, there were other ways to go about it, ways which required his living."

Zoe felt as if he'd just slapped her. Slapped her and sapped her strength. "Twelve? Why does a twelve year old kill his father?"

For the first time during his tale, James' gaze fell, his lashes obstructing his eyes from view. His reply at first confused Zoe, until she replayed it in her head. When she did, she wanted to shout, but not at him. She wanted to cry again. She wanted to both hug him and shake him.

"Because he was beautiful when he wasn't hurting me," was what James said.

Zoe's hand rushed to her mouth as his words hung in the air, still repeating in her head. She felt certain she might vomit for real; she could feel the bile rising. When she was confident she wouldn't, she unclenched her fingers and moved her fist away from her lips.

"Your mother?" she asked. The first words that made it to her mouth.

"Alive in Australia, and may she rot there. I haven't been in her presence since I was eighteen."

This was not what Zoe had meant, yet it was good to know. She didn't want to hear that he'd killed her, too.

"I meant – when he was hurting you, didn't she help you?"

His eyes slowly lifted, a cold anger in their depths. "No."

Zoe scrambled for words to convey her feeling. What she really wanted to do was strangle his mother, but she wasn't available. "So you were forced to protect yourself."

The return of the strange laugh that issued from him earlier startled her. "I suppose." He leaned back, contemplating his remaining companion. "Now you know my deepest, darkest secret. One I have never spoken of."

"Don't worry," Zoe whispered. "It'll die with me." Ominous words, she knew, but it would. What reason would she have for telling anyone? There was nothing in it for her, and the events had happened years and years ago, and…and she couldn't deny that part of her was thinking that maybe his father had deserved it.

"I hope that you won't despise me when I say that this is the only reason I told you," James said. "I'm not feeling as optimistic as you are." He reached and brushed the hair away from the left side of her face. "But I hope that you will believe me when I say that it's my greatest wish for you to live through this, regardless."

She'd already thought of that. That he told a dead woman walking.

Strangely, it hadn't scared her even more. Likely because lurking under the surface was resignation. She wasn't sure she could go back now, anyway, if she did survive. Back to normal.

Especially without Jonas.

Without all of them.

They were dead. James knew it and so she knew it. Odd how accepting it numbed a piece of her heart, her brain. But there

was one person left. One person she'd find a way to, what —
save? Maybe he'd save her.

Zoe grasped James' hand as if it were a life preserver. "I
believe you. Either way, it'll die with me, James. I promise."

"Thank you."

"Who would I tell, anyway? I probably won't see you again,
and I don't know any of your friends." She attempted a smile.

"I'm not thanking you for that."

"Then what?"

"Your conversation," he said. "It's the only thing currently
keeping me sane, I think."

She wrapped her other hand around his, gripping it with
both of hers. "Then keep talking, because…ditto."

His laugh held a bit of humor this time. "Truly now? I've
just told you that I'm a murderer."

"I don't know," came her honest reply. "I don't know exactly
how to feel about it, but whatever he did to you must have been
terrible, and — Jesus. You were a child." Her gaze dove into his
as she replayed his words, his story.

The way he'd said his father was beautiful when he wasn't
hurting him.

"I have a feeling you're sorry for it, and that's why you
seemed so nonchalant at first when you were telling me," she
continued. "You were pretending. I think it still *hurts* you. I
think if you were a cold-blooded killer, a *murderer*, you wouldn't
care. Maybe you've been trying to convince yourself you're a
bad guy ever since, but really, you're not."

James felt his senses wish to swirl yet again. Reality and
fantasy blurring.

She studied his features. "If you were a real murderer, you'd
do it again. Somehow, I don't think you have. You've been
distant tonight, but not because you're cold-blooded."

He studied her in return. "This is what you'd prefer to think.
Doubtless, I wouldn't wish to be sitting here with a murderer as

207

my last hope out of a terrifying situation, either," he said. "As my only companion."

"Okay, sure, you're all I have left right now, and I want to trust you," she conceded. "And this might slap me in the face, later, when you pull out a big knife and cut out my heart." She squeezed his hand. "But I am. I'm right. You haven't killed anyone else. You're distant because of your secrets. Because of your gifts." She very much wanted to be right. She was suddenly certain that she was. "I know you're overloaded, but can't you sense it? That I mean it?"

He searched and searched her eyes, discovering the sincerity of her words with some surprise. Given the evening's events, being surprised in this manner was a comfort.

"I thought I was the psychic," he said.

"Call it women's intuition."

A smile crept up on him, small but genuine.

"Say that I'm right," she prompted. She wanted him to *say* it.

"You're right. I've never wished anyone else dead. Not even Mother."

"I hope you're at peace one day, then. I hope you can be whole again."

She meant it. James could sense even this. It flowed through her touch.

So often, he wished for peace as well. Sitting there as they were, in the dark belly of what he would describe for the first and likely last time as true evil, he hoped peace would not come complete with moist dirt and lilies.

He then realized how true it was – that he wanted, more than *anything*, for her to walk out of this house alive. Having one confidant in the world, whether they met again or not, in some way comforted him, rather than worried him. A confidant that had the grace, even now, to find him not guilty.

Should he die, perhaps he'd remain guiltless in her memories.

"We'll get out of here, James," she assured him, and herself.

For her brave words, James could sense that she didn't fully believe it. Perhaps this was his fault, he thought. Because with her, he found it impossible to lie well.

But he attempted one, nonetheless. A pretty lie. At least, it felt like a lie. "We will."

He wouldn't rob her of her happy ending.

31

"Jonas?"

The big man's skin tingled in response to the sound of her voice.

"Jonas?"

He stopped, turned, and let the echo of his name lead him. It didn't matter that it made no sense. Didn't matter that she shouldn't be there, that he must be hearing things. That most likely it was Zoe, not –

"Barbra?"

"Over here."

Nonsensical. She was back in Seattle, finalizing that divorce he didn't want, packing up the rest of her things, no doubt.

"Jonas, I'm glad I found you."

His pace quickened. "You came looking for me? All the way in England?"

"Yes. I needed to tell you something, and it couldn't wait."

Hope sped up his heartbeat, confused as he was. "But how did you know where I was?"

"I need to tell you something, hon."

He was close to running, now. His heart skipped. She wouldn't even answer his calls, before, and now she'd flown all the way to England.

Never mind that she hadn't known the location of Grimalkin Manor. Or that she hadn't known he was leaving, or when.

She was in the manor, calling his name. She'd flown to England, and she hated flying. It must mean...

"I'm coming, baby."

~

"Fuck, what's that!" Zoe's head flew from his shoulder, her hands gripped his arms, and she looked about with wild eyes.

Had they fallen asleep?

"I don't know, I don't know," James cried.

She could feel him shaking. She was still in his arms.

They'd fallen asleep, hadn't they?

She gripped him harder. "Shh, it's okay, it's okay." His trembles were violent and it scared the hell out of her.

So did the noise.

The noises.

James' body bunched up, and he started rocking, rocking. Sounds, there were too many sounds barraging his senses. He felt like a skinned cat, raw and vulnerable.

"James, James stay with me!"

A shower of ice rained down Zoe's spine when he started mumbling incoherently.

"What, what is it?" She tried shaking him by the shoulders. "James?" A few of his words became intelligible, but this did nothing for understanding what he was spewing.

Between his now chant-like muttering and the groaning, howling, sepulchral moaning all around them, Zoe thought she'd go crazy, as well as wet herself where she sat.

It was possible that she already had.

She grabbed his face and lifted it – an attempt to find his gaze, to get his attention.

His eyes were creased shut, and his chanting became louder. As he repeated it, she had the light bulb moment, because she recognized a verse or two.

"Through me the way into the suffering city,
Through me the way to the eternal pain,
Through me the way that runs among the lost.
Justice urged on my high artificer.
My maker was divine authority,
The highest wisdom and the primal love.
Before me nothing but eternal things were made,
And I endure eternally.
Abandon every hope, ye who enter here."

This chilled her to sub zero. It made her heart gallop and thump against her breast, made it try to punch its way out.

"James, why are you saying that? Stop it!" She patted his face, not quite wanting to slap him, not yet lost to hysteria.

He continued, louder and louder.

"James!" To hell with it. She slapped him hard. Once. Twice. Again. "James!"

Mid-word his murmuring shut off. His eyelids snapped up like freed window blinds.

"James!"

He clutched her biceps. Zoe winced when his fingertips drilled into them. They'd add to the bruises she'd made before.

"I have to get out of here." A cloudy gray gaze hopped over her face. "I need to get out of here; we must get out of here!"

"How!" She shouted over the din. "Tell me how!"

His eyes jerked up.

Zoe found herself knocked back, then roughly grabbed. Unable to register what or who was doing it.

She screamed, kicked, and she screamed again until she realized James was trying to drag her across the floor, his hands at her armpits.

Panting, she tried to focus on him. "What're – you knock me over, you drag me! Damn it, make up your – "

Another scream tore her throat when a chunk of the ceiling came crashing to the floor, splintering, pulverizing the old chair that had been sitting in the spot.

The same chair they'd been on the floor next to. Except shards of wood and plaster weren't the only things there on the floor, now.

Something had fallen *through* the ceiling from above.

Zoe scrambled to her feet, reaching for James, and found one of his hands. She took it in a death-grip.

"Run!" he commanded. He broke into a pace she'd have no choice but to match even if she didn't already want to with all of her being. She thought he'd yank her other arm from its socket. She didn't know where they were running to or from what, but she didn't want to know.

For as much as she didn't want to know, she chanced a look back, and her feet tangled. She remained standing, kept moving, because James was still pulling at her. Otherwise, she'd have been hobbled prey.

The something that had fallen.

The something had legs.

It had legs, several of them, and it righted itself, shook itself.

It was coming after them. Her thoughts of Lovecraft returned with a vengeance.

Zoe's scream was louder than the cacophony of the house, which should have been impossible. She ripped her gaze from the terrifying sight of glossy black, spindly legs, red orbs, dripping spit and gargantuan features.

Surging forward, she stumbled and fell. She knocked down both James and herself. Both of their bodies lit up in pain when they hit stair steps.

Adrenaline had other ideas and goaded them on.

They were going upstairs. *Upstairs? Zoe's brain rebelled while James groped for her hand.*

"Are you crazy?" she demanded, fear twisting a high pitch into her words. "We can't go upstairs!"

James hauled her up, his grip on her arms excruciating. "We can't get out either, and that thing," he jerked his head in the direction of the scraping, screeching sounds, "isn't up *there* any more, at least." He snatched her up and pulled. "Do you really want to debate this, or do you want to get the hell away from it?"

Zoe wasted no more time debating and scurried after James as he bounded up the stairs, taking two at a time.

The pair of them sprinted down the dark hallway. James came to an abrupt halt, causing Zoe to slam into him, which knocked him into the wall.

A wall where a door should have been.

"No." It was a lament. "No!" James' hand raced over the unyielding surface. "There was a door here before; it led to another set of stairs." His palms raced over the mildewed Victorian wallpaper. Faster and harder, he moved his hands, fleshy smacking sounds against the plaster. "No! No, this should lead downstairs, to the back of the house!"

Zoe was paralyzed. Several different thoughts sped through her brain, only some of them logical.

James knew the layout. He'd known where he was going. She could trust him.

James didn't know the layout. There were no stairs there.

But she remembered the stairs, too. She was certain she did. She could trust him.

They couldn't trust the *house*.

She then saw her own hands beating on the wall next to his, as if detached from her body.

"You son of a bitch! What do you want! What..." Zoe silenced herself as another realization hit her.

It was quiet. So quiet, except for James' panicked railing.

"James." Where her sudden feeling of calmness and inner strength came from, she didn't know, but she wasn't going to question it. "James, James stop. Listen."

Still he beat at the hard surface until she thought he'd bloody his knuckles.

She clutched his shoulders and shook. "James, shhh. Listen to me." She relaxed her grip and stroked his arms. "Shhh, it's okay, it's okay. Listen. It's gone quiet."

These words reached him, for he turned to look at her. What she gleaned in his eyes wasn't encouraging, but she had his attention.

"Listen to me, James." She lifted a hand to cup his chin. He was burning up, positively on fire, but she pressed on. "I need you, James. You were the calm one, until everyone left us. The rational one, out of all of us." She could feel his sweat moistening her palm. She took a deep breath. "I can't imagine what this is doing to you, but I need you. If we're gonna survive this, I need you to calm down. You can do this. I know you can. I believe in you, James."

So close he could see her eyes, he searched them. Blindly it seemed to Zoe, at first.

"Hold on, James," she pleaded. "Just hold on, don't leave me now."

Her words penetrated. Someone needed him. His focus shifted.

"I can...I can feel our way out of this. Surely I can," he said.

Zoe gave a vigorous nod.

"I can..." He moved his head, he ran his hands over his flushed face. "The house is shifting. Has shifted. It's quiet." He looked at the only other human in his hell. "As you said, quiet."

"Is that thing still down there?"

James' chest heaved. Zoe reached and rubbed it through his sweat soaked shirt. "It's okay, James."

"It's," his head cocked, "I don't sense it."

Zoe wondered whether she should ask the next question, but she felt it necessary. "Was that real?"

"I don't know what's real!"

"Okay, okay." She reached for his hands and moved them away from his head when it seemed he was intent on pulling out his hair. She heard his trembling inhale. He squeezed her hands as if he found strength there.

"I...don't believe it was real," he whispered.

Zoe didn't know whether this was true, if he were humoring her as well as himself – or just plain guessing – but she had said that she believed in him, so she'd take it.

It was then she understood where her strength was coming from. It was seeing him in such despair, in some manner of pain she'd never experienced, would never experience, that had done it.

Her need to mother, to help, protect, just as she'd tried to protect Jonas, was strong. It gave her the wherewithal to be *his* rock when he needed it. Especially as it seemed his own mother hadn't protected him.

"Which way, James?"

Though his mind still wished to drift, and though he felt that he might faint at any moment, James stepped to the side, stepped around her, and he studied their dark surroundings not with physical sight, but his *inner* eye.

"Whether the creature was real or not, that this house has changed is evident." He took a cautious step away from her, down the hall. "There are doors missing." His feet carried him farther; his hands tested the air in front of him. "There were seven." He stopped just where another door should have been. "There are now three."

Zoe shuffled towards him. "Is it – is it closing in on us?" It seemed a preposterous question, though it wasn't as if anything else made sense, and the evidence was all around her.

James moved yet again and reached to touch the knob of a door that remained. "I don't believe that's the precise description." He tested the knob. It turned. "It's meant to deceive us. Confuse us."

"It's doing a good job of it." She rubbed her arms. "Like a damned fun house." *Oh, God. Just like Brig said...*

"Precisely." James' reply was absent, automatic, as he opened the door.

"James, wait. Where are you going?"

"There's something in here."

Then shouldn't we go somewhere else? Zoe thought, though she followed him into the room. Just where else were they going to go, back down the other set of stairs? If they were still there, that is. Go back down there and have that demonic thing reappear?

She shuddered at the thought and then spared another shudder as they moved deeper into the room.

32

"James." Zoe only mouthed his name. She had the tail of his jacket locked in her hand. It was too dark. They had no flashlights. She had to stay close to him. She wouldn't let him get too far ahead.

"Over there, there's something over there," he said.

Zoe thought he seemed *very* calm for the way he'd been losing it before. She'd wanted him to chill out, but it wasn't as if he'd popped a handful of valium – that she'd take for herself, if she had any.

"What?" She clutched the leather of his jacket harder.

"On the wall."

To Zoe, it was as if the wall were drawing him in. The way James moved in a straight line towards it, the darkness not seeming to bother him at all, unnerved her. People are cautious in the dark, afraid of tripping. They shuffle along. They test the proverbial waters.

"I don't think we should get close to the wall," she said, desperately trying to see more than black spots and dark spots.

She wanted him to stand still. She wanted to let go of him and stay away from that wall.

She couldn't let go.

"Do you have a lighter?" James asked.

Zoe wasn't sure now that she wanted to see a goddamned thing. He sounded much too interested in the stupid wall. It was just a wall. Or so she told herself.

"No. I wasn't the smoker."

James paused in his movement. "Mike was."

"Yeah, but – " Mike. They'd found his lighter on the table, not far from where they'd found the damned camera, heard the damned screaming, and they'd both avoided speaking of it. Because really, Mike could've left it there any time. There was no reason to think otherwise. Except that maybe there was...

"I, uh, I have his, I think." She fished around in her pocket, never letting James' coat free. When her fingers found purchase on the cool metal, she shivered, and that shiver danced up her arm.

She realized she had no idea when she'd gotten hold of Mike's lighter. How had it gotten into her pocket? She didn't recall picking it up. She decided that she didn't want to know. She was on the verge of freaking out about it as it was.

She opted to behave as if it were all so normal. Pretend hard enough, it might come true.

"Here." She found James' other hand and pressed the Zippo into it.

The flame bursting into life startled her and hurt her eyes. She stared at the back of James' head when he started walking again. She looked over his shoulder when he held the lighter aloft.

She nearly choked on her own spit when she saw what he was looking at. Ripping her eyes away from the scene, she planted her face into his back.

The goddamned stain. They were in *that* room, the room where Mike had last been. Weren't they? It was the same stain.

She knew that it was. The same one she and Brig had first come across together.

She could hear Mike's screams from the replay of the recording even now.

"James I want to go. Let's go."

"This is where he died," James stated too succinctly for her taste; it was too much fact for her raw nerves.

"Don't say that. We haven't seen any…any bodies." Everyone was just – gone. Pretend hard enough, it might come true.

She lifted her head just in time to see James moving his other hand. He was going to touch that filthy spot.

"Stop!" Zoe made a bid for his hand and missed.

His fingertips made contact.

But nothing happened.

Nothing happened. Zoe wanted to smack her own forehead. They didn't need to take turns being hysterical, she told herself. "Moldy water stain. Could be infested with germs." She made light of it, though she wasn't even fooling herself.

James began to turn. Her hand fell away from his coat so her arm wouldn't twist. So she wouldn't seem so desperate.

"It's full of something, assuredly," he said.

The lighter's flame cast wicked shadows across his face. For a second, Zoe wanted to back away. His words, his face, it made her uneasy. Sent a chill racing up and down her spine; it spread across her scalp.

When he started away from her, the urge was to grab onto him again. He was walking away, across the room, and she jumped into action, catching him up – but didn't throw her arms around him, as was her first impulse.

Though she did reach for him as her foot hit a solid object and she fell.

～

The walls absorbed her screech and threw it back at her as she slither-scrambled away from the corpse like a spastic lizard – away from the corpse she had tripped over, a corpse her brain tried to deny.

Not real. It's not real. It's not him, it's not, it's not. You're not seeing what you're seeing; it's too dark, and you can't see anything!

Naked flame cast its glow across the distorted features, twisting them even more, and Zoe couldn't look away, though her fingers contemplated ripping her eyes out.

"No, don't touch it!" she shouted when it registered that James had knelt, that he was holding the damned Zippo much too close to his – its face, and that he was going to touch it.

"Stop, stop," she pleaded.

But James didn't stop. The tips of his fingers skirted the edges of Mike's crusted brow. Zoe watched in horror as they explored the sunken cheeks, cheeks that appeared bruised, pocked –

"Bites," James whispered. "Hundreds, thousands of – " he gasped, and he jerked back as if connected to some invisible string, tugged by unseen hands.

Zoe couldn't move. She was still frozen in queasy shock.

"Oh dear Lord, oh dear Lord," James said, rising and backing farther away.

Zoe didn't want to know. "What?" She really didn't want to know.

James, very still, and still gazing at Mike's corpse, its mouth yet captured in wide-open terror, whispered, "They are spider bites."

Zoe reminded herself that she didn't want to know. "He was attacked by – by spiders?"

Her companion's head shook itself in slow motion. "I can't see them."

At last, Zoe remembered to blink. "What do you mean?" Her skin crawled, and she had a sudden, mad urge to shake out her clothes, swat at herself.

"I can't see anything in the residual. I could see him thrashing, twisting, hear him screaming, but I cannot see the spiders."

She looked up into the darkness of the strange Englishman's face. Damn it, she did *not* want to know.

"I should be able to *see* them," he said. "I can see the bites appearing, yet I can't see *them*."

"He was attacked by invisible spiders?" she heard herself ask, stupefied beyond fear. She then said, "Mike was terrified of spiders."

With her comment, thoughts of an earlier conversation ran through James' mind, none of which he voiced aloud. There was a sharp tug at his attention, in the direction of the stained wall, and he found himself moving towards it, as if he had no choice.

It was calling to him. It was seducing him, whispering to him, teasing him. It made promises, very appealing promises.

"James, wait, wait." Zoe scrambled to her feet. "Wait." Desperate in her need to stop him, she lunged, grabbing him just as he reached for the festering sore on the wall. "Don't!" A memory, something Brig had said to her when they were in the room before, came back. "Brig said I went away. Seemed like I was gone, that's what he said to me."

Cryptic was not a word in James' vocabulary, it seemed, as he replied, "Yes, you were, he was correct. The stain drew you. Sucked you right in." He turned towards her. "You were right. It's infested."

This gave Zoe a near violent shudder. "What do you...do you mean..."

"It came from here. They came from here. But they weren't real; they couldn't be, or I should see them, shouldn't I?" His head cocked. "I can hear them, however. I can hear the tiny feet, the hairs on their legs whispering as they slide against each other. Oh yes, I can hear it."

Zoe took a step back. "But-but…" she gave up and started over. "Are they real or not? What bit him?" She took another step back, terrified now that little eight legged monsters would burst from the seeping stain any second. That they would ooze out, swarm across the wall and leap at her with malicious intent.

She rubbed her arms. Patted them. Stopped just short of smacking them repeatedly.

James took a step forward. "It knows."

Zoe swallowed hard.

"It knows," he repeated, then moved around her and drifted towards the door. "It knows, and it caused a reaction in his body, perhaps." He carried on, to himself, the streaming thoughts of a mad scientist. "The mind is a powerful thing; when one is convinced one is on fire, for example, one literally feels the burn; why, in dream studies…"

"Shit." Zoe was not going to ask. She wasn't seeking clarification, even if half of it made a bizarre sort of sense, and he wasn't talking to her anyway, which made it easier. "Wait for me!" She glanced back as she went after James, not able to deny any longer that the dead body had a name, and it was Mike. She nearly choked on her larynx, and tears leaked from her eyes.

She may have been angry with him, but she'd never wish such a thing on anyone, not anyone, and her tears were also for the others.

Oh my God, what happened to the others? What's going to happen to us?

33

James had frozen once they were in the consuming blackness of the hallway, a blackness not born merely from lack of light, but a feeling of oppression. As Zoe's eyes adjusted, it came to her that there was a light. Dim and strange, perhaps another trick of her imagination or the house,

It knows

but she could see it; her eyes wouldn't be convinced otherwise.

She soon understood that her companion was seeing the same thing. His head was turned in the same direction. He stood motionless, gazing, gazing in a silence as eerie as the current silence of the manor.

She then realized that the space they were both staring at shouldn't have been there. Or wasn't there before. When they'd gone into that perverse room of death, there had been a wall, the wall James had beat his fists against in confused desperation.

Now there was a dim light. The type of light one catches only in their peripheral, muted on its edges, never quite bright enough. Just there in a way nearly irritating as one's eyes seek more.

It wasn't the stairway James had said should be there, either. This Zoe could see when the statue of James animated, moving in that direction as if walking through liquid amber.

Zoe felt the same as she followed. They were both met with the resistance of thick sap, yet on they walked.

Eventually they reached a room, a narrow room that immediately gave Zoe a feeling of claustrophobia, though she'd never been prone to such a phobia. No, that was Brig. *Oh God, Brig...*

Once inside, her eyes fully registered the source of the light. From a narrow window it came. The light split into dingy streaks of dull color occasionally dappled by a pure red or green or yellow as it filtered through the room.

A stained glass window; they were in the chapel.

"I thought," Zoe's own whisper startled her. "I thought this was on the third floor."

James remained silent, neither confirming nor denying her comment. He knew the room well, the room in which he'd pulled off the prank. This room where that gentle young American now –

"Ohmph." James' fist had gone to his mouth, where it pressed hard, muffling most of the sound he made when he looked towards the altar.

Zoe unconsciously mirrored the action. But the sound she made was shriller, and it was her palm that attempted to capture it. As if to scream would make it real and not imagined.

Words, yet mashed by his hand, left James. "Not this way. No, please not this way."

Zoe's hand fell away from her mouth. "What? What did you say?"

"No, please not this way," James repeated to himself, lost in a feeling, a memory.

Zoe's focus shifted to James. "What do you mean?" Her eyes narrowed. "What happened to him?"

James, his head bobble-like as he backed away, made no reply.

Logically or not, suspicion replanted its seed within Zoe. "You know!" She made a grab at his shoulder. "Did you do it, did you?"

James pushed her away, pushed away from the sudden onslaught of her emotion coupled with his own. "I did nothing."

"What happened to him?" She moved towards him again, grabbed his shoulders and shook, not registering how many times she'd done that to him in the last – the last – she wasn't sure, and it didn't matter.

"What happened?" she asked.

James stumbled away from her and hugged himself so hard that it squished out most of the air in his lungs. "I don't know, and I don't wish to know!"

But he did. He did know, or had a very good guess. One that would be confirmed, certainly, were he to touch that poor, sweet man. This man he'd come to like rather well in such a short time.

Hands clenching into fists at her sides, Zoe looked back and forth between the breathing man and the one quite clearly not. The second time her eyes landed on Aaron, every muscle in her body became rubber, and she nearly went to the floor as she gaped.

The body was bent over backwards as if someone was yet holding it down. Backwards over the altar, his face a pale ghost in the dark, mouth caught in a scream, a grimace, and his eyes wide-open. Wide-open, vacant eyes, and his tongue, blue, seemed fastened to the bottom of his mouth.

"Oh…God." Zoe oozed to the dusty, hardwood floor. Tears left white streaks through the grime on her face.

When James finally spoke, Zoe could hear the emotion coloring his words.

"He took me into his confidence in this very room," James said. "He told me why he'd become a paranormal investigator. He told me his fears."

The hitch in James' inhale brought more stinging tears behind Zoe's eyelids.

"Not being able to breathe. To die that way, this was his worst fear," James said. "Choking. Suffocating."

Aaron's face, still a portrait in her mind, flashed brighter for Zoe. "Oh my God. That's just exactly what it looks like. Like someone choked him." She lifted her eyes in the direction of James, who was a blurry outline to her. "You can...you can find out for sure."

James' own arms threatened to crush his ribcage. "I don't wish to see it. I can't, please. I won't."

Zoe rose and made her way to James, his plea so plaintive, so pitiful, that it spurned her on. "I'm sorry. Of course you don't. You don't have to."

"I've no need of touching him," he sobbed. "I can see it on his face, just as you said. I can feel it in this room. I can feel the fingers that strangled him, nearly as..." his hands flew to his neck.

Zoe wasn't certain if she should touch him while he was in the throes of the vision and so didn't. She also didn't feel like asking whether the thing that had attacked Aaron was real or imagined. So vivid for Aaron that...

It didn't matter. Their beautiful Aaron was dead either way. "James...James, let's go." A part of her wanted to pull out her hair and scream, scream, just keep screaming until her throat bled.

The other part of her was numb in its incomprehension. The numbness crept through the other half, tempering its madness. The madness of understanding, accepting, that no matter how crazy it seemed –

It was real. This was really happening.

Suddenly, James turned, and Zoe thought he'd suffocate *her* in his embrace. "I liked him, I truly did."

Zoe lifted one of her hands. She moved it in soothing circles over her companion's back. Her one friend, the only friend left in this dismal nightmare.

"Why this way? Why everything he was most afraid of?" James said. The question was rhetorical.

The words left Zoe without much thought, regardless. She parroted James. "It knows." His words after they found Mike.

James drew back his head. His red-rimmed eyes found hers.

"What are you most afraid of, James?" Zoe asked with some trepidation.

James moved away from her. *The question shouldn't be asked, it shouldn't, it shouldn't,* he thought. He attempted to focus on that negative, so he wouldn't give it away. The thing that he would most fear, a thing that had always haunted him as it was. He didn't realize, at first, that he was speaking the mantra in his head aloud, if only in a whisper.

Yet Zoe carried on, momentarily caught in her own world. "I was most afraid of losing Jonas," she said. "I thought. I mean, before all this. I mean, I wouldn't want to – "

James' slapped a hand over her mouth. "Don't say it."

They gazed into each other's eyes.

Both, by this time, understood it wouldn't matter if they said it. But they were each willing to cling to the hope that if they didn't...

James lowered his hand. "I need to leave this room. We need to find a way out of this evil, piece of shit house."

Zoe nodded.

34

"Where are we?" Zoe was lost in a way she hadn't thought possible. How could a person be so confused in a house? Yes, it was large, but it had walls. It had rooms. It was a finite space.

It wasn't behaving the way a finite space should.

This idea was unnerving, so what did she do? She repeated the question.

"Hey. Where are we, James?"

Maybe he'd have a better answer than *I don't know*. Her temerity was rewarded this time.

"Third floor, and there should be another bedroom down that way," James said.

"There's always another bedroom." *Oh, God, Brig...*

"Indeed." James continued around the corner. Zoe marveled at his ability to get around in the thick, black darkness. It was like having a cat as a guide. At least, what she imagined it might be like, which was better than imagining what the house was up to, or what they'd find in the next room.

What a ridiculous thought. Zoe squinted into the dark. Much to her consternation, she had yet to develop night vision. She went back to staring at the thing she'd stared at for what already felt like eternity.

The back of James' head.

This view couldn't keep her mind off the house, though. She had taken to referring to it – in her mind – as a third person. Just another member of their group. She had done this with (to her) alarming frequency and a sense of normalcy.

She placed a hand on her forehead. "This is so effed up."

"Pardon?"

"Nothing."

She was relieved that he didn't press the matter; he was too engrossed in feeling his way through the night. The eerily quiet darkness. Compared to the night's previous noises (that she was trying so hard to pretend she'd never heard, and which bore no connection to Cthulhu) she should've been relieved. The silence wasn't natural, however. She had never experienced such an absolute void of sound.

So, of course, she tried to fill it.

"What do you think is in the room, James?" She followed close enough to step on his heels. "That's where you're going, right? Or are you looking for another way out?"

James stopped walking. "We're on the third floor."

"Okay, so we jump out a window. Don't you want to get out of here?"

James turned to face her. She was so close that he stepped on her toes. He moved back with a soft apology.

"You are nervous," he said. "I understand this. But, my dear, perhaps we should both make an attempt to be calm and not take turns... losing it."

She looked at the floor. Or rather, in the direction of the floor. She couldn't even see that, not really. It was another dark sea beneath her feet. She was walking on water.

"How are you so calm, now?" She lifted her gaze in the direction of his face. It was pale enough to give hints of a physical presence, though she noted that it also made him appear a disembodied, ghostly head.

She didn't want to dwell on the possible irony.

"I'm not complaining," she said. She considered her next words. "I don't...I don't get you." She sagged. Her entire body sagged. "I just don't get you."

She couldn't see the way his brows creased. The lines that formed in his forehead. The small divot that formed between his eyes, above the bridge of his nose.

"Get me?" James said. "What is there to get? You wanted me sane and capable. I am, currently – the latter, at least. The former has likely always been debatable."

Zoe wanted to scratch her own face off, though it wasn't because of James. She felt like an idiot. That was the only feeling she could disentangle from the others, anyway. Of all the times to venture a discussion of his quirks. Stupid, stupid, stupid.

"Zoe." James reached out, touched her cheek. The touch was so light as to almost go unnoticed. "I understand. You're afraid and nervous. I am not judging you, so please, don't be so rough with yourself."

Zoe jerked away from his touch. Stepped back farther. Every fine hair on her back prickled, but moving forward wasn't an option. It was too intimate. He'd...

"Stop it," she said. "Stop reading me."

She couldn't see the flash of hurt in James' eyes. Or the following look of resignation, acceptance. Circumstance had thrown them together, with nobody else to depend upon. He should have known better than to think she would treat him differently than anyone else ever had. It had been a temporary reprieve.

It still hurt. It hurt that, even in a desperate circumstance, someone had rejected him, reprimanded him for being what he was. A thing he couldn't control as well as others would like.

It wasn't that he didn't understand. He wearied of understanding everyone else, without reciprocation.

"Do pardon me," James said. Words he had grown quite accustomed to saying; variations on a theme.

Zoe tried to focus on him, lost the battle, and rubbed her face hard enough to turn it pink. The flesh of her back crawled, and she wanted nothing more than to ask him for a hug. It would create a safe haven. One where she wouldn't feel so exposed.

Or maybe she could just back into the wall. Wherever it was. She was far too vulnerable.

Without another word, James turned and resumed his stroll.

"Wait!" Zoe almost ran into him again but slowed at the last possible second. "Um. Wait. Please."

"I'm right here."

She noted the tension in his tone. She wondered if it was her fault. She wasn't so lost that she was clueless as to how she'd sounded before.

Yet somehow, she couldn't make herself apologize. She couldn't bring herself to explain. Didn't he know, anyway? Did she need to explain?

It would sound like an excuse, she reasoned. There were better things, more important things, to dwell on, she told herself. But why don't I at least apologize?

"James…" She had been about to do so, until he reached for the knob of a door. Always a door. When they'd arrived at a door, she did not know. They were there, and that was that. She said his name again, for different reasons.

James paused. "What is it?"

"I think…I mean, I don't think…" She sucked in some air. "Don't open it."

Zoe wanted to tear off his fingers when she heard the sound. It had to be the sound of a knob. Metal pieces tumbling, turning. A door rattling.

"Damn it, don't, James. Just. Don't."

She wanted to kick him in the ass when it sounded as if he were tugging at the door.

"See? It doesn't want to open." Zoe shifted her weight from foot to foot. "Let's go. Find some other… door."

James was in his own world. Unstoppable. Driven, perhaps.

By what or whom, neither of them knew.

The door gave way. It was like opening an ancient tomb. It gave way, and stale air rushed at James, hammered his face. But it didn't stop there. It was determined to reach the female of the duo, and reach her it did.

Zoe gasped and covered her mouth with both hands. Then she breathed, in shallow sips, through her fingers, when the smell was too much.

James groaned, his head swam, and he groped for the doorframe to steady himself. His hands found no purchase; it was nothing but air. His groan became a sharp sound of surprise as he fell into the room. Instinct had his feet speed up, to catch up the rest of his body before it went horizontal. Instinct hadn't allowed for an obstacle on the floor, however. James tripped, his feet tangled, and he never knew how close he'd come to cracking open his skull on the lavatory basin.

"Uhhgh." James went down with a soft thud. It should've been louder. It should have hurt more, the impact. The floor didn't feel as hard as it ought.

Or as level. He discovered that he was lying on –

"Oh...God."

"What?" Zoe gripped the doorframe so hard her knuckles were white enough to glow in the dark. "What, what? I mean. Are you okay?"

James was speechless under the onslaught of a residual.

"James?" Zoe reached out like the blind woman she was, testing the air with one hand, afraid to let go of the only solid thing in reach. "James what's going on?" Epiphany struck. "Oh...I'm so stupid! Hang on, I have the Zippo."

They'd thought it best to conserve lighter fluid. They had no idea how much was left in the Zippo's rayon batt. They had no fluid to refill it if it went dry. Zoe had stowed the Zippo in her pocket, at first grateful for the lack of light, after having seen Mike and Aaron. Then she'd followed James closely, at times clenching his coattail, until she all but forgot about the lighter.

Here came a click known the world over. The scent. The stream of yellow-orange light, which blinded her in a different way than the darkness had. But only temporarily.

Not long enough.

James thought that his head would implode. He pressed his hands to his ears, though it did little to dampen the sound. Zoe's shrill screams were enough to wake the dead; indeed, James expected the body he sprawled on to rise, zombie-like, with one directive.

To shut that woman up.

35

Metal rang out, protesting the abuse as it skittered across the floor. It couldn't compete with the screams. Zoe had lost all control of her voice, her volume. Though her view of the tangled up bodies – one dead, one very much alive and trying to stand up – was damped since dropping the Zippo, it had been burned into her brain, imprinted on the backs of her eyelids.

Brig. James had fallen on top of Brig.

That, more than anything else, nurtured her screams. She couldn't see the details, which flashed through James' mind like a film, fast forward. The fact that it was someone she knew, had known for a while, and had not so long ago been joking around with – this was devastating. Third time, no more pretending it wasn't real.

James wanted to cry out under the onslaught. Her emotions. Residuals. Visions. The two-ton weight of it all should have crushed him.

Nails tearing at paper, finding plaster. "Stop, please," James said. *Brig's nails were glutted with it.* "Zoe, for God's sake..."

And flesh, Brig's own flesh, when he tore at his own throat, his own face, his – "Zoe!"

Lucky for James, her throat had become raw, and she'd exhausted herself. Her screams lessened to whimpers.

Help! Fists beating on walls. Frantic, unable to find a window. James extricated himself from the cold, limp arms and legs of the man below him. The man he'd unintentionally molested as he struggled for purchase on anything that would help him to his feet. No door, no door. The walls are closing in. HELP! Bang, bang, bam, bam, BAM. Screeeeeeeeeech.

While Zoe stood there, great heaving breaths shuddering through her body, James managed to move back and into the claw foot tub. Literally. His feet flew up in the air and there was a resounding clang as he landed.

"Damn it," he cursed. *I can't breathe! There's not enough air! Jonas! Zoe! Zoe where are you? James grappled himself back into a sitting position, on the lip of the tub.* "But there's a door."

Zoe didn't register his words. She'd stopped whimpering but hadn't reclaimed her mental faculties. Her unseeing gaze had fixed itself to the small window behind the tub.

A window where words began to form, written in fog.

James was oblivious to what went on behind him. "There's a door, so why did he…" *Wallpaper peeling, wedging itself beneath fingernails. Plaster, wood. Blood, blood from tearing nails.* "There's…what is that smell?"

The Zippo. The flame hadn't gone out. It was there, sputtering on the floor. It had ignited…

Burnt hair. A corpse's hair.

"Shit!" An uncharacteristic curse from the Brit accompanied his awkward leap. A move that landed him in precisely the spot he'd been so keen to vacate before.

On top of Brig, whose hair was alight, creating a stench the likes of which James hoped never to meet again. While details of the other man's death had their claws in him, and with Zoe trapped in her own mental hell, the flames had begun to work on flesh. Scalp. Intent on crisping it, like bacon on a grill.

Brig had used too much hair gel that morning, which only fueled the flames.

The window behind, it called for HELP. SOS.

James patted at the smoking skull. "Help me," he beseeched Zoe, who stood as before, staring at that window.

He glanced up at her, quickly surmising that she was still in shock. His eyes were watering as he dropped his gaze back to the scalded flesh beneath his hands. It wasn't so much a bonfire as a burning ember.

He'd have to suffocate the works.

James wiggled out of his jacket and flung it over Brig's head, wrapped it tight, looking much like a killer asphyxiating his victim.

Zoe's brain pieced itself back together at that precise moment.

"What're you doing?" She lunged at James, and only just kept from falling, making a true dog pile. "Get off him!" Zoe reached out, clawed at James' hands in an attempt to pry them away from their work.

James' thoughts, his senses, had fine-tuned themselves. Perhaps his gifts had their own instincts, and when let loose in an emergency, functioned properly. James didn't know. James wasn't really thinking. He was following a lead.

"Get hold of yourself, woman!"

Zoe got hold of him. Drew blood. James cursed and slapped her hand away, though for a moment it was much like battling three wildcats.

"He's already dead!" James got hold of her wrists and braced himself, squeezed hard. "Zoe. Zoe!"

She nearly went limp. Frozen in place, she gaped at James as if a third eye had popped out of his head.

He softened his voice. "He is already dead. I can't hurt a dead man."

Her first attempt at words didn't go well. She tried again. "Let go...let go of me."

She tugged, he released her, and she sat back on her ass. The floor was cold. Not that Zoe noticed. It was hard, too. But this was less important than her dead friend with the stranger's coat wrapped around his head.

"Ew... God." Zoe pressed the back of her hand to her mouth.

"His hair was on fire," James whispered. He snatched up the Zippo and snapped it shut. The room plunged into darkness.

"Light it, light it." Zoe was on the verge of another panic attack. The last thing she wanted was to be in a dark room with a dead person. She didn't care who that person was; he was dead, and that was too much. Too creepy.

James sighed but opened the metal lighter, and the flame soon sprang back into life. "There's a small mercy. It still works."

Zoe looked past the heart of the fire, which would've made her see spots, and towards her living companion's face.

"You..." Trembling, she tried to get her feet beneath her. "You..."

James brows made a swift ascent. "I...?" He didn't like what he was sensing.

On her first attempt at standing, Zoe swayed and hit the wall, landing once again on her ass. Before James could comment, or offer help, she'd scrambled up, sliding up the wall for support, and made it to her feet.

"You're too calm." She chanced a peek at Brig. "You..."

James knew where she was going in her mind. "You can't honestly..." he shook his head. "Yes, you could, but I didn't do this."

"You're such a good actor, aren't you?" Zoe slid towards the door. Or where she remembered the door to be. The room was small, cramped, and thus had been ripe for feeding Brig's claustrophobia. But she was so spun she didn't know which way was left or right.

James had no reply that felt honest. He'd been a brilliant actor when he was twelve. He hadn't been acting this night, but she wouldn't believe him. He knew she wouldn't. He'd told her what he'd done to his father.

"You made me think you were just as scared as me," she said, her voice wavering. "More scared. But you're perfectly calm, now. You know what kind of person would be calm, right now?"

James lifted the lighter in an attempt to illuminate her face. "I am not a psychopath, Zoe."

"That's it exactly. That's exactly what you are. You fake emotions." Her hands clamped over her mouth. Her head shook and shook.

James held out a hand, as if to reassure a wild animal that he meant to harm. That he wasn't about to move. And to ward said animal off.

"My dear...I think you need to take a moment to collect yourself and – "

"Why?" she all but screamed. "So you can bludgeon me to death around the next corner? Or-or..." She wished with all her might that she had something to throw at him. Something to protect herself.

"You're going into hysterics." James knew that he was on very thin ice, which itself was on the edge of a cliff. She was about to tumble over it – and take him with her, if she could just latch onto him.

"Gee, I wonder why!" She all but fell through the door and into the hall. "You told me you were a murderer. Hah!" There in the dark, James never saw the way her face blanched. "Nice one. Misdirection? Or some other psychological bullshit that I...I..."

"Please." James was careful not to make a sudden move, though he wished to stand. He felt defenseless and uncomfortable, so close to Brig. "Just take a breath and – "

"It stinks!" She gestured. "You tried to burn the evidence."

James was at a loss. He didn't know how to help her anymore than he knew why he wasn't losing his own marbles, as the American might have said, had she not already snapped.

He rose and reached out a hand.

"Stay away from me!" Zoe started down the hall.

"It's dark." James stepped over the corpse. "You can't go alone."

"Stay away."

"Zoe. Be reasonable. You don't even know where you're going."

"Away from you."

James stood in the doorway, Zippo aloft. He could just see the woman's back.

Zoe had a flash of sanity. A moment where her rational mind reminded her that she couldn't see in the dark. That she couldn't remember the floor plans. That the house didn't adhere to said floor plans, anyway.

The latter thought sent her back to temporary-insanity-ville.

"I'm not going to hurt you. I swear it," James said, though he didn't think it would matter. He went through the doorway and started after her.

She whirled and hissed at him.

He stopped.

She whirled the other way. "Wait. Did you hear that?"

James shook his head. "No. What did you hear?"

"Oh, come on, you must have." She turned back in his direction. He could just make out her wide eyes. "Jonas... it's Jonas."

James had heard nothing but his own heartbeat and her confused speech.

He didn't possess the temerity to tell her what he thought about Jonas. That he very much doubted she'd be hearing anyone other than himself, and herself, any time soon.

"There. He's calling for help!" Zoe sprinted down the hall.

"Wait!" James took off after her, the sound of her tumble on the floor reaching his ears just before he'd taken the second step. The sound suggested imminent bruises. Possibly a fracture. Her screech suggested much more.

"Are you all right?" James reached her side. "Zoe?"

"Leave me alone." She scrambled to her feet and took off once more. James didn't stop to think; he followed.

Neither made it far. The floor beneath their feet cracked open and swallowed them alive.

Zoe didn't have time to scream. Neither of them did. The maw swallowed them up fast; it sucked out their very breath. Gravity had disappeared, and they were free falling through a wall of sound without sight. A sound suggesting that the house had grown tired of its layout once again.

Or just plain grown. Creaking, crackling, crunching and settling. Stretching, snapping, slipping, sliding and yawning.

A great yawning breath, and on the exhale they were spat out. The ground rushed at them, out of nowhere, intent on one thing.

Stopping them.

Which it did, with enough force to wind each of them and leave them on the verge of mental oblivion.

At least for a time. Which was a blessing.

36

There were no snacks, no distractions, no jokes told to himself and the insects he'd not yet eaten. The program was in its third act, and getting very, very interesting. Who would win, who would be eliminated?

He didn't even have any of the childish glee that often accompanied his experiments.

It had all gotten very serious. What happened now interested him most of all. It would either destroy his mood or elevate it exponentially, and it was far better for anyone within his considerable sphere of influence, when he found his own pleasure.

Otherwise, they had to sacrifice an awful lot of their... selves.

37

Consciousness of their surroundings returned in increments. As did pain. It first snuck its way into toes, elbows, shoulders, and then, with a vengeance no human deserved, exploded to life, radiating from sources both definable and not. Through the haze of sensitized nerve endings, it was difficult to discern who, what, and where they were. The silence hindered matters. There was no creak, no whisper, not even a groan to offer direction and depth.

Until Zoe provided the groan, and James discovered that he was half on top of her. His right-brain went through a checklist, discovering that miraculously, he might be able to walk. He could, at the very least, get off the woman he was squishing.

"Are you…" All right? *seemed like the wrong question. She couldn't be all right.* "In one piece?"

Zoe groaned again and brought a hand to her forehead. "I'm not sure."

While she tried to gather herself, James attempted to get a look at their surroundings. Zoe asked the question he was asking himself.

"Where are we?"

The belly of the beast was his immediate thought. One he just refrained from blurting aloud. "I think…Dear Lord, did we fall all the way through to the basement?"

Zoe struggled to sit up, wincing in pain as she did. "No freaking way. That's…weren't we on…?"

James looked to his companion. He felt a sudden twinge of guilt for his next thought. That the fall had knocked some sense back into her. It appeared that way, at least. He reminded himself that she might spew curses at him at any moment, since she couldn't quite run away.

Yet. But running might be better than the wildcat scratching his eyeballs out.

"Third floor, yes," he replied, as he sensed her desire for confirmation. He thought to rise and was halfway to his feet when his world tilted and turned gray on the edges.

"Whoa." Zoe reached a tentative hand in his direction, just as James realized he'd landed squarely on his butt. "I don't think you should do that again. Watching made me dizzy," she said.

"You?" He brought a hand to the back of his head, and found a goose egg. "Ach. That's no good."

"Are you bleeding?" Zoe tried to look herself over, but it was too dark to make out specifics. So she started feeling her way around her limbs. "Am I, for that matter? God…I'm surprised I'm even breathing."

And then it came to James all at once. How his head had connected with her boot in the fall. That's where he'd gotten the tender lump on his head.

Not from the floor.

It dawned on him why it was that neither of them had broken bones. He didn't need to see. He was certain Zoe would find that she was rather well off for having fallen so far. Whatever bruises she had were because he'd landed on her.

It was the floor.

The floor was soft. His left-brain told him it shouldn't be so. Dirt packed so tightly wasn't soft, and would feel even harder when one was spat on it from so high above.

It was more than soft. It was squishy. The word that first came to James' mind. His brain sped off in various disturbing and imaginative directions, many correlating with his earlier, unvoiced thought.

Belly of the beast.

Zoe noticed before he could consider pointing it out. Or at least, he assumed she had, considering the shrill scream she let loose. A scream that seemed to multiply. Not an echo, but a chorus, as it careened down the hall.

A hall? It was a tunnel. James realized this in the midst of Zoe's mini-hysteria.

"What is...Oh my God...the floor, it's...James!"

"Yes."

"It's...it's-it's...squishy and..."

"Yes, I know."

"Slimy and sticky, and...James!"

"Disgusting, I know."

"It's...is it...is this...?"

"I don't know!" James closed his eyes and took a breath. Snapping at her would do no good. He opened his eyes, resolved to lower his voice. Zoe's disbelieving and somewhat wounded stare put a halt to his intended next statement. Clearly, he needed to think up different words.

"Do forgive me," he said. "I shouldn't yell at you." He paused to make a decision. "I think it's real. It certainly feels real. We weren't dashed to pieces in the fall. Even if this isn't what we think it is, our being in once piece makes as much sense as giant intestines." He heard his own laugh. His own pressure valve, pushing itself open. "The fall doesn't even make sense, so why not?"

Zoe blinked a few times. "You told me the truth."

James offered a blank stare.

"I don't mean that the way it sounds. It's hard to think straight, now." She shook her head as she rubbed her face. "I mean that you didn't sugar coat it," she said into her hands. She lowered them and looked in the direction of his eyes. "You didn't lie for my own good. Thank you."

James studied her dark visage. He was pleased that his choice to be transparent had calmed her, rather than sent her into more hysterics. A good thing, in light of his own precarious state.

People often exhibited the most interesting and seemingly contrary emotions when under stress, duress.

Shame that it didn't last.

"Oh my God..." Zoe came to her feet in one fluid motion. Further proof that the fall hadn't happened. Or that the floor was soft and squishy, just as they feared.

Or that they were crazy, and that was that.

"What now?" James followed her gaze, peering into the dark tunnel.

"Jonas." She began to move in that direction. "I'm coming, Jonas! I'm coming!"

James was baffled. He scrambled to his feet. "Wait! I don't hear anything."

Zoe was deaf to his words. She had ears only for Jonas and his pleas for help.

"Zoe!" James started after her. Noting in the back of his mind that it was slippery under his heels, he attempted to tread with careful haste. "Zoe, there is no one down there!" He stumbled over an unseen object. Something firm enough to trip him, but porous enough to make a squelch of sound upon contact.

He didn't want to think about it, not at all. He didn't wish to dissect the possibilities of what was beneath him, much more up close and personal than seconds before.

There was no stopping her, though. He may as well lie there all…night. Whatever was left of the night. James no longer had a concept of time. He hadn't for a while. He knew this on a subconscious level.

"Hold on, Jonas!"

By the sound of her, she was well away. Farther and farther away. James lurched to his feet, or tried, at least. It felt as though the floor suctioned him back down to the spot. Sucked at his feet every time he tried to gain ground.

Again, he tried not to dwell on this, on the possibilities. Convinced that if he did, the house would know and react accordingly.

He wondered what it had already gleaned from his subconscious. Those things that he knew laid in wait, that he pretended didn't exist. Or tried to pretend.

"Zoe…" James reached out, lurching forward as he did. "Zoe there's…" he fell silent. He couldn't hear her, which meant she wasn't hearing him. He was also certain there wasn't anyone down that… intestinal tract.

Why wasn't she afraid? Why didn't she see it?

Did he see what he thought he was seeing? Were they insane, after all?

When had they lost their grasp, all of them? At what point in the night? In the last few moments, or at the very beginning of the investigation? After all, did one know when they went mad, well and truly mad?

Perhaps they'd been mad to accept the invitation to the manor house to begin with. Yes, this is when they had lost their collective minds.

38

"Jonas! Jonas, I'm coming!" Zoe ran, oblivious to the state of things under her feet. All that mattered was Jonas. He was calling for help. Calling to her.

Her name. Calling her name.

"Jonas!"

James wasn't faring so well. It seemed every step he took, the floor (he kept trying so hard to think of it as just a floor) was intent on sucking his feet down. It was worse than running through sand, or water, or both together.

Tar, it was like running through tar a foot deep.

"Zoe…" James barely had breath left to call her name. He kept trying, fruitless as it was. It was the right thing to do.

She only had ears for Jonas. Closer, she was getting closer, she could tell. He didn't seem so far away. Just ahead. Just a few more feet. She couldn't see a damned thing, but it didn't matter.

Jonas was calling. His wife wasn't here, she couldn't save him, but Zoe could. Selfish but true. She'd save him, and they'd leave together.

Happy ever after. The thought filled her mind, bloomed large and bright, and if James could see her face, he'd see the smile to match these thoughts.

No doubt, she looked like a madwoman.

Still James trudged on, thinking how absurd it was, just like a dream, that the tunnel (intestine) was getting longer and longer, no matter how many steps he took.

"Zoe...for the love of..." he let out a frustrated grunt. "Damn it, why won't my feet move?" Anxiety worked its way through his nerves.

Every second that ticked by spoke more of danger, that Zoe was in terrible danger, and there he was, helpless. Helpless and ripe for the picking, himself.

"Let me go!" But the house didn't seem to care about his desires. Only his fears. He stared down the tunnel with something akin to horror and nausea written on his face, when for no apparent reason, the tunnel illuminated.

Dark...light.

He could see Zoe walking bold as you please, towards –

"Zoe!"

His voice seemed to carry only as far as his lips. He tried again.

"Zoe, stop – can't you see it!"

The ridiculous question of the frantic. It was obvious that she couldn't see what he was seeing. If she did, she would turn and run the other way, into his arms, or flat out knock him down and run him over in her haste.

Zoe reached out a hand, reached for Jonas' shoulder. Her fingertips would contact the fabric over that strong, broad shoulder any time, now, and he'd turn. He'd turn, he'd smile, and he'd take her into his arms. Into his arms, and he'd carry her out of the dismal nightmare that was the entire investigation. And he would understand. Her secret would be safe with him. He wouldn't think she was a pervert, a freak, when he found out she liked to be humiliated. Leashed. That she always thought he'd make the perfect jailor. It was a compliment, and he knew it.

"Zoe!" James may as well have been on a treadmill. Walking, walking, and making no progress.

Zoe's fingers made contact with that shoulder, but just as they did, she heard something that brought a deep frown to her lips. It set in hard lines, as if for all time.

Jonas wasn't calling her name; it was his wife's name. Barbra, Barbra.

He was holding her in his arms, his wife, and she looked right at Zoe, peeked around his shoulder right into her eyes, and laughed.

"Zoe…I'm coming…"

Jonas looked to see what had his wife so amused, and when he saw who was standing there, he laughed, too. Laughed as if it were the best joke he'd ever heard.

Zoe's hands flew to her mouth. They were laughing at her. She was the butt of their jokes. It was the wrong kind of humiliation. They were hugging and kissing – and laughing – how dare they look so happy.

Zoe's head shook and shook, disbelief pushed aside by heartbreak, defeat. Disappointment..

She'd listened to his problems; she'd lent a sympathetic ear time after time. She'd supported him in everything, in everything; she'd been there for him, she'd –

"I came to his piece of shit house for you!" She raised her arms, her hands balled into fists, intent on pummeling him, knocking some sense into him. "How could you! How can you laugh, how… how…" tears prickled her eyes, and he was a blur, they were both a blur, but she could hear them laughing…

"Zoe!" Oh my God. James gathered every ounce of will he possessed, fighting the damned floor, the human-scale flypaper, and pulled. Yanked. One foot. The other. Left. Right.

He looked down and realized that so far he'd only moved one foot, for all the encouragement in his head.

"Arrrg!" Left, left, left!

She was reaching, reaching…

"Zoe stop, stop!" Right, right, right!

Her scream split his eardrums, left his ears ringing. Because yes, it was hideous enough to draw a scream from her when she should have already used them all up.

"No!" Left...left... "Damn you! God damn you, get away from her!"

The flesh of Jonas' face swelled, bubbled, and erupted. Thousands, it had to be thousands, of many-legged black bastards with too many eyes, streamed through his pores, the widening pores of his face. From the blisters, the bubbles of flesh that popped, hairy little legs broke through. Hard, spindly, shiny little legs puncturing, making their getaway.

They streamed out like ants in a line, bees from a hive.

Spiderlings breaking out of their egg sac.

Zoe screamed again. And again. Deafening James once more.

Spiderlings breaking free of their silk Mike sac.

Mike?

Another scream ripped Zoe in half. Barbra had done it, she was the one; she was the murderess among them. She'd plotted with Smith, yes! Yes, of course! Jealous of Jonas' affection for her, jealous of the time he spent with her.

That sneaking, lying, conniving – "What have you done with Jonas! Where's Jonas!"

Barbra. Barbra with her four pairs of eyes, seeing shadow and pigment, light. Eight black and red eyes. The thing that had fallen through the floor. The thing that had nearly squashed her and James where they sat.

No, no, it was worse. Tentacles and spindly legs, suction cups and fine sticky hairs. Squid face, talons and – Cthulhu.

James saw her stumble back, back towards the gaping hole that should not exist in the floor – it was a floor, just a floor, really, there was wood – and she was about to fall into this hole, one that he knew went on and on.

One that wouldn't have a soft, squishy bottom to cushion her bones.

"Zoe stop!" At last, his feet came out of the muck. It was so sudden, and he'd been straining so hard, that he pitched forward as if from a spring. The momentum sent him down, and his face hit the floor, cracking his nose.

A bright flash of colors bloomed on the back of James' eyelids. The colors of pain. But he could hear Zoe screaming. Screaming. On and on, screaming. He couldn't be still. He couldn't give into the pain. He couldn't lie there and listen to her death.

He pushed himself up, blind with tears, stars, blood and snot.

And he ran. It didn't matter if he couldn't see. If he fell through another floor. He would not abandon her. Damn it, he wouldn't abandon her.

But he ran also for selfish reasons. He didn't want die in this hell alone. She was all he had left. He didn't want to be alone. Didn't want to die alone.

He couldn't catch her up unless he dove into the pit.

The pit she'd stumbled into and the place she'd found Jonas at last, when she landed on his putrid corpse. A husk of his former self, due to exsanguination. A corpse missing even organs.

"Jonnaaaaaas!"

The rest was silence so absolute that James broke out in a cold sweat and reconsidered his convictions.

"Zoe...I'm coming," James huffed, trying to convince himself — again — that it was a good idea. That he was man enough. "I'm coming." It was almost a whisper by now, as his will guttered like a candle in a breeze.

There was a reply, but it was a whisper. A whisper that twisted his guts into thousands of knots and turned him into petrified wood.

"You're here."

James' couldn't respond. He could scarcely even breathe. He had a nose full of viscera, and his throat had closed up at the sound of the familiar voice.

"Shall I read you a story, Jimmy?"

What air James could suck in squeaked through his esophagus and came back up in a hiccup. Bubbles formed at his nostrils, one growing and oil-slick shiny. The kind that just wouldn't quite burst.

"I'll read you a story and tuck you in."

His mind reeled. His senses told him that everything he didn't want to know, and didn't want to believe, was now irrefutable.

It was real. This was real. Every single event of the night.

Truth absolute.

"Or do you prefer James, now? Yes, James. A full-grown man and self-sufficient." There followed the laugh that had haunted his nightmares year after agonizing year. "I shall call you James."

James' vision cleared, much to his everlasting terror, giving him confirmation. There was a man standing before him, as solid as James himself was. A man who now folded his arms across his narrow chest, wearing a damnable smile that said I'm better than you are, better than anyone. Smug smile, but oh, it could be lovely. An arrogant man, but oh, he could be charming. A beautiful man, but oh, he could be ugly.

"You weren't expecting me, I see," his father said. "I must say, I find this rather, hmm. Quaint? This is what you do with your considerable IQ? You, hmph… hunt ghosts?"

James swiped at his nose and whimpered with the splinter of pain that shot up into his brain. A pain he'd felt before. The one time dear old pop had gotten angry enough to hit him in the face. Always before, he was careful not to touch his son's 'angelic features', but one time, he'd gotten particularly impatient.

Dear old Dad laughed that goddamned beautiful laugh of his again. That silken, congenial laugh. The one he used to charm the pants off other men, and occasionally lift the skirts of other women who were not his wife.

With James, he used a different sort of charm. A different manner of sweet talk. But that one time, when James had attempted to defy him, he'd lost his patience and broken his nose.

James had told his mum a lie, for fear of having something else broken. Even though, by this time, he knew that she knew better. She knew better, but didn't seem to care. She had her standing, her social circle, her mansion and her husband's wealth.

It wouldn't do to have a scandal. No, it wouldn't, and so she turned the other cheek, plugged her ears, or drank herself into a state where no such things existed.

Dear old Dad had not hit him with such force before that particular night. Not until after he was ten. After he'd already been sneaking into his room for a good five years.

"Don't you have anything to say to your father, James? It's been so many years; you must have something to say."

Words had abandoned James. Just as motor reflexes seemed to have done. All he could see in his mind was the bed. Pause, repeat, rewind, play. The four-poster bed. Four posts with which to anchor the ropes that he would tie his son up with, spread eagle, sometimes face down. Suffocating in a pillow, night after night.

But it was better than looking into his father's beautiful face. The face that could beam down upon him a bright, loving smile. That sometimes much-too-salacious smile. The smile that twisted and shifted when pleasure wrote its story in his father's features.

A son should never have to see such tawdry pleasure on his father's face.

"Well?" Dad lifted a slender brow, the action elegant. He always was elegant, even when he was sodomizing him. A ludicrously elegant rapist.

It was an absurd thought. James laughed. The snot bubbles burst over his upper lip.

Father waved an equally elegant hand in a stupid gesture he had no right to own.

James laughed again. The pitch spoke of imminent hysteria.

"You're a sight. Don't you have a handkerchief?" Daddy reached for his breast pocket, where a white silk handkerchief was folded into a neat pocket square. "I suppose I could lend you mine."

James laughed again. A twisted, winding sound, liken to an oboe played by an amateur. "Of course, even dead, you'd be impeccably dressed."

"And you, in life, so filthy." Father freed the silken cloth with a flourish, and held it up for his son. "Might I entreat you to wipe your face?"

"Do I disgust you?"

"It's most unbecoming."

"Indeed? I think I rather like that. Keep your precious silk."

"Oh, James. You're far too pretty to be covered in blood and oozing mucus." He held out the expensive cloth.

James didn't reach for it. He'd snapped. It was audible, at least, in his mind.

Too pretty to be covered in mucus.

Father would say this when James cried. You're too pretty to cry so hard, James. You'll make your eyes swell and be swimming in mucus. That pout, however – I do so like that pout.

James took a step back.

His father took a step forward, brandishing the silk handkerchief. "Come, now. We can't have you looking a mess."

"For...for what?" It was the timid question of a five-year-old boy.

"Your starring moment, of course, Jimmy."

James' feet propelled him backwards, but instinct had him stop just short of running into something.

Someone.

"Do as your father says, Jimmy." Dear old Dad, still offering the fucking handkerchief.

A shriek of panic would've left James, if it weren't for his swollen throat. He turned and ran.

Ran into Father.

"James, James, James. This will be so much easier if you don't resist."

So much easier if you don't resist.

James gagged on his own swelling tongue. "Ohg…gods…" Again, he whirled and made a break for it. This time, progress was his friend. This time, he went several steps, each one getting him closer to, if not freedom from the house, a good distance from the one thing he most feared.

This wasn't necessarily his father. It was his own past he feared most. His own past, now come back to haunt him in a way it hadn't before.

Now it had a real voice. A tangible body. A symbol of everything bad in his life. The man stood for everyone who had ever shunned him, or abused him, because of his talents. Everyone who'd hurt him, because they thought him strange. Father even represented the Mother who never wanted him.

And Father represented his fear of love, of closeness, because Father had always said that he loved him. That what he did, he did in love, for he so loved him, his pretty boy. His lovely, intelligent, wonderful boy.

James had believed him, which was why it had scarred his psyche so deeply. James, who even then was sensitive, had understood it through his father's touch. That this was how his father showed love. It was right to him, and so it was right to James.

That is, until the night James decided he didn't want love, if that were the cost of it, the price he had to pay. It was the night he began to escape in his mind and plotted over and over a way to end it all, to snuff out this love forever.

Nothing else had worked. When he'd protested too strongly, he'd gotten hurt. Protestations earned him bound wrists and ankles. Fighting back garnered worse positions and humiliations.

A broken nose.

James ran and ran; it felt like forever. He didn't dare a look over his shoulder, afraid he was being chased, or worse – not. If not, who could say where Daddy dearest was?

Progress was not his friend for long enough.

James fell back, hand flying out to break his fall, and his wrist sprained on impact.

"Oh God, oh God." He tried to look away, but it was so difficult, so very difficult, when there stood Aaron.

Aaron, that sweet American man he'd started a friendship with, one who'd flirted with him and told him a secret.

Aaron, whom he'd seen dead some time ago – wasn't it? He wasn't certain. Time slipped through his fingers like water.

"You're not real," James rasped. "Not real!" James shook with a sob. Would've remained on the floor sobbing if not for the sound of Father's voice behind him.

"Darling, let me help you. It wouldn't do to have bruises."

In front of him, Wraith-Aaron said, "Of course I'm real. I came back for you."

"Aaron? But I saw you…" James pressed the heels of his hands to his eyes and looked at Maybe-Aaron through a rainbow of spots.

"Saw me what? Oh…you mean after I was strangled?" Aaron's look turned accusatory. "Why did you tell? He knew exactly what to do to me."

James pulled at his own hair. Some of it came away, stuck under his nails, though he never noticed the pain. He flew off the ground and lurched forward. Closed his eyes and kept going, like a battering ram, not knowing if he'd hit a solid body or…

Air, it was nothing but air, and he sluiced forward. He came to an abrupt halt when the thinking part of his brain asked him where the exit was.

"Jimmy, let Daddy help you…"

39

"No!" James did a spastic shuffle, looking in every direction, desperate for a way out. He even looked up, seeking the hole they'd fallen through. He and Zoe. *I'm so sorry, so sorry I failed you!*

It wasn't there. Maybe he was standing in the wrong place. Maybe it had all been in their heads. It had to be. Basements weren't fashioned out of human tissue and digestive acid. They weren't made of stomach lining and, and, and...

"I've gone mad." James laughed a nervous laugh. "That's it, I've gone mad." He directed his gaze up to the ceiling once more. "Even if I find the hole, how do I get up? I have no rope." He laughed again. "If I did, I could hang myself and be done with it."

His fingers skirted his lips, as if they could touch yet another laugh.

"Where is it you think you're going, Jimmy?"

A squeal of surprise jerked through James. Father was right behind him. It didn't matter where he ran, be it in circles, he couldn't abide being so close to the man who'd made the darkness a waking nightmare, and then had stolen even the daylight from him.

Daddy had spied on him, caught him skinny-dipping with his best friend. He'd followed them. He'd never forget how Daddy described, in lascivious detail, what he'd do to that other boy should he catch them in the pond again. What he'd do to James in private, later.

His skin crawled for the umpteenth time. It felt as if bugs creeped just under the surface. He wanted to rip his face off.

Yet again, he ran. To where, he didn't know. If he could run long enough, perhaps he'd get somewhere, eventually.

As if reading his mind, which it may have been all night, the house offered up a set of stairs that he swore weren't there before. But he stopped dead, just at the foot of them, because – stairs? Why should he trust this was real? If they were real, why should he trust the manor? It hadn't done anything to help him before this, so why should he take the stairs, now?

"No," he whispered. "It's a trick. If I take these stairs you'll... You're a serial killer."

"James!"

That wasn't Daddy.

James swallowed over the lump in his throat. Morbid curiosity demanded that he look. That he look in the direction of yet another familiar voice. Just as he did, hands were on him, the grip strong, too strong for smoke and mirrors, ghosts and shadows.

"There you are. Where the fuck were you guys?" Brig shook him. "Do you have any frigging idea of the hot mess that is this house?" He gripped James harder, to the point James almost cried out. "I yelled and yelled, why didn't you come? Dude, I think..."

James was staring at him in abject horror, eyes large round Kewpie-doll eyes.

"What? Why are you looking at me like that?" Brig said. "I'm the one who just had the piss scared outta him. But oh, wait until you hear the story. I think I got some good evidence. You guys are gonna shit yourselves."

James was stunned that he hadn't done that very thing, already. He didn't think that he had. He tried to work himself free of Brig's grip, before just such a thing happened.

"But-but-you're-you-"

"Hah, spit it out, man. Didn't figure you for the hysterical type, James."

James studied Brig's face. Brig, who looked perfectly normal, and appeared quite alive. It didn't compute. James had seen the body. He'd seen it, and he'd relived how Brig had died.

"Brig, you're..." James reached for the muscle man's shoulders. "Get us out of here." As he said the words, his hands sought purchase on solid, warm flesh. Perhaps the dead body had been the trick. The ghost. Maybe Brig was warm and alive, and he could touch this warmth.

But this wasn't to be. James' hands sank into clammy, cold, scabby flesh. Along with the sensation came the scent of burnt hair and cooked meat.

James screamed. The scream threatened to black him out, what with the pressure. His broken nose, his shock.

"Get away from that boy, James. You're mine."

Brig, hair on fire, scalp sizzling, gave James a quizzical look. "Who's that?" He reached for the top of his own head. "And wow, is it warm in here, or is that just me?"

With a raw grunt and wail, James made a bid for the stairs, no longer caring where they went, as long as it was away. Up, up, up, it seemed a never-ending prospect, but on he trod. Anything was better than being down there.

"James, where are you going, dear boy? I didn't excuse you."

He ran. Trotted. Stumbled. Ran. Panted and huffed. On and on he went. Convinced he heard footfalls behind him, constant, echoing footfalls, he pushed and pushed until he was ready to fall over.

But there was no stopping. To stop was to suffer a worse fate than his lungs burning, his thighs turning to jelly.

The toe of his shoe caught when his feet grew too heavy, his legs too limp, to lift. He fell, stumbled, and whacked his shin. Tears filled his eyes. Exertion, fear, and memories brought them about. Spilled them over his cheeks.

"Pl-pl…" he made a desperate, raspy bid for air. It felt like sucking through a needle thin straw. "Please…"

Footfalls. Footfalls. Click, tamp, click, tamp, click.

Then came that final gasp of adrenaline. The one that would move him up those last few steps, if indeed there were a few more stairs. It lifted James up; he crawl-walked up a stair, and another, one more, and just one more…

He nearly wept again, this time in profound relief, when he realized he was on flat ground. Smooth flooring. A landing. A hall? Another story. How many stories up? His thinking mind couldn't parse it. For all the running, he wouldn't have been surprised to find himself atop the Shard in London.

But of course, he wasn't, much as he wished he were. He could yet hear the footsteps, mocking him, teasing him, taunting and chilling him. Maybe he was in the Shard. His father was the type to snag an invitation to its grand opening, its ribbon cutting.

Father had the respect of his peers and the business world, even if some hated him, as well. They hated him because he was so damned good at what he did.

Fooling people. If they had only known.

James let go with a torrent of tears. He didn't have the strength to fight them, though he couldn't spare the strength to weep, either.

40

"There, there, you're making a mess of your face. What will mother think?"

As far as James could tell, she didn't think much at all, at least not about him or the state of his person. She thought about her tea parties and her next gin.

James felt the cool, smooth touch of silk on his face. He hardly registered the sting when his nose was wiped. His head was pounding as if a marching band resided in his skull. The barometric pressure had long since broken the gauge. Along with his blood pressure.

"That's better," his father purred.

"No, please. Don't touch me."

A sigh. "You sound as if you have a mouth full of cotton and a head full of insulation. I can't understand a word, James. Enunciate."

James wanted to scream, but he was beyond it. Even screaming in his head hurt, in a dull, hammering sort of way.

"Let's get you up. Things to do."

James felt hands at his armpits. He wanted curl up into a fetal position and stay there until it was over. He, by habit, began to surrender.

Those nights on his bed, that was the worst. He couldn't hide. He couldn't fold in on himself, couldn't get away from those penetrating eyes, that covetous stare. James had not felt so utterly nude and vulnerable in all his life as he did on those nights.

So he'd go away, in his head. He wasn't certain when he'd started to surrender. When it was that he realized it was easier, if worse in other ways. Surrendering to dear old Dad sped things along.

It also meant he didn't suffer the restraints. Unless he curled up into that ball. Surrendering meant not curling up, not hiding, not hindering access.

James was forcing his legs to remain straight, going away in his head, or trying. He couldn't find the happy place. It once was the pond, which he thought was his secret, until Father spied on him, and made a point of explaining in great detail all the times he'd seen him, followed him.

He tried to go to his other place, the dark place, the one where twelve-year-old James had plotted and planned, had taken private joy in the thoughts there, the thoughts of ending it forever.

He couldn't reach it. He'd already done it. He'd already killed his torturer, but it wasn't forever. The man was here, in the flesh, trying to drag him to his feet and do God knows what. It made more sense to stay on the floor, unless Father had decided he'd prefer a new angle.

James had killed him, but Father had come back. How could he get rid of him, now? Homicide hadn't worked.

He became conscious of his father's breath on his ear. Whispered words, soothing words, so like those whispered to twelve-year-old Jimmy, *Jimmy*, how he loathed that nickname. *Jimmy you're so beautiful, Jimmy I love you, don't fight it, Jimmy, you know you want this, too.*

He lost it. The deep, primal part of James broke, and sprang to life. A part that liked living and liked doing so on its own terms. A part that would rip his father to shreds with teeth and nails, if it could.

He wiggled and writhed, slithered across the floor like a snake, in an effort to escape the clutches of those wicked, soft, pampered, evil hands.

"Now, don't fight me, Jimmy."

The feral part of James found the strength to swing a leg, to kick. Where the blow landed, James the man did not know. He was up and moving before he registered that he could. That he was free.

Then Father said precisely what James had always feared.

"You can't escape me, James."

Maybe not, but he was going to try, or die trying.

"Why make this difficult, son?"

James dashed down the hall. Doors, there were several doors, opening to only the house knew where. He tried the first he ran into. Resistance. It was as if something on the other side pulled when James pulled, determined not to let him win.

A split second passed. He wasted no time fighting it. There were other doors.

"Jimmy..."

Another knob. Stuck. Locked. Unyielding.

"I think you owe me, James. That was my favorite mount."

James' feet rebelled at that. His brain rebelled. Just when he'd been thinking that perhaps he hadn't snuffed out his worst nightmare after all, that maybe he had been insane since he was five, Daddy said it.

He referenced his own murder.

So it was true.

James lunged for another door, convinced now that Father wanted revenge and would take his sweet time getting it from James' hide.

Father always liked going slowly with things that were worth the time.

"Was it really so bad, Jimmy? I loved you; I still love you."

James let out a twisted, high-pitched laugh. "Love?" But it was true. He'd felt it. His father's sick idea of love.

He scrambled to the left, to another door.

"We can work this out. I shan't tell anyone what you did."

Bile rose in James' throat; he burped it up. Zoe, he'd told Zoe that he'd murdered his father, and she had taken it to her grave.

He was certain of it. As certain as he was that when he reached for the next door, it would open. Clarity of senses had struck like a cobra. Both horrid and welcome.

It was true. Everyone was dead save James, and he wanted to remain not dead, because he was suddenly quite positive that dying in this manor meant an eternity of bearing Father.

Perhaps all of them. Anyone who had ever died here. Sophie. The men, three generations...His co-investigators. People he didn't yet know of.

"Open, open, open," James muttered, prayed.

The door opened, just as he felt the breath of the other man on the back of his neck.

Impossible, impossible, that a ghost should be so solid, yet James knew better. James had experienced ghosts in this manner before. Some so powerful, so good at gathering energy... They just hadn't been related to him.

"I will not surrender to you, not ever again!" James rushed through the door and into the room. He grabbed fistfuls of his hair when a frantic assessment told him that there was no exit.

"I'm losing my patience, James."

James took comically large strides across the room. Towards the boards. There was a boarded up window and the smell of fire. Old fire. Old soot.

The section he'd seen from outside. There had been a fire in this section of the house. As soon as it registered, the scents gagged him.

Mold, from water, water mixed with ashes; it was a veritable soup. Musty, sooty brick, burnt wallpaper, and...

"Bodies..." James' hand flew to his mouth in an effort to stop the vomit. Hands on his shoulders sent it back down the other way, and he choked on the swallowing of it.

"I say, that's about enough of that, James. You're not a common street urchin."

James wished, he wished hard, that he could convince himself that it wasn't real. Or, at least, that it was just a ghost and that a ghost couldn't hurt him.

But James knew better.

He reached for the blackened boards, praying that they were as rotted as they ought to be after so much time, or at least weakened. He reached and got purchase on the edge of one, and he winced at the instant splinter.

Father behind him, pressing his face into the back of James' hair, he kept his hands working, damn the splinters. He pulled and scraped, his hands slipping repeatedly, his breaths coming in shallow, short bursts.

It was a replay of Brig and a bathroom closing in. The clawing, the need to get out. The claustrophobia.

"Jimmy...I could see my way to forgiving you, if..." Devil Dad's hands moved up the sides of James' body.

James cried out in pain and panic. All he could see were those four posts. He could feel the restraints. He could taste the cotton pillowcase and hear his own muffled cries.

He gasped; he sucked at the air, again, again. It was a near mimicry of a chapel and a tall American, struggling for air.

"Jiiii-mmeee..." A kiss pressed to the back of James' jaw, just below his ear, sent creepy-crawlies racing along his skin, under his clothing, over his clothes. Thousands of scampering, tickling, itching, horrendous legs, all spawned by that kiss. That one little kiss.

James wanted to tear the flesh from his own bones, and he let out great sobs but managed to instead claw at the wood. Still the wood, only the wood.

It was close to a replay of man named Mike, who had an irrational fear of spiders. But Mike hadn't managed the wood.

"Please, James. I'm sorry. I'm so sorry, do forgive me."

James paused. The tone. So familiar.

"Don't leave me here all alone. I beg of you."

James began to turn his head, to look.

"After all, you sent me here, you know. The day you killed me."

James shivered with a cold flash that came from within.

"But I forgive you." Father laughed his most charming, harmless, laugh. "I would even say I'm proud. You were always so brilliant, and you proved it yet again. Really, well done, James."

James caught sight of his tormentor in the corner of his eye. Like Zoe and her need to mother, a part of James had wanted to help Father. He had wanted to be the one to fix things. He had wanted to believe that Father could love him in a proper fashion, and that he was the one good thing in Father's life, because they all knew that Mother didn't love him.

He wanted to believe that Daddy was ill, and misunderstood. It was his fault that Father did what he did, wasn't it? And so, he would make it better.

A guttural yell shook through James and he turned back towards the boards, the boards that surely still hid a window, dear God, let the window still be there, and he yanked, and clawed, and ripped and pulled with a hell-borne fury and vengeance that welled up from deep within and erupted when he had a spark of understanding.

The understanding that he'd been so close, too god damned close, to falling for it once again. To forgiving Daddy, once again. To believing him. James loathed himself, as he had back then.

"Ahaha...ahaha. Oh, James. You can't escape me."

"Yes...I...can!" Light. Dim, but there. So very dim, but to James, a supernova. "I can, I can, I can." Wood creaked. Cracked. He placed a foot on the wall for more advantage, prizing the board away with a resounding snap.

"James, please don't leave me."

"I will not be like Zoe, I will not." James chanted these words; it was a drone.

"Zoe? James, if you want Zoe, she can stay with us, too. It will be just like before. Our little family."

James' heart threatened to explode in his chest, or punch its way out and expire at his feet, flopping like a fish.

But then another board snapped.

Knuckles bloody and torn, nails ripped and full of wood chunks. So close, adrenaline spiked again. Hope was a powerful thing.

"James! Don't leave me!"

One more board. Stubborn, that last one. He had hold of it, though, and wasn't about letting go for anything, not even the sick, morbid desire to look upon his father's face one more time, to see what lay in those blue-gray eyes.

The board threatened at every second to fight back. James rocked with it, like rubber, boing boing, back and forth. Something, had to give, it had to –

"Very well. Enough games."

The blood in James' veins frosted over. Hands tugged at him, forced his body slowly away from that last board.

But James, like a pit-bull, refused to give it up. Perhaps couldn't give it up. His fingers were stuck in claw-like form, the joints locked, rigid.

Snap.

Between this sudden freedom and Daddy's hands turning him, James was whirled in his direction with great speed, and it dizzied him.

James closed his eyes as hands came to his chest.

Gravity abandoned James for the second time in one night, then. But much more violently than before, considering the shock to his system when his back struck wood and glass, and glass and wood pierced cloth and shoulder, lower back and thigh, making a veritable pincushion out of him.

And then he fell.

Time

Eyes too intense in their darkness – even the sclera appeared to bleed black, though it reflected the light from the news broadcast on TV – took in the words without aid of sound. He found lip-reading enjoyable at this moment, and he could hear the words plainly enough as if spoken to his mind, in any case. Easier now that he was so invigorated.

The reporter spoke of five Americans missing now for two weeks, their last known whereabouts Bristol, England, for that is where their plane had landed. A hotel clerk recalled two black vans delivered to the hotel for some of its guests, and having enquired about this, remembered that they were paranormal investigators. They had said something about investigating a property, though they were not at liberty to discuss it, they had said. But then one of them had later asked the clerk if he knew the address of an estate, which he did not.

Mr. Smith smiled a crooked smile at the T.V. He had anticipated that. People can never keep their mouths shut. But no matter. It did not concern him.

Abnormally twisted fingers tapped at the arm of his flesh-toned chair as he watched a while longer, waiting for word of the psychic, though he did not expect such. He was waiting for confirmation of what he surely knew. Mr. Trussart did not keep close ties with anyone in particular, least of all his mother. No one would be looking for him, thought Mr. Smith.

A reason he chose him.

Mr. Trussart preferred blending in as much as possible. Mr. Trussart found it difficult to form close ties.

Mr. Trussart, ah, such a lovely specimen. Such a gifted, pretty, tasty little specimen.

Such a delicious secret within that tempting flesh. Smith was very proud of him.

Confirmation came when no man from London was mentioned, no gifted historian connected to this investigation noted in the broadcast, though in London it had been reported by co-workers of his that he had not shown up for his duties in some time. A separate broadcast, that. One James Avery Trussart was missing.

Mr. Smith laughed a laugh so hideous it defied description. He might have to dig this one up later, yes indeed. That one was too much fun, too delectable. He had survived the longest, not as delicate as he appeared. He was not so fragile in the end, that one. But he would let James' body rest a time...a time. Allow him to heal a bit before driving him down the emotional rabbit hole once more, Mr. Smith decided. Anticipation was such a wonderful thing, and beginning fresh was so much fun – not to mention, if he pushed him too far too soon, there would be nothing to drink in, nothing to absorb from the young man.

He was only human, after all. Even Mr. Trussart could be pushed only so far before breaking. He'd give him time to recoup.

And then place another bet, though he hadn't minded losing this one. Even when he lost, he won – in some instances, anyway.

He and the old hag exchanged a glance.

"I told you," she said.

"Yes, yes."

Smith switched off the TV, grinning maliciously over the last words from the news anchor.

"When police arrived at the scene, two black vans were found abandoned in a desolate estate some fifty kilometers from the village. There seems no trace of the missing persons as of this broadcast, and Commissioner Barden admits bafflement. The remains of the mansion appear undisturbed, innocuous and sterile as ever. The trail, it seems, has gone cold."

Epilogue

The lithe young man wandered aimlessly down the sidewalk, scarcely aware that he was even moving. He'd walked quite a distance, all of it in the same dream-like state, though moments ago, at the very beginning of this journey – it may have seemed like moments to him, anyway – he had been running, the state nightmarish.

Here and there, passersby cast him curious first glances and second glances, some thinking him perhaps homeless, though he was dressed rather well. But he'd been wearing the same clothing for some time now, and it was mightily soiled.

Not to mention he had the look of one used roughly and left to wallow in a culvert. Then there was the limp. Surely he appeared in need of help.

A couple passersby thought perhaps something ailed him – that something had happened to him, but they couldn't be bothered to stop and inquire as to his state. They had their own affairs to attend.

At least one person regarded the young-looking man with a suspicious eye and maybe a touch of wordless fear. But most passing him didn't even notice him. Or rather, did their best not to notice him. There was, in their subconsciouses, a wordless understanding that it might be best to stay away. That the young man was mad, not just dirty and injured. This wordless warning over road the urge to offer aid.

As the haggard looking waif of a man paused by a café, one person, one very kind person, took one look at him and felt compelled to approach, ignoring the wordless warning. "Do you need assistance?"

Eyes blue-gray and haunted slowly shifted to the stranger, though to the stranger it appeared that the poor boy didn't understand.

The elderly gentleman laid a hand on the other man's arm. "I say, can I lend you hand? Are you all right?" And as he looked into the young man's eyes, he realized those eyes appeared very old in their way. As if they had seen too much, far too much in a life that otherwise appeared relatively short.

For the first time in his life, James Avery Trussart felt and saw *nothing* from the touch of another, and a sound that began in a deep pit within him percolated, eventually bubbling up, up and out into the chilled night air. This sound alarmed the elderly man, who took an involuntary step back. *This chap is mad*, he thought. *That's a mad man's laugh. Whatever he's witnessed, it has made him insane!*

"I should think that I am *not* all right," James replied to no one in particular, his voice quietly tense, and this tension wire sounding as if it would snap at any second.

The old man took another step back, a hasty step.

But he needn't have worried.

James returned to his nightmare, never noticing when it was that he began walking once more, nor quite certain where it was that he was going.

"But I am alive..." he murmured, entirely unaware that he had spoken aloud.

Acknowledgements

Wanda. It was so wonderful to meet you. Thank you for the mini ghost hunt and the opportunity to handle the meters. Come back soon. Melissa Hopkins, as always, for reading version after version of everything. Between you and me, QUORK.

A CHAPTER FROM S. ROIT'S

PARIS
IMMORTAL

THE FIRST BOOK IN A SERIES
OF THE SAME NAME

AVAILABLE FROM SNOWBOOKS

Chapter One

Monsieur Lecureaux is heading for my office. My guts want to knot, which is unnatural for my usually confident self, but I've heard a lot about him. Butterflies, I have them. I've stepped into an entirely new world, and I don't merely mean moving to Paris.

They say he's charming. They say he's handsome. Most use the word *beautiful*. They say he's eccentric. They say when he gets angry, it ain't pretty. When he gets agitated, there's something disconcerting as hell about it. It's like a child's tantrum on steroids.

That's what they say.

They being new coworkers of mine, whom I barely know, but boy, do they have a lot to say about this particular client.

I've never heard of anyone as rich as he is.

My co-workers spoke in hushed tones about the new husband. He's only graced them with his presence twice. I don't know what to make of it. Everyone has different details and none of them jibe. I brushed it off as mostly gossip, deciding whoever knew the entire story had their lips glued shut. The only thing I knew for sure was that they fired the last guy, and I was in his old office.

Imagine, trying to extort money from these clients through a family estate. Stefan was obviously lacking in the common sense department. You don't fuck with rich people's estates, especially not one that ancient, not to mention the evidence was right here in the computer.

Fucking idiot.

Mind you, I'd never do such a thing, but I'd be a hell of a lot smarter about it if I did. Stefan's lucky he isn't in jail. He sexually harassed Lecureaux's husband on top of everything else. What nerve, eh? Sounds about as sharp as a bowling ball.

This all remains hearsay, of course.

I knocked back a small amount of scotch to steady myself and got up, heading for the door. I'd greet my client immediately, yeah, that would be good. I couldn't contain myself and ended up opening the door just to have a peek into the hall. What I saw stunned me speechless. No doubt I looked like an idiot standing there. I sure started to feel like one.

This is no golden blond. This is not the one named Michel.

This is his husband coming towards me. Damn, who has hair like that? The overhead lights reflect off the long thick strands like a spotlight on dark metal. The pale color of his skin confuses me. There's something unusual about it. It seems so smooth and —

Fuck, I don't have a word for it. I notice during his slow advance that maybe he isn't as tall as I first thought. Maybe six feet, but he's quite slender, which makes him seem taller. Looking at him brings to mind reeds, slender reeds.

Shit, look at those eyes. Jesus. Who has eyes like that? No one does. Eyes like gems, like emeralds. I swear the temperature in the hall is dropping from his cold gaze.

His mouth, it makes my own mouth water, and I could rest my tongue in the sexy cleft of his chin for hours. His bone structure would inspire artists by the hundreds. Gee, is my jaw on the floor yet?

He either hasn't noticed the way I'm sizing him up, or doesn't care, because I'm sure I'm being obvious.

This doesn't stop me from taking in more details.

Dressed in elegant suits the other two times he visited the offices, so I heard, his attire stuns me. His black shirt looks stretchy and takes a deep plunge from the neck. A shimmery shirt. A good-sized teardrop shaped stone rests between his sculpted collarbones. It's dark ruby, maybe, but no, wait. Did the red just move? It shimmers too, seems like.

My eyes can't stop moving down to where his shirt stops – above his navel. His pierced navel. Plenty of pale flesh shows down to the pants he wears. His flat belly inspires visions of tongue baths. I can't will my eyes to move up, 'cause I see more black hair, wisps of it. Holy shit, his pants defy gravity, and Jesus Christ, you can guess his religion.

Ehemm, yeah, enough of that. Two words come to mind in the moments I can't move or look away. *Murderously beautiful.* He is the most beautiful thing I have ever seen, male or female. Exotic, androgynous, and the word *ethereal* comes to mind.

Apparently he really *didn't* care one way or the other about my staring, because he stopped in front of me and all he said was:

"You would be *Monsieur* du Bois?"

I tried to find my voice, and my cheeks got hot when he spoke, 'cause I realized I was still staring at his crotch. When I looked at his face it wasn't much better.

"Yeah. That's me."

Be professional, Trey. Speak French, it's a reason they hired you. "*Enchanté de faire votre connaissance.*"

I held out my hand, hoping it wasn't trembling, hoping he wouldn't notice that my palms had started to sweat. His long black lashes lowered, and he stared at my hand. It seemed he was considering. I was about to withdraw my hand when he reached out and grasped it, the touch light. My fingers trembled from the unexpected coolness of his skin, but it wasn't just from that. The touch itself, it was —

"A pleasure." His eyes lifted as he spoke. Mine wanted to dart away, but that green, green, green caught them and they couldn't. I managed to let go of his hand.

"We need to take care of some business, I hear."

His face was smooth. "*Oui.*"

"So...yeah, come on inside, I've got all your files here." Oh so professional, Trey.

"*Merci.*"

I realized he was waiting for me to go back in first.

"Excuse me, yes, come right in." I forced myself to turn around and headed straight for the desk and my computer. Sanctuary in files.

He followed me and stopped in front of my desk. He checked out the office, standing with his hands clasped behind his back.

If he looks like this, what does Michel look like?

I quickly looked back at the monitor when his eyes shifted in my direction.

"Did Robert inform you what needs be done?"

I nodded. "Yeah, I'm opening the files right now. Don't worry, this'll be taken care of in no time."

"This is what I like to hear, *Monsieur* du Bois."

Man, his voice is so — "That other guy wasn't much of a file keeper."

Stone cold silence is what I received for that comment.

I need more scotch.

"Seems to be the preferred drink of those in law," he said, breaking the oppressive silence.

I looked up. I noticed him staring at the bottle of scotch behind me on the shelf. "Oh, the scotch. Come to think of it, I've seen a few lawyers drink it."

"The misguided file keeper you spoke of seemed to like it well enough." His eyes shifted back to me and pinned me to the back of the chair.

"I found it in here, actually."

He studied me, and I mean studied. That's what made me nervous about his eyes. Like he was looking into me one moment and through me the next.

He went silent again. I don't feel a need to fill every silence, but I was ready to squirm.

"I guess he left in a hurry," I said, and someone stole half the volume of my voice.

"I should think so," he replied.

"Well, that's none of my business, right? I've got his office, that's all, and his mess to clean up," and someone stole the rest of my voice.

He heard me anyway. "I am certain you heard gossip."

I didn't even try to reply.

"I know how people gossip," he went on. I swear he almost smiled.

Almost.

"He attempted to steal something important and I found him vulgar. Certainly not as fantastic as what you may have heard." He didn't sound angry, just stated it as a fact.

I shook my head. Yeah, I managed to do that.

"I'm only vulgar when the situation calls for it," I heard myself reply.

And almost crawled under the desk to die. He probably won't appreciate my humor, I was thinking as I shrank, but then I heard him laugh. It was just a little, but it had a nice tone. It was soft, clear and deep, just like his speaking voice, which was also wonderfully French.

His French – it was different and I couldn't place it, though I understood him well enough. What was it? I hadn't heard anyone speak French that way before. Of course, I was in Paris now.

I ventured a look at him. His eyes appeared brighter.

"Will the paperwork take long?"

Paperwork.

"Oh no, not once I get going. Which I'll do right now. Sh- I mean sorry, where are my manners? Have a seat."

God, I'd left him standing. I watched from the corner of my eye as he flowed gracefully into the chair. Posture that perfect I'd only seen on ballet dancers. He folded his hands in his lap.

My head wanted to spin. He looked like sin and acted like a well-bred gentleman, probably raised as one, I thought. The clothes on the other hand suggested...well they suggested all kinds of things. Looks can be deceiving, they say. Somehow I thought the look wasn't as deceiving as the mannerism.

Say something and stop staring.

Try again, Trey.

"Would you care for some scotch?" I asked, thinking his comment before might have been a hint.

"No, I would not, thank you."

Okay, well at least I offered. "Water?"

He almost smiled again. "No, thank you."

"For me to get to work?"

His smile finally formed and I felt giddy for it. Small it may have been, but it was a smile.

"If you please, but I will keep you company."

Oh yeah, just make me more nervous. How ridiculous am I right now?

"I will not mind if you imbibe."

Is he reading my fricking mind, or what? He's just being polite. Don't drink any more scotch, Trey.

"If you really don't, I honestly wouldn't mind having some, that's for sure. Long day, all that."

He nodded.

Guess I'm drinking more scotch.

I grabbed the bottle and tried to pour enough, yet not pour what looked like too much. His eyes drifted over the room and I found myself staring at him yet again.

Right. Open file type, idiot. He might not be so patient if I keep him here too long being – what was I being? A teenager with a sudden infatuation? Jesus Trey, he'll like you far better if you get this done, if he likes you at all.

"*Monsieur* Lecureaux, you'll be happy to know I already had most of this done in the event your husband arrived to see to the matter, so really, this won't take long at all."

He looked at me before I could look back to the file. "Wonderful. You must be very industrious."

"I don't believe in wasting people's time."

"Then we should get along well."

"I hope so *Monsieur* Lecureaux. My chances of keeping this job depend on it." I tried to give my best inside joke sort of smile.

Oh man, he smiled that little smile again. Two for two.

"You may call me Gabriel."

I may?

A smile and a first name basis. Starting to feel a little better, here. Scotch not so important now. Well, after he leaves it probably will be again.

"Thank you, Gabriel. Okay, here come the printouts. I'm getting in touch with the bank computer, now. I already called Rinoche when Mr. Bouchet gave me the short version. He knows you're here and will be waiting for the faxes."

"Marvelous." He leaned back in his chair a little. I suppose for him this was relaxed.

Nah.

I bet he relaxes in other –

Shut it, Trey.

"I do not much care for business, Trey. I may call you Trey?"

You can call me anything you – "Of course."

"I do not care for business, Trey, therefore the fact you appear to have handled this so thoroughly and quickly, pleases me."

"That's what I'm here for." To please you.

Don't go there Trey.

Mental shake.

Think about his French. It has a different cadence.

"So, the paperwork," I said.

He gave me an affirmative by way of the barest nod, and went back to studying me.

I turned and grabbed the papers. "Read these over and then just sign those top four, Gabriel. Simple." I smiled as I slid them across the desk to him and then found, thank God, the good pen I hadn't chewed on yet, and held it out.

His movement was fluid when he took the pen from me. He skimmed the papers fast.

"Sure you don't want to read it more carefully?"

"I trust you have been thorough."

Okay. I hope he isn't one of those who doesn't read, then gets pissy about something later.

I watched him sign. Long, delicate fingers. Piano hands and he's left-handed. That must be his wedding ring. I couldn't get a good look before he held out the pen, which I carefully took without touching him. With his right hand he slid the papers back to me. Wow, that's some rock. What kind of stone is that?

The papers, Trey, the papers. I looked through them to make sure he signed them all. Man, even his handwriting was beautiful, elegant. He's fucking elegant. Not just elegant, *fucking* elegant.

"Just one more thing, Gabriel. Quick talk with Rinoche."

"Yes, that is how it is all set up. The password, he wishes to hear me authorize it."

I nodded and dialed the number. "I'll just step outside."

He took the receiver and I willed myself out.

Didn't want him to think I wanted the password but I didn't want to go. I could only stand there in the hall staring at the floor and imagine –

Nothing, nothing at all, right.

I almost jumped when I felt someone tap my shoulder.

"Finished?" I managed to ask.

"Yes."

"Well that's it, really."

His head inclined slightly to the left. "Truly. That is all?"

"Scout's honor."

"You were a scout?"

I swore it was a genuine question, and I laughed, then felt bad for laughing. He didn't react, just waited.

"Um, no. Just an expression."

He slipped to English. "I know. I simply wonder how many were scouts who say this."

I couldn't help laughing again. "Few, I bet."

His head straightened. "Most likely."

He stood there what felt like forever, really still. It was almost eerie.

"Thank you Trey, this was the most pleasant visit I have ever had here."

"I won't let it go to my head since it's only your third time."

Shit, that sounds like gossip. How do I know that, right? He's going to wonder why I said that.

His face held no expression when he spoke again. "The third time is a charm, no?"

"That's what they say."

"They say a lot of things."

Shit. "Yeah, they do. Most of the time it's crap."

Third time's a charm? Yeah, he smiled again. This time it was bigger. I relaxed a little.

"You speak French very well, but in English your sound is far different. From where are you?"

I found the way he phrased that enchanting.

"New York."

"There is a different quality from the accents I have heard."

"Lots of people think of the City when I say New York, but I'm from Upstate. I have a little NYC in there, though, a little."

"Ah, yes I can hear it now. Yet I think I detect something else."

I wasn't sure what to say to that. He remained silent.

Any chance of blinking, dude?

"Were you born in Paris, Gabriel?"

"No."

That was it.

"Elsewhere in France, then." No shit. But maybe he'll say where.

"Yes."

That was it.

Okay. Man of few words. I'm generally good at conversation, but right then I was at a loss. It felt like asking a normal get-to-know-you question was prying.

"It was a pleasure, Trey. Good evening."

I guess I was right about prying.

"Okay, well have a good evening, Gabriel."

"*Merci*." It was an implication of a bow, the way he inclined his head before pivoting oh-so-gracefully and walking away.

I found myself watching – tight ass.

Shut it, Trey.

I watched until he was gone, literally slapped my forehead, and went back into the office to gulp scotch. The encounter was both disconcerting and exhilarating.

I couldn't imagine anyone being more beautiful, but I still hadn't met Michel. Words like hot, magnanimous and outgoing bounced around the office in connection to him. Animal magnetism, those were some more. I suddenly asked myself if I was going to survive working with them. Holy shit, I about fell into Gabriel's eyes, it felt like. In fact, they were still haunting me more than anything else.

Wait.

Had I seen eyes like his before?